He spoke against her mouth.

"Does this feel like bullshit? I wanted you before I could see you. And now that I've seen you . . . I want you even more."

His words sapped her lingering will-power. She couldn't stop herself. She lifted her hands and grabbed his neck, her fingers curling through the strands of hair at his nape, pulling him closer, drawing him in. And still it was not enough. Still not close enough. She wouldn't be close enough until she had managed to crawl inside him.

There were distant sounds. A dog barking. A car starting somewhere down the street. The sudden burst of wind stirring the heated air and wrestling with dry leaves in trees. All this was muted background to the roar of blood in her veins for this man. For his mouth on hers. His tongue sliding past her lips. For the hard plane of his chest mashing into her.

He made a growling sound of approval.

By Sophie Jordan

The Devil's Rock Series
FURY ON FIRE
HELL BREAKS LOOSE
ALL CHAINED UP

Historical Romances
WHILE THE DUKE WAS SLEEPING
ALL THE WAYS TO RUIN A ROGUE
A GOOD DEBUTANTE'S GUIDE TO RUIN
HOW TO LOSE A BRIDE IN ONE NIGHT
LESSONS FROM A SCANDALOUS BRIDE
WICKED IN YOUR ARMS
WICKED NIGHTS WITH A LOVER
IN SCANDAL THEY WED
SINS OF A WICKED DUKE
SURRENDER TO ME
ONE NIGHT WITH YOU
TOO WICKED TO TAME
ONCE UPON A WEDDING NIGHT

FURY ON FIRE

A Devil's Rock Novel

SOPHIE JORDAN

WITHDRAWN

AVONBOOKS

An Imprint of HarperCollinsPublishers

FURY ON FIRE. Copyright © 2017 by Sharie Kohler. All rights reserved. Printed in the United States of America. No part of this book may be used or reproduced in any manner whatsoever without written permission except in the case of brief quotations embodied in critical articles and reviews. For information, address HarperCollins Publishers, 195 Broadway, New York, NY 10007.

First Avon Books mass market printing: February 2017

ISBN 978-0-06-242375-7

17 18 19 20 21   QGM   10 9 8 7 6 5 4 3 2 1

For Angela Hanna:
Thanks for the wine, the laughter and the friendship—not
necessarily in that order! You're good for my soul.

FURY ON FIRE

ONE

*I*T WAS MOVE-IN day.

Faith had been waiting for this her whole life. Okay, maybe that was a slight exaggeration. As a child she had been perfectly content sharing a roof with her family, but at the age of twenty-six she was overdue for getting her own place.

Propping her hands on her hips, she took a satisfying look around. She was a homeowner.

She knew she could continue to live with her father forever (he would love that) or at least until she married. She stifled a wince. Not that there was any prospect of that happening. One usually required a boyfriend first.

"You sure about this, Faithy?"

Her brother posed the question. Hale was a little sweaty from hauling all her things from the back of his and Dad's trucks. He wiped a forearm against his brow.

She smiled and shook her head. It was a little late to be asking. The mortgage was signed. The down payment made. Her stuff was everywhere, surrounding her inside the two bedroom, two and a half bath, including all the new furniture she'd bought—the most money she had spent on anything excluding her car.

Although it wasn't as if Hale had never asked the question before. He'd asked. Every step of the way he had grumbled his disapproval. Apparently it was fine for her brother to have his own place, but his sister? Not so much. As far as Hale was concerned she was still the baby of the family. Never mind that she went away to college all by herself. Four years in a dorm and then two more in graduate housing was apparently different.

She'd probably encouraged her family into thinking she was going to live with Dad forever. When she finished her grad program she had moved back home right into her old bedroom with its Hello Kitty curtains. For the last two years she had resided with her now retired father and worked as a social worker for the city of Sweet Hill. It had been easy. Comfortable.

She went to work every day and then came home

and made dinner. Hale would join them a couple nights a week. It had been just like when she was growing up. The only thing missing on taco Tuesday was her other brother, Tucker, who was an Army Ranger fighting somewhere on the other side of the world.

Ever since her mother died, Faith had attempted to fill the void and take care of the men in her family. Her father and brothers had come to expect it of her—and she had let them. She'd expected it of herself even.

After grad school, it was easy to fall back into the lifelong pattern. Less easy was breaking the pattern, but she was doing it. Finally.

She needed her own place and she was finally making it happen. A social life, *dating*. She was claiming that for herself because God knew a hovering brother and father wasn't conducive. Hard to invite a man back to your place when you lived with Daddy. Even harder when Daddy was the former sheriff.

"Are you sure about this, Faithy?" Hale repeated.

She winced at the lifelong nickname. Lifelong or not it made her feel like a little girl. As long as she lived at home, her family would always treat her like a child.

Standing at the door of her new duplex she smiled at her father and brother as they gathered on her porch.

"Yes, Hale. I'm sure." She propped a hand against the doorjamb. "For the hundredth time, yes."

Her older brother eyed her house, turning slightly on his heels to survey the surrounding neighborhood—as though he hadn't examined it the moment she'd first picked out the property over a month ago. His steel-eyed gaze hesitated on the duplex next door. A truck was parked in their shared driveway.

"Well, let's leave her be." Her father clapped Hale on the back. It was funny actually. She had two brothers and a father, but Hale was the most protective. Kind of hard for Tucker to be protective when he wasn't around. And Dad probably figured he didn't need to be as long as Hale was doing such a bang-up job.

"Dinner next week?" she called as her father moved down the driveway between her car and the neighbor's.

Dad didn't glance back at her as he moved toward his truck parked along the curb. He held a hand up in a quick wave. "Sure thing," he called, his manner brusque, even for him.

She couldn't help noticing that he wasn't meeting

her gaze. With a farewell tug on his baseball cap, he pulled open the driver's side door and climbed inside the cab, still averting his stare as he started the engine and drove away.

Hale lingered on her porch. He, on the other hand, had no trouble looking at her. His deep-set eyes were probing. "He's trying to act like he's okay with this."

"Hale," she said, her voice pleading. She didn't want to feel guilt over doing this. Guilt had kept her home for the last two years. It had taken a lot for her to announce she was leaving. A lot to buy a house and actually go through with it.

He held up both hands, palms face out. "I get it. I do."

She nodded. "Considering *you* moved out and have had your own place for years now, I'm really glad to hear that."

"It's different with you," he countered.

"Why?" she demanded.

"You're a girl . . . a daughter."

She puffed out a breath and waved to his truck in the street without any real heat. "Go on with you. Take your sexist double standards and get out of here."

Hale dug a hand in his pocket and he moved toward his truck. "Take it easy, sis."

"Seriously, you're a caveman," she called. "It's like you stepped straight out of the nineteen fifties!"

His typically stern expression cracked with a grin, reminding her that the majority of the ladies in town had his name knitted on their pillows. Her brother was a heartbreaker—even more so because he rarely dated, and when he did it was never anyone in the local community. He never let any of the nice girls of Sweet Hill get within twenty feet of his bed, insisting they were only after a ring. She knew he was off and on again with a woman in Alpine. A CPA that worked long hours and apparently wasn't looking to get said ring on her finger.

"See you at dinner next week," he called.

"I don't remember inviting you!"

"Of course you did. I just broke my back moving you in. You owe me." He winked at her as he ducked inside his truck. "Make your chicken parmesan."

"I'm making liver and onions . . . or something vegetarian," she called after her carnivore-loving brother.

He hung out his open window, his broad palm skimming the side of his door as he replied, "Funny. *You* don't like liver. Neither does Dad."

"I can learn to like it." She planted her hands on her hips.

Chuckling, he started backing out of her driveway. "See you next week."

She waved grudgingly. Overbearing or not, she loved him and she knew he loved her, too. She knew he even understood her need for her own place and her own life or he would have dug his heels in much more than he had.

Closing the door to her house, she turned back around to face her new abode.

It was perfect. An open-concept space with a kitchen that looked out into the living and dining area. She imagined entertaining in this space. Hosting Sunday dinners with her father and Hale—Tucker, too, when he came home. Maybe one of her brothers would eventually settle down with a girlfriend or wife.

She carried the image a little further and saw herself cooking for a few of her friends, maybe even a boyfriend. She winced. She had the friends. Now she just needed to work on getting the boyfriend. Easier said than done.

The good thing about growing up as the sheriff's daughter was that no one screwed with you.

The bad thing about being the sheriff's daughter was that no one screwed with you.

A chastity belt could not have been more effective. No one dared mess with her. By the time she was a junior in high school, Hale was already one of her father's deputies and giving MIPs to her classmates every time he caught them drinking at a party. As far as those high school parties were concerned, no one handed her a beer. No guy even attempted to touch her. Half the time they didn't even invite her, too afraid that the party would get busted.

No, Faith never had a prayer. She was a social pariah, and that did something to a girl. Watching guys turn tail when they saw her coming cut into her confidence when it came to the opposite sex. That lack of confidence had followed her through life.

By the time she got to college, she was woefully lacking in experience and kept to herself. She landed her first boyfriend in her last year of college. She dated Chad for eighteen months. He was an engineering student. Sociable and outgoing, he put her at ease. Sex, when they finally had it, was nice if not exactly rock-your-world. She figured that would get better with more practice. However, their last few months together they hardly practiced. No, they spent more and more time at school and work than with each other. When Chad broke up with her, explaining that he wanted to see other people, it wasn't so surprising. Maybe even a relief.

They were hardly seeing each other at that point. She couldn't say she truly loved him. She thought she had, in the beginning at least. But it had never been passionate between them. Not like she always imagined love to be. It was never a chest-squeezing, giddy and breathless kind of thing, but maybe that was simply the remnants of her teenage self hoping for something that belonged on the pages of a romance novel.

Rolling up her sleeves, she got to work unpacking her kitchen and putting everything in its place. Coasters on the bar counter. Oven mitts on their hooks. Trivets in the drawers. Dishes in the cabinet. Her spices in the rack that hung on her pantry door. The tall pepper mill that had belonged to her mother and still cracked pepper better than any pepper mill she'd ever encountered took position by her stove.

She eyed the ancient stove, vowing to look into upgrading it. A good oven was essential. Faith liked to cook. She had been doing it since her mom passed away and it became apparent that if she relied on her father and brothers, every day of her life would consist of frozen pizza and scrambled eggs. Badly scrambled eggs. Bone-dry and crunchy. If she wanted to eat anything better for the rest of her adolescent life, she'd concluded that she was going to have to be the one to prepare it. She'd found peace working in her mother's kitchen. It was like she was connected to her somehow, surrounded by her pots and spices, using her recipes.

She ran a hand over her gleaming new refrigerator. Tomorrow she'd have to go to the store and buy groceries. Right now she had a few basics. Opening her refrigerator, she peered inside and assessed if she had enough ingredients to make her mother's chocolate chip scones.

Satisfied that she did, she tightened the band of her ponytail and got started. Soon she was shaping doughy crescent scones onto a well-seasoned pan, the place smelling like the childhood of her memories. With three kids, two of whom were teenage boys that topped six feet, her mom had constantly been cooking. Setting the timer on her phone, Faith wiped her hands off on a dishtowel.

Content, she sank down on her couch and turned on the television, relieved that her cable was already up and running. She flipped channels until she landed on a comedy. She saw enough grim realities at work. When she vegged in front of the TV, she preferred lighthearted fare.

She abandoned the episode of *Modern Family* when the timer went off. She sprinkled the tops of the hot scones with sugar until their golden-brown crust sparkled with sugar crystals. Leaving the pan to cool, she returned to her couch.

It wasn't very long before the sound of an engine outside drew her attention. It must be her neighbors. Sharing a driveway (not to mention a wall), she imagined she would hear them whenever they came and went.

Her Realtor hadn't imparted any information about her neighbor the few times Faith had looked at the house. Curious, she stood and peered out the peephole, glimpsing a body moving to the front door before disappearing out of sight. In that split second she identified it was a male body. A very *tall* male body. She marked his height, the curve of a well-muscled shoulder covered by a black T-shirt and a gold-skinned arm roped with sinew. His dark hair was on the long side, obscuring his face. There wasn't enough time to see his features, and she felt an uncalled stab of disappointment.

She heard the key in the lock. She listened as he entered the other side of the duplex. The door thudded shut. For a moment, she absorbed the fact that only a wall separated them. Only a wall divided her from a stranger. But he was her neighbor. He wouldn't be a stranger for long. Not once they met.

She stood there for some moments, thinking, debating how she should go about introducing herself.

Reaching a decision, she moved back into the kitchen and grabbed a plate. She carefully chose the best four scones and placed them on it. Without bothering to don her shoes, she walked outside and strode along the duplex's shared porch, stopping in front of her neighbor's door. She knocked twice. Nothing.

She waited several moments and then knocked again. Louder. Maybe he was at the back of the house and didn't hear her.

Knocked again. Nothing. Staring at the peephole, she wondered if maybe he was in the shower. Several seconds ticked pass and she lifted her hand to knock yet again.

The sound of a car pulling into their driveway had her turning around. A beat-up Honda parked behind her car, blocking her in. She watched as a bombshell of a redhead climbed out of the car. She was wearing ripped-up jeans so tight they were painted on. A yellow Rainbow Brite graphic tee so thin you could see the dark leopard-print bra underneath it completed the ensemble.

She slipped her keys into her back pocket as she

walked up the drive, her thick-lashed eyes landing on Faith.

"Hey," she greeted.

"Hi," she returned, wondering if she should say anything about the woman's car blocking hers, but then decided against it. Faith wasn't going anywhere tonight.

"What you got there?" Redhead nodded at the plate in her hands.

Faith glanced down, a little flustered in face of this confidant, sexy female. "Uh, scones," she answered.

"Scones?" she echoed like she had never heard the word.

"Chocolate chip," she added.

"Damn." The girl bent at the waist to breathe them in. "Sounds good. These for North? You here to see him?"

"North?" Was that her neighbor's name?

"Yeah. North Callaghan."

Faith jerked a thumb to her new place. "I just moved in. Thought I would introduce myself to my neighbor." She motioned to the door she had been knocking at.

"Oh. Ain't that nice. I'm Serena." Serena picked up a scone off the plate. She sank her teeth into the crust and then moaned in delight. "Oh my God. These are amazing. Promise me you'll make these all the time."

Faith shrugged uncertainly, wondering why she was asking. Because she lived here with North? Or was she simply a frequent guest? "I like to cook," she offered.

Serena nodded. "You moving in is a very good thing. Or bad." She laughed harshly. "My ass doesn't need to get any bigger."

From what Faith could see, Serena's ass was very nearly perfect.

"Do you live here?"

"With North?" She laughed. "No. No one lives with North. I'm just a friend. I pop in . . . you know, whenever the mood strikes. North." She chuckled again and this time the sound was throatier, as though she'd just taken a bite into a delectable piece of pie and was reveling in it. "He's always up for a good time."

Faith's cheeks burned. Serena's meaning was unmistakable. The two of them were friends with benefits. Fuck buddies or whatever.

Serena sniffed the scones again. "Maybe I'll come by even more now if you keep supplying him with baked goods."

"Oh, well." She motioned lamely at the plate. "I was just going to say hello—"

Serena's eyes glinted with amusement. "Have you seen North yet?"

Faith shook her head.

That eating-a-slice-of-fabulous-pie look came over her face again. Only this time Faith knew it had nothing to do with food and everything with this North guy. "Well, you'll be baking more scones for him once you do. Trust me."

"Why do you say that?"

"Let me do you a solid. I'll give him the scones. Tell them they're from his new neighbor. You introduce yourself to him another time." Her thick-lashed eyes swept up and down, surveying her. "Once you've done something with yourself." She whipped her finger in a small circle at Faith. "I suggest you start by losing the sweatpants. You're tall. Wear something short and show off your legs."

Faith groped for speech, shooting a quick glance down at herself in baggy sweatpants and a T-shirt. She plucked at her shirt, pulling it away from her chest. She wore a sports bra underneath, so her breasts were mashed into one nearly nonexistent uniboob.

"Don't look so offended. You'll thank me later."

Feeling embarrassed enough, Faith mumbled something incoherent and abandoned the scones to her. Whirling around, she stalked back into her duplex without another glance behind her.

Once inside, she vowed not to think about the mortifying exchange. She dove back into unpacking, determined to get the rest of her house in order, telling herself that the encounter with her neighbor's guest wasn't a reflection on him . . . necessarily. So he had vulgar friends. It didn't mean this North guy was going to be a bad neighbor. He was probably perfectly civil. Polite and courteous. The kind of guy who would loan her a shovel or hose or ladder.

After showering in her new bathroom, her contentment returned as she slid beneath the sheets of her bed. She stared up at the ceiling at the hypnotic spin of fan blades.

Her ceiling fan. Her shower. Her bed. Her home.

It had been a long time coming. Nothing could ruin this for her.

The noise started slowly. A gradual thumping . . . steady thuds against her wall. Like wood striking wood.

She sat up and cocked her head to the side, listening. She turned and stared at her headboard, her wall close behind it. It was coming from the other side. She pressed a hand to the wall, felt the vibration of every thud through the plaster and paint.

Then the moaning started.

Her face caught fire, understanding exactly what was happening.

Sex. Sex was happening on the other side of her wall. Mere feet away Serena was going at it with her neighbor. The mysterious North.

Serena's moans twisted into wails, the volume increasing with every bang against the wall. "Oh God! Oh God, oh God, oh God!"

Not just sex, Faith amended. This was down and dirty fucking. Her face burned nuclear-hot.

She dropped back on the mattress with a gust of breath. "Fabulous," she muttered. It couldn't last long, right? It had never lasted long with her and Chad. She winced. Nothing about what she was hearing next door resembled what she had with Chad.

She laced her fingers over her queasy stomach and stared up at the whirring fan blades, waiting for the racket to subside.

Minutes passed. The thumping continued.

Serena stopped crying out pleas to the Almighty and reverted to keening wails, broken up with intermittent pleas to North.

"Don't stop. Don't ever stop. North! North! NORTH!"

Faith's eyes grew so large and aching in her face that she had to force herself to blink. That tantalizing glimpse of a muscled arm and too-long dark hair flashed through her mind.

The thumping grew louder. Harder. She marveled that his headboard wasn't knocking the plaster off her wall at this point. His wall probably resembled swiss cheese.

Faith grabbed a pillow and pulled it over her head. It didn't help.

She picked up other sounds, too. Over the headboard slamming against her wall, she thought she heard the sound of bodies slapping together. Through it all, North never said a word. She never heard his voice or his cries. Unlike Serena, he was a quiet lover. She had a flash of a faceless man, naked and hard bodied, thrusting between the redhead's curvy thighs like a man possessed.

Serena was screeching like she was on the verge of death. Faith couldn't believe it. She couldn't believe a woman could be reduced to such sounds. What was this man doing that was so amazing? Every man had a penis. What made his so spectacular?

"Incredible," she muttered.

She couldn't believe she had moved next door to *this*.

She couldn't believe sex could last this long.

And she couldn't believe that *she* was starting to get turned on from it.

It was undeniable. The throb was there, deep between her legs, a pulsing beat. She pressed her thighs together, trying to kill it. She wasn't this perverse. She didn't even know what he looked like. She hadn't even heard his voice. How could she be getting aroused? How would she ever face him after this?

Because eventually she would. They were neighbors. They would eventually come face-to-face and she would have to act like she hadn't heard him hammering some woman on the other side of her wall. She moaned and rolled onto her side, still suffocating herself with her pillow.

Finally, Serena released a scream that sounded faintly like one of those jungle monkeys you hear at the zoo.

The banging stopped.

Faith lifted the pillow off her head and expelled a breath like she was the one who'd just finished a sweaty bout of marathon sex. Her thigh muscles relaxed. Her knees sagged. Her breathing eventually slowed as the night rolled in and darkness stole across her room, sliding in between her blinds like creeping hands.

Voices briefly carried through the wall, indistinguishable murmurings, and then silence fell next door. The only sound Faith heard was the rasp of her breath in the dark.

TWO

NORTH DIDN'T LINGER. He never did. He lifted himself off the bed, not sparing a glance for Serena. For now the ache, the never-ending pressure in his chest, had eased. It was only a temporary fix. He knew that, but for as long as it lasted he'd take it. When the pressure returned and work and booze weren't enough to kill it, he'd hook up with Serena or someone else. Nothing like sex to chase away the demons.

"Well, that was nice," Serena chirped, still breathless. She peeked over her shoulder at him.

Fortunately, she wasn't one of those clingy types that needed cuddling after sex. He gave a swat to her perfect ass and moved away. He knew it was more than nice. Women like Serena didn't settle for anything less. They were a lot alike. She didn't do relationships either. She was in it for the sex. A quick fuck, hard and satisfying, short on the foreplay and zero on the sweet talk.

He slid on a pair of jeans, snapping the buttons. He'd been out of prison for two years and he was doing okay. He had a job. A house. Sunday dinners at his brother's place whenever he wanted it—which wasn't as often as Knox would like. There was only so much marital bliss North could witness between Knox and Briar without feeling nauseous. He forced himself to go occasionally just so Knox wouldn't show up on his porch determined to play big brother.

"You should try one of those scones I left on the kitchen table," Serena suggested behind him.

"Scones?" He glanced back at her. She was wrapped up in his sheets like some artfully arranged centerfold. He wasn't dumb enough to think she was posing like that, one knee bent halfway to her chest and a generous hip thrust out, accidentally.

"Yeah, chocolate chip."

"You baked? Never pegged you for much of a cook."

His brother's wife cooked. Last time he'd visited them out at the farm, she'd baked a chocolate pecan pie that could make a grown man cry. Briar Davis—correction, Briar Callaghan—was a fucking girl scout. She was a nurse, a great cook, and even though he wasn't supposed to notice it, she had a nice rack. Oh, and she loved his brother. The same guy who went to prison with him . . . whose hands were as bloodstained as North's.

Knox had been there with him at Devil's Rock. Except for those last four years. Then it had just been North. Alone. That was the difference.

Apparently, those four years made all the difference.

Knox was able to have a normal life with chocolate pecan pie and a wife.

Four additional years at the Rock made North fit only for booze and meaningless fucks.

Serena pouted. "Maybe you don't know everything about me, North Callaghan."

He looked her over appraisingly. "I think I know you pretty well."

"Just because we've gone to school together since kindergarten."

"We took Home Ec together freshman year," he reminded her. "You almost burned down the classroom when you tried to cook a quesadilla."

"Oh my God." She giggled. "I forgot about that. Well, I've learned a few things since then."

He scanned the luscious swell of her backside. In high school, she had been a tease. No guy got in her pants, but she'd enjoyed fooling around and tying them up in knots. Quite different from the girl she was now who worked four nights a week at Joe's Cabaret.

"I know you have," he admitted. They had all learned a few things since high school. In his case, nothing good.

She stared at him for a long moment and he was pretty certain she was thinking about how much they had both changed. She worked as an exotic dancer. He was a hardened felon—a far cry from the clean-cut kid he used to be. Tatted, scarred up, hair too long, his body a honed weapon, he bore little resemblance to the guy who'd sat across from her in Home Ec. Not only did he know how to take a beating, he knew how to give one.

He knew how to kill.

He slammed a heavy metal door shut on those thoughts. He'd just gotten laid. He didn't want to lose his after-sex buzz by traipsing down memory lane.

"I'm gonna go work out back," he said, tugging on his shoes, already done with this conversation and craving his space. Solitude. It was a downside to having sex. Sometimes they wanted to chat afterward.

Indifferent to his announcement, Serena continued, "Your *new* neighbor baked the scones."

"Huh," he replied noncommittally. He'd noticed the car in the driveway. He knew the place had been sold. The FOR SALE sign had come down a week ago. The duplex next door had been vacant almost three months after the old man who lived there moved in with his son's family. Various Realtors had traipsed in and out of the house with prospective buyers in that time. He'd stopped paying attention.

The last thing he needed was a nosy neighbor bringing him baked goods.

Serena stood, indifferent to her nudity. "She seems like a nice lady." She held his stare.

He shrugged.

She rolled her eyes. "She *is* your neighbor. You might want to introduce yourself."

"What for?"

"It's called civilized behavior."

He laughed once. A harsh bark. "Does that sound like me? Civilized?"

She stepped forward and patted her fingers against his chest. "No, darling. That's why I come to you. Nice men . . . well, they don't fuck like you do." She sighed. "Pity."

He reached for her hips and hauled her against him. She was talking too much. Words he didn't want or need to hear. If she was going to stay, she was going to have to shut up.

She continued, "Sometimes, whether you like it or not, you have to engage with other people. You have to speak to other people."

"I talk when I need to."

She smiled crookedly. "Sure you do." She sighed and shook her head with an air of defeat. Which was just as well. She didn't want to fix him. She liked him just the way he was. Always up for a good time between the sheets. "You should meet her."

Nice. He didn't do nice. He didn't have *nice* in his life. It wasn't that he didn't want it. He just wouldn't know what to do with it if he had it. For the majority of his life, he had been swimming in shit.

He reached for the shirt he'd tossed on the recliner in the corner of his room and pulled it over his head. "Let yourself out."

"I always do." Rolling her eyes, she sighed. "I guess this is my cue to go."

He shrugged. "I didn't say you had to go."

"Didn't you?" She slipped on her underwear and hooked on her bra. "You know someday I'm gonna get offended at your wham-bam-thank-you-ma'am attitude." She grabbed her T-shirt. "Fortunately for you, I just want you for your body." Reaching between them, she fondled his dick. "And for what you can do with this." Grinning, she stepped back and finished getting dressed.

"Really?" he smirked. "Someday?"

She sniffed and rubbed under her eyes, where her mascara had smeared. "Not today apparently."

"Night, Serena." He turned to leave the bedroom.

Her voice stopped him. "You should come by the club. My friend Marcy was asking about you."

"Marcy?" he asked blankly.

"Yeah. The other redhead. The fake one." She tossed her mane of red hair proudly. "She said she'd like to be on your list."

North winced. He didn't like it when Serena referenced his "list" like he actually kept a running catalog of women on hand to access when he needed a quick fuck.

Don't you?

He only ever did one-night stands. It was never messy that way. No one became entangled. Occasionally, those one-night stands were repeated. As with Serena. Sleeping with the same woman was sometimes convenient.

Turning, he passed through his bedroom door. Serena followed him down the stairs. She slipped on her high heels where she'd kicked them off near his kitchen table and motioned to the plate of scones.

"You should try one. They're amazing."

Homemade scones. So fucking domestic.

He stared at the plate. He owned a few dishes, but he usually ate off paper plates that he bought in bulk. He didn't own a plate like this—cream colored with tiny little flowers edging the border. Briar would own plates like these. His brother would eat off a plate like this. Knox could pretend he was someone else. That he'd never been kept inside a cage.

Not North.

She sighed. "Fine. Be stubborn."

He didn't look up from the plate as Serena pressed a kiss to his lips and slipped out of his house. He heard her car door slam in the night. The engine started and faded away. He began to turn, intending to head out back to his welding shop, but then he was spinning around. He had plenty of work to finish—his own freelance and custom pieces he was hired to do for the garage where he worked—but first he had to deal with this. He snatched up the plate and pulled open the front door.

He stalked across the shared front porch. The

light was on and he could see there was already a welcome mat in front of the door. *Of course.*

Bending, he set the plate with the three remaining scones on the mat.

He didn't want to make nice with his new neighbor. He didn't want homemade scones. He wasn't that man. His time at Devil's Rock had seen to that. Twelve years turned men into animals, and he was nothing less than a fucking brute. Scarred inside and out.

Two years free on the outside didn't erase that. Nothing could be undone. Nothing was ever erased.

He knew it. He wouldn't pretend otherwise.

He couldn't if he wanted to.

SHE WAS STILL awake when she heard the back door open and slam shut next door. The slam reverberated for moments, traveling into the bones of her house. It was strange that she was connected to another person like this, sharing and sleeping within one actual structure, only a wall dividing them. And yet they hadn't met yet. She didn't even fully know what he looked like. *Just the sound of him fucking.*

She bounded from her bed and made it to her bedroom window in two strides. She peered through the blinds, craning her neck to get a better view of the figure striding across the backyard.

It was him. North Callaghan. The guy who had just made a woman scream like a porn star. She shifted in place on her feet, suddenly feeling itchy inside her own skin as she observed the way his jeans hung low on his hips . . . the denim hugging his ass perfectly. Her already alert girl parts clenched.

From her position at the second-floor window, she could see into both her yard and the neighbor's, a fact she had noticed when she initially viewed the property. A work shed of some sort sat at the far back of his yard.

Usually the double doors were shut, but tonight they stood open, revealing various tools, machinery and equipment inside.

She sighed as he disappeared into the shed. Out of sight, out of mind. Well, not exactly out of mind. She was standing rooted to the spot, still staring after him like he was the hot lifeguard at the community pool the summer she turned thirteen.

God. She was hard up if the sight of a man's back got her this flustered.

Yes, she wanted to date and meet Mr. Right, but maybe she should focus a little less on finding her forever guy and more on Mr. Right Now.

Would hot, meaningless sex be so wrong? How

hard could it be to get laid? She knew the thought would traumatize her father and brothers. But wasn't that why she wanted her own place? To lead her own life without interference or judgment from her family?

The privacy and freedom to do whatever she wanted—*who*ever she wanted.

It was something to consider.

Lights sparked and flared from inside the shed, spitting out into the night. It sounded like a blowtorch. Maybe he was welding? She wasn't exactly sure about stuff like that. She'd grown up around guys. Changing the oil in her car, mowing the yard. Anything mechanical. Her dad and brothers handled that. Guy stuff might have rubbed off on other girls, but not Faith. Those things never interested her. She'd stayed inside in the air-conditioning and read her books and watched *Barefoot Contessa*.

Turning from the window, she moved and sank back onto her bed. Sliding under the covers, she listened to the distant sounds of a welding torch. It wasn't nearly as distracting as the sounds of sex. It was almost pleasant. Like white noise to lull her to sleep.

She pulled the pillow to her chest and tucked it between her legs. White noise or not, her mind drifted back to him. To the sounds of him having sex.

She jammed her eyes shut. So the walls were thin. Serena wasn't a girlfriend. By her own admission, she had told Faith that. Tonight wouldn't be a daily occurrence. So loud sex would only happen sometimes. Occasionally. She'd deal with it. Having a place of her own, her first home, still outweighed the annoyance.

Rolling on her side, she prayed for sleep to come.

THREE

*F*AITH WAS RUNNING late. It hadn't been as easy as she hoped to fall asleep last night. Even with her eyes closed, images flickered across her eyelids of Serena with the hard-bodied, faceless North Callaghan.

Not at all how she imagined spending her first night in her new house.

She winced as she stubbed her toe on a box coming out of her closet. Tonight's order of business? Finish unpacking.

Of course, she could chalk it all up to the fact that it was Monday. It was cliché, but true. She was never very good the first day of the workweek. She barely had time to apply a quick coat of mascara and lipstick and cover up the pimple on her chin before getting dressed and shoveling a Pop-Tart into her bag to eat on the drive to work.

She swung her satchel over her shoulder and then secured the lid on her coffee mug before she scalded herself with hot coffee. That would be the perfect way to round out her morning. Snatching her keys off the table, she opened the front door and stepped outside into the already muggy morning.

Crack.

She glanced down.

"What on earth . . ." Crumbled bits of chocolate chip scones littered the ground alongside the cracked remnants of her plate. Aside from the scone Serena had eaten, it appeared as though all three were accounted for.

And her plate was broken!

She snapped her gaze to glare at his door. What kind of neighbor returned a plateful of scones?

"Jerk," she muttered.

After stepping back inside her house, she dropped her stuff onto a kitchen chair and snatched up a roll of paper towels to gather the mess.

Squatting, and now certain she would be late for work, she started picking up pieces of plate and scone, noticing the ants swarming her mat. At least someone enjoyed the fruits of her labor.

As far as she was concerned, this said it all. She and North Callaghan were never going to be all warm and fuzzy borrow-a-cup-of-sugar neighbors.

The most she could hope for at this point was that they could stay out of each other's way. She ripped off more paper towels with a vengeance.

When they did cross paths, hopefully they could act civil. She was accustomed to coping with difficult personalities at work, after all. This would be no different than that. And really, how often would she have to see the guy anyway?

NORTH SWUNG BY Joe's Cabaret on his way home from work. Not because he was especially into hanging out at strip clubs, but because he'd made a promise.

Joe was a middle-aged man with a gland problem. That could be the only explanation for his perpetual sweating.

North had spent twelve years at Devil's Rock, smack in the middle of West Texas. The summers were brutal and inmates spent a good amount of time out in the yard. That said, North had never seen anyone sweat like this poor bastard.

Joe reigned over his establishment like a cock ruling the roost, and despite the blast of air-conditioning, sweat stains bled through the cotton fabric of his polo. His office was located near the back door, a large glass window allowing him to look out over the seedy business of his club. Calling it a cabaret, as though it were some classy establishment with highly choreographed music and dance routines, was wishful thinking on his part. He would stand at his glass window, mopping his brow with a handkerchief. According to Serena, he was an adequate boss. Fair. He never made the girls do anything they didn't want to do. That was important. He needed to know that. For Piper's sake.

He inhaled and then regretted it as the stink of the place assailed him. Stale body odor and the sickly sweet smell of the fog machine.

North was most assuredly flawed, but he'd made a promise, and his word was all he'd had for so long. When he was without a home, family— freedom—he'd just had his word. His fists. And the allies he had formed in prison.

Cruz Walsh had been one of the few he could call friend after Knox and Reid left him. He'd stood with North when others circled him, sniffing out his sudden vulnerability. North owed him, and he wouldn't break his vow to him even though two years had passed.

He stepped deeper into the dim confines of Joe's. Only two areas were lit—the bar and stage. It was purely for purposes of profit. You had to see the booze and the girls. More conducive for customers to give up their hard-earned cash that way.

A few of the waitresses greeted him, recognizing him from previous visits. He might even have slept with a few. He couldn't be sure. When he first got out, those days were a blur.

It was a Wednesday night, but you wouldn't know it. The chairs edging the stage were full. Construction workers and suits alike were salivating over the dancer dressed like Little Red Riding Hood. All that remained of her costume was the red cape and basket she swung provocatively as she strutted down the stage in a pair of fuck-me red stilettos.

He hadn't noticed her before, but her eyes zeroed in on him standing at the edge of men circling the stage. Her hands swept over her belly and up to fondle her breasts, her eyes all the while fixed on him.

"North!"

He turned at the sound of his name. Piper rushed forward, balancing a tray of drinks with one hand. She stood on her tiptoes to hug him. Even in her high heels, she was a tiny thing. Nothing like her big bruiser of a brother.

"How are you?" she asked.

He nodded. "Good."

"Haven't seen you in a while." She looked up

at him with a sunny smile. "Not that I blame you. You could do a lot better than hang around this place." She shot a glance around with a sniff.

Her reminder stabbed at him. He hadn't been in Joe's in a while. When he first got out of prison, not a week passed that he didn't pop in to check on her—and threaten any bastard that looked at her wrong or got too handsy.

She'd resented his presence at first, insisting she didn't need looking after, insisting it was going to cut into her tips, but she soon realized that his glaring persona contributed to even better tips. She stopped complaining at that point. She needed the money too badly. For herself and her sister.

"Been working a lot."

"Mm-hm." She propped a hand on her hip. "Serena loves to share that she sees you plenty outside these walls. Makes the other girls jealous."

"I see her occasionally," he allowed with a shrug.

"Uh-huh." She nodded at the table closest to him. "You staying for a bit? Want me to get you a drink? The usual?"

"Sure." He nodded.

"Serena's not on tonight, but Little Red Riding Hood is totally giving you the eye."

He sent the dancer a quick glance. "I came here to check on you. I didn't come for that."

She shook her head with a chuckle. "No, you never come here for that, but funny how you always seem to find it."

Still laughing, she walked away, weaving between tables. He glanced back to the stage. Red was definitely giving him a solid fuck-me stare, and not just because it was part of her job. He knew *that* look and he knew the real thing. This was the real thing.

Piper returned soon with his beer. "Place is pretty busy tonight or I'd stay and chat."

He lifted the beer in salute. "I understand. How's your sister?"

"Good. Doing great in school. On a soccer team now."

A smile tugged at the corner of his mouth as he imagined Piper's fourteen-year-old sister tearing up the soccer field. Like Piper, she was a little thing, but also like Piper, she had spunk. "Glad to hear that. Cruz must love that."

Her smile dimmed a little as she said with a little less conviction, "You know it."

"Piper!" The bartender shouted her name and pointed a table waving for a waitress.

"Gotta go. You should text me and come by for dinner."

He nodded. "Will do." Except he wouldn't.

Rare were the occasions he ate dinner with the Walsh sisters. It was just like when he took dinner with Knox and Briar. Sitting at a table, sharing stories, acting civilized, laughing . . . it wasn't easy for him.

The blonde finished her dance as the music ended. A new song kicked on. She exited the stage, but not before sending him another smile over her shoulder, this one full of promise. Settling back in his chair, he watched Piper work, making sure no one got too fresh with her. Several of the customers felt his stare and sent him wary glances, probably assuming that Piper belonged to him. He let them think that. Their relationship wasn't anyone's business. She was Cruz's sister. That made her like a sister to him, too. Almost like Katie.

At the thought of his cousin everything went cold inside him. The twisting mass in his chest pushed harder, making his lungs constrict, air difficult to draw in and out. His grip tightened around his beer bottle.

"Hey, there." Little Red Riding Hood dropped down in the chair opposite of him, bringing with her a sour waft of nicotine. "I get off in an hour."

His fingers lifted and flexed around the sweating glass of his bottle and he deliberately chose not to think about how kissing her would taste like an ashtray. He wasn't particular. He wasn't looking for anything—*anyone*—permanent. "Ten."

"Ten?" She cocked her bleached blond head to the side as though she wasn't familiar with the number.

He leaned forward, balancing his elbows on the table. "I'm leaving this place in ten minutes." He lifted his beer and gave it a little slosh side to side. "The time it takes to finish this beer. Either you leave with me." He shrugged. "Or you don't."

She stared at him, a slow smile curving her lips. "I'll go get my things. I suddenly think you're worth any dock in pay I get."

She hurried from the table. He watched her go. His only concern was in lightening that pressure in his chest so that he could breathe easier again.

HOLDING BAGS OF groceries, Faith kicked the door shut with one foot and rushed to set them down on the counter before she dropped them on the floor. Her favorite hot sauce was in a glass jar at the bottom of one of the bags and she didn't want it to crash everywhere.

It was her third night in her new house. She'd yet to meet her neighbor, although there was evidence aplenty of him. Twice now she'd returned home to find her spot in the driveway already occupied with his bike. She'd had to park on the street. She understood if he'd felt free to use her portion of the driveway while the house was vacant, but it was occupied now. It was occupied and he knew it, which only seemed to further signify that North Callaghan was an ass.

Today had been a good day at work as far as days went. She'd checked in on some of her cases and the children were doing well. They were safe and thriving. She didn't have to remove anyone from an abusive or neglectful environment. She didn't have to sit through a tedious court hearing.

And Brendan Cooper had finally asked her out. Wendy, who sat in the cubicle beside hers, had insisted he was going to, but Faith had her doubts. She couldn't help thinking that moving into her own house had brought her a little luck. They'd worked in proximity for over a year, after all. It took him this long to ask her out.

Deciding to treat herself, she fished her phone out from her bag and ordered chow mein from her favorite Chinese place. And what the hell. She ordered a side of egg rolls and crab rangoons, too. She'd go to the gym tomorrow. As much as she hated it, she dragged herself there a couple times a week.

She'd met Brendan several times at the court-

house over the better part of a year. Even Hale
knew him and had nothing but good things to say
about him, which was something, since Brendan
was a criminal defense attorney. She'd noticed
him right away because he was one of the only attorneys without gray hair—or rather *with* hair—
wandering through the halls of the courthouse.

She kicked off her shoes and started putting
away her groceries with a goofy smile on her face.
He said he'd call her to make the arrangements,
but they'd both agreed on this Saturday.

The other night she might have rashly decided to
have meaningless sex rather than keep waiting for
Mr. Right. Madness. Clearly. Mr. Right might be
closer than she thought. She shouldn't give up on
her dreams because her ears—and other parts—
had been burning up from the sounds of wild sex.
She could have both. Wild sex and Mr. Right. She
wouldn't give up.

After stacking her last Greek yogurt on the top
shelf, she closed the door. She'd meant to get to the
store yesterday, but she'd had to conduct a home
visitation that ran late. She hadn't gotten home
until after seven. At least now she had food for
breakfast.

The doorbell rang as she turned for the stairs,
intending to get out of her work clothes and into

something more comfortable, preferably with an elastic waistband, for the night.

She opened the front door to the already dark night and accepted the piping hot bags of Chinese food, then paid the deliveryman. After shutting the door, she set the bags on her coffee table. Skipping up the steps to her bedroom, she hummed lightly under her breath. She stripped off her blazer and hung it back up in her closet. She tossed her blouse and slacks into her laundry hamper and slid on a pair of well-worn yoga pants followed by a T-shirt.

Faith snatched up a hair band from where she had discarded it on her nightstand and pulled her hair up into a messy ponytail. She started out of her bedroom door, her steps light and happy. She had a date on Saturday night and Chinese food waiting downstairs. Life was good.

Until it started again.

No, not *it*. Him.

He was at it again.

She twisted her neck around to scowl at her bedroom wall where her neighbor's headboard was slamming with a vengeance. *Again*.

"Oh, c'mon. Seriously?" she muttered, turning to glare at her bedroom wall. Propping a hand against her headboard, she pounded on her wall with the side of her fist. It didn't seem to matter.

The activity on the other side of her wall didn't subside.

It hadn't even been a full three days. For heaven's sake, it was a Wednesday night. Then she winced, realizing how very *old* she sounded. As though sex could *only* happen on weekends at a designated time in the evening. Was it Serena? Was she back again or was it someone else?

Almost in answer to her thought, she heard a woman's moans. Different than before. More whimpery. It wasn't Serena this time. Faith had that sound etched in her ears.

She shook her head. The guy must have a revolving bedroom door. She glanced at her bedside clock. It wasn't even eight o'clock. This couldn't be a regular occurrence. Please, no. That would be awful and . . . uncomfortable.

Uncomfortable?

Yes. Merely uncomfortable. Not bothered. *Not* hot and bothered.

One thing was for certain . . . it was time to meet her neighbor. Maybe if he realized her bedroom was on the opposite side of his, he would exhibit a little more restraint, because this was just ridiculous.

She toyed with the idea of knocking on his door, but given his current activity that seemed destined for awkwardness. Clearly, they needed to meet, but not tonight.

Tomorrow, she would descend on him. Turning, she fled her room as the sounds grew louder. She took refuge on her first floor, relieved she could no longer hear the activity next door nearly so well.

Tomorrow would be soon enough.

FOUR

*T*HE FOLLOWING DAY, Faith stepped outside into the early-morning light and observed North Callaghan's truck in its usual place—and his bike inching over onto *her* side of the driveway. The guy knew no boundaries. Annoyance punched her in the chest. *Just another point of contention to be discussed.*

She swung her gaze to glare at his door for a long moment in the already humid morning. The cicadas' song congested the air as the moment stretched. She plucked at her silk blouse to keep it from sticking to her skin. Pencil skirt. Fancy blouse. Heels. Today she'd gone all out. She had to testify in court and had dressed for the occasion. There was also the chance she might run into Brendan.

She continued to glare at that door. At this early

hour, she didn't know if his guest was still visiting or had left sometime in the night. There was no strange car parked along the street, but that didn't mean anything. Perhaps North Callaghan drove her home—or not.

Last night, she'd eaten her chow mein downstairs and watched *Chopped* at full volume, but that didn't stop the faint sounds of opera sex from trickling down and attacking her ears. Honestly, she didn't know how many more nights like that she could endure.

Seized with sudden impulse, she dove back inside her house. In her kitchen, she scrawled a quick note on a piece of paper. Finished, she stared at it for a moment, making certain it said everything she wanted it to say.

We need to talk at your earliest convenience.
Faith Walters, your next-door neighbor (833-555-1201)

Polite. Succinct.

Nodding to herself, she swung her purse and satchel back over her shoulder and exited her house, heels clicking on the concrete. On her way to her car, she stopped and stuck the paper between the windshield wipers of his truck. Feeling pleased with herself, she dusted her hands and climbed inside her car.

Now she only had to wait.

Once in her car, she went straight to the courthouse. It was only a fifteen-minute drive from the outskirts of Sweet Hill to the city's small downtown area. Fortunately, she was the first witness called in to the custody hearing over eight-year-old Noah Grimes. Faith had worked his case upon moving back to Sweet Hill after grad school. The parents, in and out of jail for various drug charges, had failed to send him to school—despite all their promises. A bus picked up within walking distance of their home, so that wasn't an issue. He should be in the second grade by now, but he was at a kindergarten reading level. He knew his alphabet and a few common sight words. That was it. No more. His math ability was deficient as well.

In addition to the truancy matter, prior to removing him from his family Faith had noticed he looked thin. Too thin. When she offered him a granola bar, he'd eaten it without taking a breath. The boy's maternal grandparents were applying for custody and had already been vetted as appropriate guardians. They were loving grandparents who had effectively lost their daughter years ago to her drug addiction and just wanted to save their grandson.

They sat in the courtroom now, solemn-eyed and attentive to the proceedings. After delivering her testimony, Faith stepped down from the witness stand. She mentally sighed as Noah's mother buried her face in her hands and wept. They were always sorry. Always remorseful. Her husband, a tall, cadaverous-looking man whom Faith knew to be twenty-eight but looked more like thirty-eight, pushed up abruptly from the table where he sat. The action sent his chair banging to the floor.

His attorney placed a restraining hand on his arm but it did no good. His eyes bulged as he stabbed a finger in Faith's direction. "You got it wrong! You don't know nothing, bitch! I'm a good father! You did this, you stupid bitch!"

The judge banged on her gavel, calling for order. Court officers swarmed him. Faith hurried from the courtroom, shooting a quick, encouraging smile at Noah's grandparents. Mr. Grimes wasn't the first angry parent she'd ever encountered. She knew better than to take it personally. At the end of the day, when she looked in the mirror, she could take comfort in the fact that little Noah was living in a safe and loving home. That fact made suffering one asshole parent bearable.

She left the courthouse and was back at the office by 10 A.M. Unfortunately, she hadn't come into contact with Brendan at the courthouse, so the special care she had taken with her wardrobe and hair for his sake turned out to be a waste of time.

She spent a little over an hour answering emails and catching up on work before Wendy popped her head inside her cubicle. "Hey, let's go get some lunch."

"I've got an interview at Washington Elementary at two—"

"Plenty of time. Frank's right outside."

Faith reached inside her drawer and grabbed her purse. "Well, why didn't you say so?"

One of Sweet Hill's favorite taco trucks was parked outside the building. She was surprised she hadn't noticed everyone stampeding outside. CPS shared office space with several other government entities.

There was always a bit of guessing where Frank's would be from day to day. It was early yet. They were lucky that the line wasn't too long.

"So?" Wendy asked as they sat side by side on a concrete bench eating their tacos. "Excited for your hot date Saturday?"

She chewed her last bite of pulled-pork-and-pineapple-slaw taco, covering her stuffed mouth with her fingers. She nodded assent.

"Brendan Cooper." Wendy whistled. "Girl, he's a catch."

Faith nodded, finally swallowing her bite. "I know. I've been hoping he would ask me out for a long time."

"Well, c'mon. It's not easy for any guy in this town to get up the nerve to approach you."

"What do you mean?"

"Your dad is the retired sheriff. Your brother is scary as all get-out and he's the *new* sheriff. Your other brother is like a flippin' Green Beret."

"Army Ranger," she corrected, using a napkin to wipe at her lips.

"Whatever. Not much distinction. He can still kill a man with his bare hands."

She nodded. "This is true." Hale, for that matter, could do the same. He'd served in the Army as well, before returning home to work with Dad.

It was the same song and dance from when she was a teenager. She thought it didn't matter so much anymore. She thought that any man worth his salt wouldn't be so intimidated. Not if he really liked her. At least that's what she always told herself.

"So. Where are you and Brendan going?"

"I don't know. He texted me this morning to ask where I would like to go to dinner."

"Oooh. I hope you said someplace really good. Like Ruby's Steakhouse," she suggested, naming the expensive restaurant

Faith toyed with the edge of her taco. "Not sure if I want to eat an enormous steak dinner on our first date."

"Oh, that's right. You wouldn't want to feel stuffed and bloated if you get naked."

She snorted. "I think you forgot a key phrase there. First date."

Wendy stared at her with wide, solemn eyes. "You never know. You haven't been on a date in a good while and he's a good-looking man. He might make a move. Just saying . . . you better be sure to shave above the knee."

She tried not to let Wendy's words fluster her as she went back to work. She wanted a relationship. She wanted love . . . and sex. Now there was a prospect of that on the horizon. She should be thrilled. She *was*.

She blamed it on this clash with her neighbor. It hung over her like a thundercloud. Hopefully by the end of the day all this could be sorted out and put behind her. Maybe even by the time she got home, he would have read her note and be ready to clear the air between them.

HE FOUND THE note on his windshield.

It was midmorning. He wasn't clocking in at work until one o'clock today.

He exited his backyard through his side fence, carrying the large copper-and-aluminum sculpture he needed to deliver to Dr. Perry, a local dentist who'd hired North to create a piece for the waiting area of his office. He existed primarily on his salary from the garage, but his freelance work was gaining momentum and starting to bring in a nice bit of income. His reputation was growing. Three months ago he'd created a sculpture for an agent in Nashville, so word was getting around. A year ago he'd developed a website featuring his work and he received a steady amount of inquiries. It kept him busy. Busy was good. Kept his mind from thinking too much, from going places he didn't want it to go.

Grunting, he lifted the heavy piece into the back of his truck, managing not to wrench his back, when he noticed the paper stuck there, fluttering in the barest breeze. Grabbing it, he read the note on some kind of soft green stationery.

At your earliest convenience . . .

So fucking proper. Only a woman who baked
scones would use such a phrase.

Faith. Even her damn name was proper. She was
probably old and matronly . . . living with a bunch
of cats and scones. That's probably what she fed
her cats. Her day-old scones.

He was sure she had some gripe or complaint.
Why else would she have left a note on his windshield? He speculated for a moment, wondering
what had prompted the request. He kept to himself. He wasn't particularly loud. Unless—

Ahh. Red. The dancer from last night. He wasn't
loud, but she, on the other hand . . . she had been
very loud.

The minute they'd finished he had regretted
bringing her back home with him. Even if it took
the edge off, he just wanted to take a shower and
go to bed. *Alone.*

He wasn't much into kissing. Kissing was too
personal and he didn't want that kind of intimacy
from the women he took to bed. He just wanted a
quick release.

That said, women always wanted kissing, so he
did his part and gave them one or two at the beginning. Red had tasted like the ashtray he'd pre-
dicted and her whimpers reminded him of a kicked

puppy. Her speaking voice wasn't much better. It was nasal and overly loud. He was relieved when she didn't stick around and he didn't have to be the asshole and ask her to leave. The worst was when they wanted to cuddle. Things really got awkward then.

He glanced down at the note again, staring at the looping handwriting. It was pretty. Elegant. Nothing like his chicken scratch. It made him wonder. Holding the note in his hand, he wondered at the scone-baking woman who wrote it. He looked over at her duplex—sharing a wall with his own. He winced. Naturally she had heard him banging some woman whose name he didn't even know.

Damn it. He guessed he had to talk to her. Later.

For now, he hopped in his truck and dropped off the sculpture. He was gratified at how pleased Dr. Perry was with it. He loved the piece and assured North he would have more work for him again soon. He also told him that he had even recommended North to one of his friends who wanted a smoke pit for his backyard.

Feeling pleased with himself, North headed to the garage and spent the rest of the day working on the custom bikes awaiting his attention there.

By 5 P.M. he called it quits and headed home.

He slowed as he turned onto his street. Both

driveways were empty. Apparently he had time to take a shower and get the stink off him before he knocked on Faith Walters's door. At least he then wouldn't offend the proper Miss Walters with his smell.

He took his time, showering for a long while, letting the warm water spray over his body. He never got tired of having his own shower. No water shutting off when the allotted time was up. No COs, no other inmates. The privacy meant never having to watch his back.

When he finished he grabbed a towel and chafed his head with it, rubbing the long strands of his hair dry. Walking from the bathroom, he noticed a message on his phone. He pushed play, then grimaced at the sound of his brother's voice inviting him to dinner. Again. He was overdue. He'd have to stop dodging him and go soon.

After setting the phone down, he peered out the blinds of his front living room window and stilled at the sight of Faith Walters's familiar car pulling into the driveway. The day's fading sun hit her windshield, making it difficult to see within. He could only make out that someone sat behind the wheel. A smudge of a shape. No distinguishable face. No features.

He waited, a strange anxious energy filling him

as the door swung open. Time crawled as he leaned forward slightly. He held his breath, dragging a hand over the faint stubble on his jaw as Faith Walters emerged, her face obscured. She was talking on her phone, her face tucked awkwardly into her shoulder to keep the phone from falling to the concrete. Even as concealed as she was, he could tell she was young. Not the matronly type he had assumed.

The sleek fall of her hair concealed the side of her face that was facing him. He couldn't make out any of her features.

Her hands were full, carrying a purse, briefcase bag and coffee mug.

Frustration rolled up in him. *Turn. Look at me.*

Not getting his way, he shifted his perusal to the rest of her. She was tall and slender, wearing one of those high-waisted snug skirts that stopped just past her knees, with a blouse tucked in. The blouse's pale fabric was shimmery, the kind that would get snagged on his callused palms.

He'd had his share of spinners, but it wasn't what he preferred reaching for in the middle of the night. He was big, and he didn't like the feeling, irrational or not, that he might break a woman. This one looked just right. Perfect. She looked like she would fit him.

His cousin had been a small girl. Petite. His hands curled into fists at his sides as memories of Katie flooded him. He tried not to think about her. Ever.

He tried not to think about how that bastard had *enjoyed* breaking her and then bragged about it to all his friends. He tried not to remember how he and Knox had made him pay for that.

North shook his head. He didn't *want* to think about her. He wanted to forget.

He refocused on his neighbor.

She wasn't very well-endowed, but her blouse draped over her slight breasts like a lover's hand, and his palms tingled, itching to mold their shape.

She carried herself toward her door, her high heels clicking over the concrete as she talked on her phone. Even without her heels, she would be tall. He wouldn't have to bend down very far to claim her mouth. Her long legs would wrap around him and anchor him nicely.

Her shoes were sexy as fuck—nude, a shade darker than her legs. He imagined gripping those heels, flinging them over his shoulders as he wedged himself between her thighs. He would slide his hands along that infinite stretch of skin as he drove inside her.

Obviously he had been with all body types. When

he first got paroled he couldn't get enough sex. Any-where, any woman, he was down for it. Women and good barbecue. For the first few months he indulged himself in both at every opportunity. He had twelve years to make up for, after all. Twelve years of jack-ing off and eating crap food on a tray. Understand-ably, he gorged himself.

Except lately his appetite had been tapering off. Instead of sex every night, once a week was enough. Same went for barbecue. Although a brisket sand-wich sounded good tonight. Staring at those legs through the blinds, he decided getting laid didn't sound too bad either.

His gaze skimmed the long lines of Faith Wal-ters. He felt his cock stir. It wanted. Without even seeing her face, it wanted her. Her body was built for taking everything a man could give and giving it back.

He stopped abruptly at the thought, killing it. He didn't need to be thinking this way. He didn't want to be thinking this way. Not about her. There were other women out there to fuck. He needed to forget about this one.

He glanced down. Too bad his body wasn't of the same school of thought.

He still hadn't dressed. His cock jutted out, hard

and aching, the head flushed a hungry reddish hue. All for a woman whose face he hadn't even seen.

Once upon a time, he could have been with a girl like her. He'd applied to a half-dozen colleges and planned to attend Texas A&M alongside Knox, who was there in his second year. Their lives took a different turn, however, the night they went after Mason Leary.

Now, a woman like her wouldn't so much as touch him. He scoffed. She wanted to talk to him *at his earliest convenience*. He shook his head. Fuck that.

He avoided trouble. Ever since he'd been paroled he had managed to stay out of trouble, and he intended to keep it that way.

Granted, his impulse control was low when it came to women, but he hadn't broken any laws. No, it was simply fucking—trouble of a different sort, but the good it did him, the need it served when he slaked his lust in a woman's body, far outweighed any risk he courted.

Suddenly the idea of meeting her was a sour concept.

He didn't want to exchange niceties. Some sixth sense told him to avoid her, and he had long ago learned to trust his instincts.

She was his neighbor, so it wouldn't be an easy matter to escape her. She was proper . . . what Uncle Mac would have called a lady. She was the type that would want to cuddle with any man to warm her bed.

His partners were women into casual sex. Women that didn't mind shacking up with a former con. One look at this female told him that she would *very* much mind that. There was nothing *casual* about her. She probably only ever fucked tax attorneys and men who played golf on Sunday afternoons—oh, and it wasn't fucking for her. It was making love.

Turning from the window, he grabbed a beer out of his fridge and marched upstairs to get dressed, deciding he would forget all about her.

He rubbed at the center of his chest where the dull, twisting ache was flaring up again. It was his earlier thought of Katie. It chased him like a fog that would never fully fade.

His cousin was dead and it was partly his fault. He knew he wasn't to blame for her attack, but what he'd done afterward to Mason Leary . . . yeah, he was responsible for that. Killing Leary hadn't been right. He knew that now. Not that he and Knox had set out to kill the bastard. They'd wanted him to admit what he'd done to Katie, but things had gotten out of hand. Especially once Leary started mouthing off and calling Katie dirty names.

Killing Leary wasn't what Katie needed to heal. She had needed North and Knox to be around to support her. She needed them to *not* go to prison.

North had been closest in age to his cousin. She'd talked to him about everything. Confided in him. He still remembered when she had told him about her upcoming date with Mason Leary. She had been so excited, and he'd been happy for her. She'd tried on and modeled her outfits in front of him that night. They had both agreed that the blue shirtdress with boots was the way to go. The old familiar bile rose up in his throat when he remembered the state of that dress after Leary was finished with her.

North and Katie had a special bond, and he'd turned his back on her—*abandoned* her—when he and Knox got arrested.

The last thing she'd needed to hear was a judge pronounce them guilty for manslaughter and sentence them to prison. It had been the final cut. The thing that pushed her over the edge. As wrong as he was for taking Leary's life . . . his greatest crime was what he had done to Katie.

A heavy sigh pushed out past his lips. As for Faith Walters, he needed to forget about her—

pretend as though that house was still vacant and continue on with his life as usual.

Stopping, he stared at himself in front of his dresser mirror for a long moment—and did the exact opposite of that. He thought about his neighbor.

His cock was hard, the skin still flushed an angry red, tight and pulsing with hunger. Before he could quite think about what he was doing—or why—he wrapped a hand around himself. Lowering himself on the bed, he sank onto his back and pumped his dick, working it almost savagely from the base to the head, desperate for release . . . for something to take the edge off.

His eyes drifted shut and the image that rose in his mind was of a sleek body in an ass-hugging skirt. Long legs propped up on nude-colored heels. He saw all of that as he fisted himself. Thinking about her wasn't hurting anything. It was simply a convenient image that got him off. That was all.

That was it.

He closed his eyes, feeling a flash of frustration at the vagueness of her face in his mind's eye. He could envision parting those thighs well enough, but when he reached for her face, he had nothing. He went back to the memory of her body, the curve of her ass, the straight fall of her hair.

His breathing grew ragged and his balls drew up tight.

He visualized fisting those strands with one hand and gripping that ass with the other, his fingers digging into tender flesh. In his mind he was spreading her thighs wide and driving the swollen length of him into her. He came with a head-tossing groan. His spine arched on the bed as he shot out over himself, rattled in the aftermath.

He was certifiable. Just the thought of some faceless woman had him jacking off to the best release he'd had in months. This shouldn't have felt so good. It shouldn't have shattered him so much. Masturbating should not be better than the reality of an actual flesh-and-blood woman. Maybe he was tired of the women he'd been spending time with . . . maybe he wanted something else. *Someone.* Maybe that's why nothing—*no one*—seemed to help take the edge off lately.

Dropping his head back down on the bed, he stared up at the ceiling, his heavy breaths slowing, wondering what the hell that meant for him.

Decision reached, he quickly rose from the bed and cleaned himself off. That done, he strolled naked downstairs and snatched Faith Walters's note from where he'd left it on his counter. He crushed the paper in his fist and pulled the front door open in one smooth move. North stepped one foot outside on the porch, then twisted sideways and tossed the note in the direction of her door. It bounced once on her mat before rolling and settling to a stop.

Let her see it there tomorrow. She'd get the message.

His earliest convenience was never.

FIVE

*H*E DIDN'T CALL. He didn't text. He didn't knock on her door as she assumed he would. As a normal, responsible person would do when they found a note on their windshield from their neighbor.

By the time Thursday evening rolled around, she accepted that he didn't care. Not only was she living next to a sex-hungry deviant, he was rude, too. *Rude.* A cardinal sin in the South. The memories she had of her mother were vague and not exactly plentiful, but she remembered her mother telling her over and over again that rudeness was unacceptable. If another girl was mean to her on the playground, it was not right to be rude back. Maybe he wasn't from around here and such basic courtesy hadn't been infused into his baby food.

When she returned home Friday afternoon to find his bike encroaching on her spot, she pressed down on the brakes and stared, idling in the street, tapping her fingers in annoyance over the steering wheel before going ahead and parking her car.

Their combined driveway was built for two vehicles, not two and a half. She had to roll her far left tires into the grass in order to fit her car, but she was feeling stubborn and unwilling to give up her rights to the driveway by parking in the street. He had to be aware that he was infringing on her side. He couldn't be that oblivious.

Slamming her car door shut, she marched up to his door and knocked. The television played quietly inside, but he didn't come to the door. She told herself it was because he didn't hear her. He wasn't looking out the peephole and ignoring her. He wasn't *that* rude. No one could be that big of a jackass.

Grumbling under her breath, she marched inside her house and wrote him a second note.

Please keep your bike to your side of the driveway or park it on the street.

She grudgingly signed her name and included her phone number (again), her mother's words playing in her head. *Just because someone is mean to you doesn't mean you can be mean back.* She stepped back outside and tucked the note in his windshield wipers once again.

Stomping back toward her door, she noticed a crumpled ball of paper at the far side of her welcome mat, practically in the neglected corner of her porch. As though it had been thoughtlessly tossed and then blown there by the wind. Dread pooled in her stomach.

She stopped, her gaze narrowing on the familiar pale green paper.

No, he did not.

She advanced on the crumpled paper. Bending, she scooped it up, already knowing, already recognizing. It was her note. Her dread took a hard turn into indignation. He'd read her note and tossed it aside. That was how little he thought of her. That was the kind of neighbor she was dealing with. One who banged women silly, rejected her scones, destroyed her notes and parked in her spot.

Inside her house, she changed her clothes, then turned on her television and went about making dinner, inhaling through her nose until she felt calm and composed. She stood in front of her pantry, inspecting its contents. She felt like she deserved a little bit of comfort food, so she went with pasta. At first she started making enough for two. Old habit left from when she lived with her father.

Suddenly, loneliness stabbed at her. She sniffed back a sudden burn of tears and returned half the pasta to its box. What was wrong with her? She'd wanted independence, freedom.

She still wanted that, she reminded herself. Rude neighbor not withstanding, she loved her new place. She just hadn't thought about what being alone would *feel* like.

Even when she was in college and grad school she'd had roommates. She shook off her longing for the sounds of her father walking down the creaking hallway of her old family house—or the sound of a baseball game on the living room television punctuated by Dad's occasional shout. She smiled ruefully at the memory and then gave her head a swift shake. She would be visiting home on Sunday and baking his favorite meatloaf and mashed potatoes. Hale would be there, too, doubtless shouting at some game on the TV alongside Dad. She'd get her fix of home and family.

Besides, she reminded herself, she had a date tomorrow night. Whether Brendan was Mr. Right or not, she was getting out there. She'd find someone eventually. She knew she had a lot to offer. She didn't have to be alone forever. Not if she didn't want that for herself. Life was full of choices. She was in control of her fate.

She returned her attention to the sauce for her pasta, tossing in bits of bacon into the bubbling concoction of olive oil, milk, and parmesan cheese.

While the sauce finished simmering, she poured a glass of wine. This evening had become about comfort and indulgence, after all. It had been a long day. Sitting with a bowl of creamy pasta in her lap in front of her television, she found an episode of *Modern Family*. Burrowing deep into the thick cushions of her couch, she scooped up a big spoonful of spiral noodles and took a bite, moaning in approval.

The episode was almost over when she heard her neighbor's door open and shut. Without getting up, she pushed the mute button and angled her head, listening as keys jangled. She heard North Callaghan's steady tread over the concrete of their shared porch.

She resisted the impulse to go to the window and spy on him through her blinds. Along with fighting down that impulse, she crushed the flare of curiosity over where he was going, what he was doing—*who* he was doing. None of her business.

She sat rock-still on her couch, her fingers clutched tightly around her spoon. He had to have seen the new note by now. She waited, imagining him grabbing it off his windshield. She envisioned the tall length of him standing in their driveway as he read it. Maybe. Probably. Perhaps now his conscience would prevail upon him and guide him to her door. She listened for a knock.

An engine started. That was a no then. He wasn't coming to her door.

She gave a sigh of disgust, unmuted the TV and went back to watching her show where everything was laughter and everyone was happy and life was full.

SHE WAS A persistent little thing. Well, not *little*. He'd seen enough of her body through the blinds to know that.

He crumpled the paper into a ball and tossed it toward her door like he had done before. Hopefully she would find it later on her front porch. It was for the best. Let her get the message that he would never be in the running for Neighbor of the Year. The best way to kill his interest in his mysterious neighbor was to scare her off—all within legal means, of course. He wasn't going back to jail for any reason. He'd die first, because that's what prison would be the second time around—a death sentence.

Once in his truck, he drove to Bob's BBQ Shack and ordered some brisket, ribs and sausage to go.

He also ordered a side of potato salad that rivaled his aunt Alice's. He'd spent many a summer eating potato salad and fried chicken, crowded around his grandparents' kitchen table, his future a distant rose-tinted mirage. He smiled faintly. Those had been good times. Not every memory of his past was a bucket of shit.

Climbing back behind the wheel, he set a brown bag full of smoked meat on the seat beside him. The delicious aroma filled the cabin of his truck as he made his way back home to eat his dinner alone.

SIX

$\mathcal{F}$AITH WOKE TO a persistent knocking, broken up by the swift pings of her doorbell. A quick glance at her clock revealed it to be half past midnight.

She stumbled groggily from her bed. Rubbing at her eyes, she paused as she caught a glimpse of herself in the hallway. She'd looked better. The day she took a softball to the face her freshman year she had looked better than this. Her hair stuck up in a haphazard bun, strands sticking out wildly from every direction on her head. A T-shirt that had belonged to Tucker, circa 2005, complemented a pair of baggy pajama bottoms that she would never get rid of on threat of death.

The doorbell rang again, prompting her to action.

The pièce de résistance was the green avocado mud mask she'd applied to her face for the night. Her former roommate Bonnie swore by the stuff, and since Bonnie's mother was sixty years old and looked thirty-five, Faith tended to believe all of Bonnie's beauty tips, as they had all been passed down from her mother.

Flattening her hands on her door, she peered out the peephole. The low glow off her porch light illuminated Serena standing in front of her door. Or rather swaying in front of her door.

Faith frowned. Maybe the woman was fleeing from Faith's jackass neighbor? Maybe he was a brute. An abusive brute. Faith had seen horrible things as a social worker, and she had heard stories all her life in whispered undertones between her father and mother, and then later between her father and brother, about events they had witnessed in the course of their day-to-day work. What did she really know about North Callaghan, after all?

She quickly unbolted the door and yanked it open. "Serena? Is everything all right?" She surveyed the woman with an eye for injuries, searching for any evidence of abuse.

Serena blinked. Dropping her chin, her gaze started at Faith's feet, slowly working her way up to the top of her head with wide eyes, not missing a single thing. "You're not North," she finally proclaimed.

It took a long moment for Faith to register this

declaration and what it signified—along with Serena's booze-laden breath. "No. I am not North." Annoyance pricked at her chest. "Are you looking for him?"

"Ohh!" She smacked her forehead hard enough to make Faith wince. "You're the scone lady! Hey . . ." She took an unsteady step forward, inching inside Faith's house. "You got any more of them in here? Those were gooooood."

Faith lifted her hands and set them on Serena's shoulders, giving her a gentle push back to keep her from entering her house. "No. I don't have any more scones. Sorry. Is there something I can help you with, Serena? Are you hurt?" Faith swung a quick glance sideways, as though she expected her neighbor to jump out from the shadows.

"Hurt? No! I'm not hurt." She attempted to step inside again, saying, "You got North in there? North! North! Come out!"

"Wh-what?" She shook her head in bewilderment. "No, he's not in here. Why would you think that he's in—"

"You're in his house." She blinked and tilted her head back to look up at Faith. "If he's not here, then where is he?"

"I . . ." Faith stopped and took a breath, understanding dawning.

She looked out to the street and where Serena's familiar car was parked haphazardly. The ass end stuck out onto the street. The front of the car was wedged right up behind North Callaghan's truck, barely a hair separating the two vehicles.

"Serena," she drawled, her stomach twisting sickly. "Did you drive yourself here?"

She nodded sloppily. "Yes." Leaning forward, she whispered loudly, one finger pressed over her lips as a gust of booze-laden air escaped her, "I've had a few beers."

"A few?" It seemed like she had more than a few.

"I always get horny when I drink so I thought I'd take myself here." She splayed her arms wide, nearly losing her balance. "North is always up for a good time."

As in another sex marathon. "Well, *here* is my house, not North's." She jabbed a thumb to her left. "There is North's house."

Serena's eyes grew comically large. "No way!"

"Yep." Faith nodded. "You've knocked on the wrong door." She shrugged. "It happens." Especially when intoxicated.

Serena slammed both hands over her mouth. Sputtering sounds still managed to escape, however. The woman was on the verge of hysterical laughter. "For real! I'm sorry! That is hilarious!"

"It's quite all right," Faith said. "Happens more than you'd think."

Really, it never happened. But living next door to Mr. Sexy Fun Times, it might become a thing.

Dropping her hands from her mouth, Serena stepped closer, squinting. "Is that guacamole on your face?" Wrinkling her nose, she stuck out a finger as though to test for herself.

"No! No, stop that." Faith swatted at her hand, bobbing her head out of Serena's range. She felt her hair flopping on top of her head, strands falling onto her forehead and getting stuck in the avocado mask.

Suddenly a yellow glow flooded the porch as the neighboring porch light flipped on and the door to the left pulled open.

Oh. No. *NoNoNoNoNoNo*. She wasn't going to finally meet him now. Not like this. She wasn't going to finally come face-to-face with him looking this way.

She resisted the urge to run inside and slam her door shut. So what if he saw her with a green avo-cado mask on her face and dressed like a thirteen-year-old girl at a slumber party? She wasn't out to impress him. That ship had sailed. And clearly he was not out to impress her. He didn't give a damn about her. Inexplicable anger sizzled through her at the ugly thought. The feeling was mutual. At least that's what she tried to tell herself . . . that's what she tried to convince herself.

Regaining her composure, she turned to face the neighbor who had been ignoring her notes, ignoring her—who did not have the courtesy to park in his own driveway or keep the sounds of fornicating to himself like any other respectable human being.

And then she saw him. Truly saw him.

Melting brown eyes. Dark hair hovered over naked shoulders, the strands uneven and layered, all the more appealing for the effortless nature of the style. This guy didn't go to a salon or dump product in his hair.

And then there was his body. His body with all its curves and hollows. His abdomen with those tight ridges. He belonged on billboards advertising Calvin Klein underwear. He turned at the waist and his muscles bunched and danced in unbelievable ways. Her mouth dried and her heart kicked painfully against her chest. She'd seen a hint of this when he entered his house and when she'd spied on him in his backyard. But nothing had prepared her for the real up-close-and-personal reality of him.

His face was a study in beauty, too. Square-cut jaw and a beautiful well-carved mouth. Eyes so rich and deep. Eyelashes criminally long. A woman would throw down good money for those lashes.

None of this beauty was marred either by the jagged scar running down his face and ending at his jawline. It might have ruined another face, but not his. No, it added to his masculinity. Gave all that prettiness a hard edge. A half inch to the right and it would have sliced his eye, too. He must have been pretty once, but now he was this. A man whose face both drew and repelled. Enticed and intimidated.

He was the embodiment of her every sexual fantasy. Scratch that. He was the embodiment of *every* woman's sexual fantasy. She could almost cry. Or laugh. She wasn't sure which of the two was the stronger impulse.

His deep brown gaze skimmed over Serena before landing on Faith. She supposed they were both in bad shape, but Faith would probably win the prize for biggest freak show. Which was saying something considering Serena was swaying on her feet with bloodshot eyes and definitely looking like roadkill.

The world seemed to fade away as they assessed each other. It felt as though she had been barreling toward this moment for a long time rather than the week she had been living in her new house.

She was certain, of the two of them, she was the only one feeling this way. She probably never even crossed his radar. Especially considering he could never do the right thing and introduce himself to her or answer the damn door for her or pick up the phone and acknowledge any one of the notes she had left him. No, she was certain she was the only one who felt as though the world were fading away and leaving just the two of them standing in it.

His gaze swept over her. Instantly she wished she was wearing a bra at the very least. She felt vulnerable without one until she remembered that she was wearing the world's baggiest T-shirt and her breasts were practically nonexistent anyway.

He was much bigger in the flesh. Taller. Broader of shoulder. And speaking of *in the flesh*, he had on a pair of boxer briefs. Nothing else. Her gaze devoured tan, muscled skin that bunched and rippled as though it was possessed with its own life.

So. Much. Skin.

God. *OhGodOhGodOhGod*. This wasn't happening. *Say it wasn't happening*. Please. God. Not like this.

His eyes narrowed. "Faith Walters?"

So he knew her name. So he wasn't so indifferent to her notes that he didn't file away that little tidbit. Although he didn't look thrilled to see her.

But he was definitely seeing her. His gaze crawled over her face, leaving a path of fire in its wake.

"North Callaghan, I presume?" Did she actually say that? Like she was in some sort of Alfred Hitchcock movie?

He chuckled. "Great. So we know each other's names. Glad we got that out of the way."

"Yeah, well, how would I know anything about you? You won't acknowledge the notes I left for you. Or answer your door whenever I knock."

Serena laughed. The sound jarred Faith. For a moment she had forgotten her presence. "Oh, North? He's not very social. He wouldn't know the first thing about being neighborly. Or small talk, for that matter." She staggered forward until she fell against him. Her hands made good use of the proximity, touching and stroking that delicious chest of his. The irrational urge to step forward and yank Serena's hand off him seized her. She quelled the urge as Serena continued talking. "But you don't need small talk with North. That's the nice thing about him." She giggled, her clumsy fingers sliding south on his chest. "Well. Not the *nicest* thing."

He didn't crack a smile, and she imagined she saw a flash of irritation in his dark eyes. He grabbed Serena's wandering hand and stopped it from roaming.

Serena clucked her tongue and pulled a pouting face. "Aw, you're no fun."

Faith could well understand the irritation. Indignation filled her, bubbling in her chest like when she ate too many peppers on her nachos. Which was absolutely crazy that she should feel like that. She should not feel offended on his behalf. He was a rude, inconsiderate neighbor. If he was okay with being treated like a piece of meat, then who was she to care?

"Your friend Serena here has had a few drinks."

"Yeah, I see that," he said without taking his gaze off Faith.

"Yeahhh, so. It appears she drove herself here. Drunk."

Serena's head whipped around to glare at Faith. Apparently she wasn't so out of it she missed the reference to herself. "I'm not drunk!" she protested.

North sighed and dropped his head back briefly to look skyward. "Christ, Serena."

"North," she whined. "Don't be mad at me!" She turned to glare at Faith as though she were the one responsible for loverboy being annoyed with her.

"Sorry if she disturbed you." He turned Serena in the direction of his door, guiding her away from Faith. "I got this now."

Something snapped inside her. Her temper finally let loose. "Do you?" she called after his back. "Do you got this?"

Because clearly there were other things he did not get. Since the day she moved in there were several things he did not get.

He stopped and turned to face her. "Do you have something to say?"

It was almost laughable. He posed the question mildly. Only she felt like a line had been drawn in the sand. Actually that had happened some time ago. He simply didn't realize it. Or perhaps he simply didn't care.

"Norrrrrth!" Serena whined his name.

He turned around briefly to snap, "Go inside, Serena."

She gave a huff and then disappeared inside his house.

He faced Faith again. "You were saying?"

Yes. She was saying. She was saying something. Exactly *what* she couldn't put into words when he stared at her with such a steely gaze.

She sucked in a sharp breath and forged ahead. "For days I have wanted to introduce myself to you. It seems we are well past friendly introductions now though." She swallowed, fighting against the golf-ball-size lump in her throat. "Aren't we?"

He stared at her for a long moment, not responding.

"Hello?" she growled. "Are you listening to me?"

Finally he came to himself as if shaking off a daze. "I'm sorry. I was mesmerized by that green shit all over your face."

Ohhh. As if she needed the reminder of how terrible she looked in front of him.

She mustered as much composure as she could and pointed at the door to his house. "I would appreciate it if you had a talk with your friend." Now would be the perfect moment to insert that his friend needed to control the volume of her orgasms. The perfect moment. And the worst moment.

He arched dark eyebrows over deeply set eyes, waiting for her to finish.

She inhaled. "I realize your booty call is important to you. God knows it's been a couple days." Yes. Those words had come out of her mouth.

Something like humor glinted in his eyes. "Keeping track, are we?"

"Hard not to. Our walls aren't very thick, you know?"

"Apparently not."

She waved back to his house where Serena waited. "Driving drunk, as she so obviously did, not only put her life in danger but countless others, too. I'd appreciate it if you would emphasize that point to her. For everyone." Not the outrageous things she had thought to say, but no less important, no less true. She had grown up her whole life surrounded by law enforcement. She had heard the stories. She'd seen the look on her father's face the morning after he had to scrape some poor soul off the highway because some idiot decided to get behind the wheel of a car after he had one too many drinks.

He waited a moment before replying, still looking at her, still assessing, still making her feel like a bug squashed beneath his shoe. "I'll do that."

She tried to read him, to see if he was mocking her, but she only sensed that he was being honest in his reply.

She gave a nod. "Thank you."

Still clinging to the scraps of her dignity, she spun around on her bare feet, feeling the bun on top of her head start to slip.

She fled inside her house and slammed the door behind her before her hair took a complete tumble. She fell against the door, her back flat against its surface, her chest heaving as though she had just completed a marathon.

She finally got to meet him. They finally had

a conversation. Unfortunately it went nothing as she had anticipated. She closed her eyes in a weary blink. A deep heaviness settled in her stomach and she knew this wasn't over between them.

As if there were any doubts to that thought, something crashed next door that sounded suspiciously like a lamp, followed by Serena's shrill, drunken laughter.

Faith strained to listen, stepping into her kitchen area and jerking as several thwacks hit the wall beside her table.

Stepping forward she pounded back on the wall. "Keep it down!" She was done playing nice. So what if she sounded like some old prude. She wasn't in college anymore. She didn't have to put up with loud neighbors anymore.

She heard the deep muted tones of North's voice, his words a distinctive rumble. *Great.* Now she would hear their shenanigans all night. She winced at that idea. The notion of North having sex with an inebriated woman seemed wrong. She wanted to think better of him for some reason. Which was very strange. Serena clearly wanted some action. That was why she came here. She had said as much. Serena's hands making a direct beeline for his junk left little doubt of that.

What was so disappointing was that North Callaghan was likely prepared to give it to her.

Snorting with disgust, Faith pushed away from the door and headed upstairs. She climbed into her bed and settled back on her pillow, hoping to fall back asleep so that she would not have to endure the sounds of marathon sex coming through the walls again.

For once, her wish came true, and she fell fast asleep, sparing herself the sounds of whatever was happening next door.

SHE HAD GREEN shit all over her face. He had no idea what it was. Clearly some part of a beauty regime that women felt necessary. Women like her. Women not for him. Women who cared about skin care and had careers and dated men with careers. Not felons who worked in garages and fooled themselves into believing they were artists. She would never get her pristine hands dirty with someone like him.

He dropped his head back against the flat expanse of his front door and released a mirthless laugh at the memory of her green face. He still didn't know what she looked like underneath that mask. Unbelievable. He was dying to know, dying to see her for himself. It was messed up. He lived next door to her. He knew it was as simple as knocking on her door and playing the role of nice neighbor. Introducing himself properly. Apologizing for whatever he had done. He grimaced. He could start with apologizing for his drunk friend showing up at her door in the middle of the night.

He could be charming if he decided to. There had been a time in his life when he had been a well-liked guy. Affable. Full of smiles. Teachers had loved him. Coaches had only ever praised him—not just for his athleticism but also his positive attitude. Parents had wanted their daughters to date him. North Callaghan had been a name that meant something, that held value. He'd been a prince in his corner of the world—Sweet Hill, Texas. Granted, it was a small corner of the world . . . but he'd been a prince nonetheless.

If he pretended to be that guy again, if he channeled him from the grave, he could probably smooth things over with Faith Walters.

She had stood toe-to-toe with him, her eyes flashing under the light of the porch, ready to take him on. Ready to let him know just how little she thought of him.

Crazy as it seemed, that just made him want to

engage with her further. But as himself. As the guy he was now, not the ghost of the boy he had once been. Which was the complete opposite of what he had planned to do. Pretend she didn't exist, pretend the house next door to his was still vacant. Locking horns with her was not the plan.

One thing for certain: she was unlike any woman he had ever met. He couldn't remember conversing with another woman for any length of time without sex as the end result.

Not that he "met" many women. They weren't exactly plentiful where he worked. Of course his sister-in-law had suggested setting him up on a few dates. He winced at that idea.

He glanced to where he had deposited Serena's drunk ass on the couch. She was getting to be too much trouble. It was one thing to have a convenient fuck every now and then, but when it stopped being convenient . . .

There was also the not-so-minor fact that when he stared at her, he felt nothing. Not the slightest arousal. Even a hot mess, she was undeniably attractive. Her skirt rode up to reveal an enticing view of her black-thong-clad backside. He knew that body. Had felt it under him, above him, countless times. She was a great lay. And he felt nothing.

Christ.

It couldn't be any clearer. They were done. It was no longer fun. Sex with Serena—hell, with anyone lately—hardly took the edge off anymore. He didn't know what could, but he had to find it. The idea of not finding anything to ease the pressure, to dull the pain, to distract . . . it was unthinkable.

Serena lifted her head from the couch. He grimaced at the large drool stain she'd left on his cushion.

"North!" Her bleary gaze fastened on him. "C'mere! Why aren't you naked yet!"

He approached the couch. "Shh. You don't need to shout."

Not that he had ever cared before. Suddenly he was very conscious of the woman living next door to him.

Serena popped up and started shrugging out of her clothes, her movements determined.

He grabbed hold of her hands. "Not tonight, Serena."

She wrenched away and collided with the lamp on the side table, sending it crashing to the floor. She gawked at the wreckage for a moment before bursting into laughter.

"Shit," he grumbled as he moved to pick it up

and set it back on the table. It listed to the side, the shade mangled. This was stupid.

He glanced back to find Serena topless and squeezing her tits like she was working the stage at Joe's Cabaret. "Come on, baby," she called, her voice loud enough to be heard down the block. "You know you want to play with the girls."

His gaze drifted to the wall as though he could see through it to the woman undoubtedly listening on the other side.

He sighed, feeling suddenly far older than his years. Serena was fine as long as she wasn't drinking. Fortunately, this was only the second time he had to deal with her like this. But he was thinking two times was two too many.

He snatched up Serena's shirt and pushed it at her to take. "C'mon. Get dressed."

She grabbed the shirt and tossed it across the room with a cowgirl yell. Hopping to her feet, she wobbled unsteadily on the couch cushions, her arms jerking wildly at her sides in an effort to balance herself. Her lack of balance didn't stop her from bouncing like it was a trampoline.

"You're going to fall and break your neck," he snapped.

She continued to bounce, her hand slapping

the wall with every jump. "C'mon, North! This is fun!"

"I'm going to pass."

Thump! Thump! "Keep it down!" Faith Walters's voice carried through the wall, her agitation coming through loud and clear.

"Serena," he snapped. He caught her hand and tugged her down from the couch. She decided to accommodate him by launching herself in his arms. He caught her neatly.

"Aren't you strong? Like a fucking tank," she gushed, pushing her giant breasts against his chest, her hands snaking over his shoulders. "Speaking of fucking, take me up upstairs."

He sighed. There was no sense talking to her when she was in this condition. He'd let her down in the morning. Be as kind as he could, but there would be no confusion. They were done. Hopefully there wouldn't be any drama. They weren't a couple. This wasn't a breakup, after all.

He carried her upstairs and deposited her on the bed. She rolled onto her back on his mattress, stretching like a cat. Her eyelids drooped to half-mast over her glassy gaze. She extended one hand up to him, inviting him to join her.

"I'll be right back," he lied.

Turning, he marched back downstairs and helped himself to a beer, confident that she was close to passing out. Leaning against the counter, he waited, staring hard at the living room wall, wondering what Faith Walters was doing now.

For some reason it bothered him that she thought he was in here banging a drunk woman. And that was senseless. Stupid even. Why should he care what she thought of him?

Whatever the case, it didn't stop him from thinking about her. From wondering. Did she go back to bed? Did she sleep in that green mask? Did she fuck wearing it, too? Shaking his head, he released a little laugh.

He didn't think she was married. There hadn't been any evidence of a husband or live-in boyfriend. She appeared to live alone. Meaning she wasn't getting any. At least not recently.

Well, maybe she should. Maybe that would help loosen that stick up her ass. Maybe then she wouldn't care about what sounds she heard coming from his house at night. He took a pull of beer and wondered why he was suddenly so interested in Faith Walters's sex life.

He let another ten minutes pass before he headed back upstairs. As suspected, Serena was asleep, sprawled across his bed, fresh drool falling. Grabbing the top blanket on the bed, he gave it a yank and took it with him as he headed back downstairs. He didn't feel like sharing a bed tonight.

He dropped down on the couch, rested an arm over his forehead and pulled the blanket up to his waist. Rolling his head sideways, he stared at the wall until he fell asleep.

SEVEN

$\mathcal{F}$AITH WOKE THE next morning feeling resolved, if not rested.

A sudden shout from outside and the slam of a door didn't even faze her.

Of course. Why wouldn't last night's drama carry over into the morning?

Bowl of cereal in hand, Faith moved to her kitchen window and watched the redhead storm out and jump in her car. Serena took off with tires squealing. Apparently last night's fun didn't extend into the morning hours. Shrugging, Faith moved back into the kitchen. She rinsed off her bowl, spoon, and set them inside the dishwasher.

She was done. She would leave no more notes asking North Callaghan for anything. She was a Walters. That meant she had resources. Normally, she didn't like to pull strings, but it was time. Time to cast her principles aside for a greater purpose.

The next time she wanted to communicate with North Callaghan, she would not rely on notes. She would not beat on walls. She would not knock on his door just to have it go unanswered.

She would be heard. She'd pick up the phone and call him directly.

So if her resources happened to involve calling Doris, her brother's dispatcher, on her way to work, no one needed to know. She would be happy to help Faith. Doris had been sneaking her candy from her desk drawer ever since Faith was three years old and Doris worked dispatch for her father.

When her cell phone rang midmorning as she was coming out of a meeting, she identified Doris's name as the caller. She reached for the pen on her desk, ready to copy down North's phone number. "Hey, Doris," she greeted. "Were you able to get me that—"

Doris cut right to the chase. "Why do you want this guy's number?"

"Uhh . . ." She hadn't bothered to explain *why* to Doris. They'd both been in a hurry this morning and it just hadn't seemed necessary. Asking Doris to keep it under wraps and not mention the request

to her brother hadn't seemed a big deal either.
Doris understood Hale's tendency to interfere and
she was totally in Faith's corner.

"Tell me you're not dating this guy, Faith."

"No!"

"Whew. That's a relief. Your brother wouldn't
like that."

"Why, Doris? What's wrong with him?"

"He's got a record, Faith. His rap sheet is ugly.
This isn't the kind of person you need to be around.
Who is he to you, Faith?"

North Callaghan was a criminal? Hadn't she
thought that beautiful body a weapon? The type
honed not in a gym but rather on a battlefield?

"Um." Now probably wasn't the time to tell her
they were neighbors. "No one, Doris. I just wanted
his number."

Doris sighed, accepting that Faith wasn't going
to give her the full story. "Okay. Just be careful,
Faith."

Faith nodded, jotting down the numbers Doris
recited and vowing not to ask Doris the particulars
of North's record. It conveyed a level of interest
she did not want to project. From here on out, she
would do her own digging.

And it was time she learned everything she could
about North Callaghan.

ALL DAY FAITH stared at those digits scrawled on the slip of paper on her desk, not getting nearly enough work done. She finally caved and typed them into her phone for safekeeping. Under contacts, she hesitated and then typed in **Asshole Neighbor.**

She giggled, pleased with herself. That kept things in perspective.

Okay. So she lived next door to a felon, but he'd served his time. She had no reason to be scared of him. He'd roused several emotions in her since she moved in, but fear wasn't one of them.

He'd been out for two years and he had lived a clean, crime-free life since his release. It wasn't as though he was a pedophile or rapist.

No, just a convicted murderer.

She winced. She wasn't a fool. Even though she had discovered all she could about North Callaghan and his crime, she knew living next door to him wasn't an ideal situation. Her brother or father could not find out. They'd have a U-Haul in front of her house before she could blink.

She didn't want to move. She wasn't going to.

North Callaghan had been convicted of killing his cousin's alleged rapist. *Alleged* was a kind characterization. All the media she uncovered did not paint a favorable picture of Mason Leary. He and his family had waged a strong campaign to prove his innocence, hiring fancy lawyers out of Lubbock, but she'd read Katie Callaghan's testimony and the testimony of the doctor who attended her when she was admitted into the hospital. No female would want to be hurt in that manner.

Everything she'd unearthed pointed to the fact that North and his older brother inadvertently killed the young man, beating him in an attempt to get his admission of guilt. North had been eighteen years old at the time. His brother not much older. Their actions weren't right. She wasn't condoning them, but she could see how something like that could happen.

The fact remained: she did not believe herself at risk from her neighbor. Her ears might throb from the sounds drifting from the other side of her bedroom wall, and she might feel stabs of annoyance when his motorcycle crept onto her side of the driveway, but that wasn't reason enough for her to sell her new house and move. He'd served his time and was entitled to a place to live. Wasn't that how the system worked?

She moved through the rest of her day in a fog, making calls and filling out paperwork as her mind churned over this new development.

She took a late lunch outside on one of the benches in front of her building, not even tasting the ham-and-cheese croissant sandwich she had packed. The birds found her. They always did. She broke up bits of the bread from her sandwich and tossed them out for them.

She snorted at the image she must make, a single woman tossing food for the pigeons. The only thing missing was a shawl and an old-lady hat. She needed to get out more. Maybe if she was socializing more, making new friends and dating, she wouldn't care so much about one neighbor, felon or not.

She straightened her spine and reminded herself that she had a date coming up. Maybe things would start looking up and changing then.

"Hey, Faith," Wendy called on her way inside the building. "Drinks tonight at Willie's! Flor and I are going. They've got a hot new bartender. Something nice to look at as we drink our margaritas. You in?"

She hesitated, chewing and swallowing her bite. "Sure," she called out. It beat going home and staring at her walls.

"Thata girl! See you inside. Staff meeting in thirty."

Faith smiled slightly as her friend disappeared inside the building. She finished the last bite of her croissant sandwich and dusted off her hands, then headed into the building. She just had to make it until Saturday.

SHE FELT RELAXED by the time she got home from Willie's. She wasn't much of a drinker and since she had been driving, she hadn't overindulged. She wasn't about to pull a Serena move, but one mango margarita was enough to put her in a more relaxed state. Additionally, Wendy and Flor had kept her in stitches. Hard to be tense when you couldn't stop laughing. Flor, twice the bartender's age and mother of three, had flirted shamelessly with the younger man. She was inspiring. Faith needed half that woman's confidence.

North Callaghan's bike was missing from the driveway. At least she wouldn't hear him having sex again. She snorted at that.

She entered her house and dropped her things on the table. After kicking off her shoes, she moved into the kitchen and grabbed a bottle of wine. She was home now. Not driving anywhere. She might as well continue with her state of relaxation.

After changing into shorts and a supersoft T-shirt, she took her glass of wine and dropped down on her couch, where she channel surfed until she landed on a rerun of *The Big Bang Theory*.

During her second glass of cab, she decided dessert was in order. She'd shared some wings and nachos at Willie's with the girls, but there was always room for something sweet. Grabbing an ice cream sandwich out of the freezer, she settled back on the couch for an episode of *Cupcake Wars*.

A bike growled outside. Faith jumped up, holding her wine glass out in front of her so that the liquid didn't slosh over the rim. She hurtled herself to the door and pressed her eye against the peephole. Sure enough, there he was. She glimpsed the large dark outline of him through her window before he passed out of range. The door clicked shut.

Huh. She stood back, her blinds snapping into place. Alone on a Friday night. That must be a first for him.

She stood there for some moments, listening. It was silent on the other side of the wall. She tossed back her wine, then moved into the kitchen and poured herself a third glass. Or was it a fourth?

Shrugging, she set the bottle down on the counter with a satisfying clink. She wasn't going anywhere. If she wanted to get soused in the privacy of her own home, then that was her right. She had tomorrow to sleep in, after all, and all afternoon to recover before her date with Brendan.

EIGHT

NORTH WOKE UP sweating with a curse on his lips. Sitting up, he swallowed his gasps and ran a hand through the loose strands of his hair.

He dragged his hand down his face to his chest, stopping directly over his heart. He pressed his palm there, where it pounded with frenzy beneath his perspiring skin. Moments like this reminded him of before. Of all those nights in his cell. Sometimes he'd wake to the sounds of men crying, being beaten or assaulted. His cellmate was neither friend nor enemy, but the same couldn't be said for everyone else. For other inmates, nights were the worst. The longest. When the strong preyed on the weak.

He lifted his hand from his pounding chest and dragged it over his face. He should be over this shit by now. He wasn't locked up inside there anymore.

He didn't have to look over his shoulder. He didn't have to stand silent witness as others were broken.

His breathing gradually slowed and evened. He shifted on his bed, the mattress creaking slightly. The sheet slid low on his hips, rasping against his skin.

He slept naked. That was the luxury of being a free man. He could sleep naked. Walk around naked. Eat leftovers in front of his fridge buck-ass naked. Walk in his backyard and stare at the moon without a stitch on if he wanted. He had the freedom and privacy to do whatever he desired in the confines of his own property. So why the fuck did he still have nightmares?

Suddenly his bedroom felt claustrophobic. After flinging the covers back, he rose from the bed and walked downstairs. The nightmares were the same in that they always varied.

Sometimes it was Katie, sobbing, wild-eyed and shell-shocked in her ripped-up dress. Sometimes he was with Knox and they were beating on Mason Leary, North's knuckles stinging and covered in blood. That was a common-enough nightmare. Leary under him, taking his punches and blows, but then the bastard would transform into someone else. Often it was Katie. Sometimes it was his brother. Sometimes North himself.

Other times he dreamed of the riot at the prison—the one that nearly killed him and left his face cut up. At the time, he'd thought he would die in that riot. The swell of writhing bodies had been like a storm around him and he thought surely it was the end. But it hadn't been. He'd survived.

Scarred, but not dead.

The worst days actually came after the riot. Knox was gone; paroled. Reid, the leader of their crew, escaped Devil's Rock, abandoning North, too.

The crew he ran with was weaker, more vulnerable to the other gangs in the prison. It was a testing period, to see how North and the remnants of Reid's crew could stand up to attacks without Reid or Knox. North had survived. At a price. There was always a price.

He pulled open his fridge and grabbed a beer. Shutting the door, he turned and headed out back. After opening the back door, he stepped outside into the night. Dry air crackled around him as he walked through the yard, indifferent to the sensation of his bare feet crunching over dry grass. A slight wind stirred his hair and rolled over his exposed skin. He took a long pull on his beer. With a sigh, he stretched his neck muscles and looked up at the night, at the blanket of darkness studded with stars. He'd never seen a view like this from his prison cell. He was always shut in before dark fell.

He stood there, slowly nursing his beer, enjoying the sensation of air moving over his body. Freedom. As close as he could get anyway.

Gradually a prickly sensation worked up his spine. He knew better than to ignore it. Paying attention to that sensation had kept him from getting shanked in prison. He wouldn't ignore it now even situated in the seeming safety of Small Town, USA.

He turned slowly on his bare heels, his sweating beer clutched in one hand as he surveyed his yard. He missed nothing in the flat expanse of grass—he probably needed to mow again—or in the quiet slats of fence boards staring back at him. His gaze drifted upward, scanning his house and then drifting over to his neighbor's house.

That's when he saw it. Not *it*. Her. Faith.

He watched her outline standing in the upstairs bedroom window. The blinds were open and she was backlit from a source of light somewhere in her house. Again, he couldn't make out her features, just the long shape of her.

But he felt her stare on him. On all of him . . . naked as a jaybird.

He had no idea what she wore. *If* she wore anything at all. There was the chance that she was as naked as he was. The idea aroused him. There was no denying it.

He took another long pull from his beer, his gaze never leaving her window. Never leaving her shadow. He couldn't imagine her face. But he heard her voice in his head. He saw her shape. He imagined those endless legs.

He felt her eyes on him. He knew she was watching him. She probably thought she was invisible to him up there. He smiled slightly, his free fingers resting on his abdomen, sliding down incrementally. He wanted to shock her. Maybe somewhere deep inside she was getting excited, too . . . watching him. Watching him touch himself in front of her. For her.

His cock jutted out at full mast. His hand slid lower, closing around himself. Hell, this was for himself, too.

He knew what he was doing was messed up. She could call the cops and lodge a complaint. They could be knocking on his door in under twenty minutes. That was the last thing he wanted, but he couldn't move. Couldn't stop. He couldn't go inside. He couldn't stop tormenting her. Tormenting himself.

He gripped hard. Felt his balls pull up tight, begging for his hand to move up and down, fast and rough. But even that wouldn't be enough. It wasn't what he wanted.

He didn't want to simply jack off. He wanted to sink deep into a woman's softness. He wanted long legs wrapped around his hips. He wanted the mystery of her face resolved.

Christ. He was about to lose his load like some teenage boy with his first girl. This was insane but he couldn't stop himself. Not as long as she was watching. His fingers tightened around himself, squeezing until his dick throbbed harder.

He registered that. Processed it. She had not moved away from her window. She was still standing there. She couldn't be too repulsed. Could she? Maybe she was touching herself, too. From this distance, with the obstruction of her blinds, it was impossible to know. But God, that thought got him more aroused.

He was close just like this with one hand squeezing his cock. The only thing more appealing to him than getting himself off was the thought of jumping her fence, yanking open her back door and marching inside her house. Finding her. Claiming her. Riding out his climax inside the woman watching him.

Christ. He didn't even know her. Not her face. Not anything about her. He dropped his hand, that glaring truth scalding him.

He still felt her stare. It practically peeled the flesh from his bones.

It was the nightmare. That was the only explanation for this sudden dive into insanity. The nightmares always put him on edge. Made him as anxious as a long-tailed cat in a roomful of rocking chairs.

With a curse burning on his lips, he strode back inside his house, letting the back door slam shut behind him. He was done with this crazy fixation on his neighbor. She was just a woman with all the usual parts. Same as any other.

He was going to bed. Tomorrow he would get laid. Find some willing woman to slide inside and take off the edge.

One thing was for certain: after what had just happened, he doubted he would ever have to face her. She would be giving him a wide berth from now on. He snorted. Hell, she would probably be calling her Realtor to move first thing in the morning.

And that, for some reason, rubbed him in all the wrong ways.

NINE

Holy hell, what just happened?

Her neighbor had stood naked as a jaybird in his backyard. Looking right at her window. Almost like he could see directly through the blinds to her. Even though she knew that wasn't possible.

No, he wasn't just naked. He was naked with a full raging hard-on, which he gripped in that big fist of his. A fist not so big, mind you, that she missed how large his . . . er, member happened to be. It was as impressive as the rest of him.

And then he stopped. He walked inside his house like nothing happened. He'd turned away. Not Faith. No, she had stood there gawking, peeking through her blinds, her breathing raspy, unable to look away.

"So unfair," she muttered as she marched downstairs and refilled her wine glass—even as she contemplated digging out Mister Perfect from her nightstand drawer.

Mister Perfect was the name she had given her vibrator. Like North Callaghan, her vibrator was impressive in size . . . but Mister Perfect was battery operated. At the moment, that did not offer much enticement. Not after staring at the flesh-and-blood form of North Callaghan.

She swigged back her glass of wine in one more gulp and then grabbed the bottle to top it off again. Her head was spinning—and it wasn't just because of the alcohol.

He was even sexier fully naked. Naturally. She snorted in disgust. *Her* best look was when she wore jeans and a turtleneck. She lived in Texas. So she could pull that look off two days a year. So unfair.

Life was unfair though. She was living next door to a man who looked like *that*. And the man happened to be a felon. And a jerk.

She sighed.

Taking her wine, she plopped back down on the couch. Muttering under her breath, she picked up her phone off the coffee table and scrolled through her contacts until she found his name. Or at least what she had decided to name him before.

With one final sip, she deleted **Asshole Neighbor**

and changed it to **Cock of Wonder**. That produced a fit of giggles . . . all alcohol induced. Probably. Or perhaps she was losing her ever-loving mind.

She had just finished saving the change when a text popped up on the screen.

> Like what you saw?

She squeaked and flung the phone across the room. It was an instinctive reaction born of horror and shock.

He was texting her. How on earth . . .

Understanding dawned. She had seen the crumpled notes on her porch. *Her* crumpled-up notes that he had tossed on her porch. Evidently he had saved her number from those earlier notes. Apparently he wasn't so indifferent to her attempts to communicate. He had thought to save her number.

But why? And why was he texting her now?

Her fingers were shaking as she gathered up enough composure to text him back. You're horrible.

> So you were watching.

She winced at his reply, instantly regretting revealing that tidbit to him. She could almost hear the smugness in his voice. I walked by the window and glanced out.

Sure you did.

She replied with: I should have called the police. Masturbating naked in your backyard had to be against the law, right?

But you didn't. You won't.

I wouldn't be too sure.

He didn't know about her ties to law enforcement. She'd hang on to that information. It might be useful later. If she dropped it on him now he might read it as a threat. She wasn't big on threats. Besides, she had long ago vowed not to rely on her father and brothers to fight her battles. They'd done that enough in her life already.

Although it would serve him right if she called her brother right now. Knowing Hale, he'd drive right over. If she told him the specifics, he'd handle North Callaghan himself—and it wouldn't be through the proper channels. She grimaced. Forget about arresting him. Her brother would go old-school and wipe the floor with North Callaghan. Or he'd attempt to anyway. She wasn't so confident that it would be an easy fight for Hale. He might be six feet five and made of muscles, but North Callaghan had come out of prison. And he was built, too. She'd hate for her brother to get hurt.

No, she would handle North Callaghan herself.

Feeling bold, she texted him back. No company tonight? Or you just felt like putting on a show for the neighbors?

Tilting back her head, she downed the rest of her glass. "God, I really am an idiot," she muttered. Even half lit, she knew better than this. Drinking and texting did not mix.

Her phoned buzzed in her hand and she glanced down.

Just one neighbor. Just you.

The smug grin on her face faltered and her stomach dipped in a way it had no business doing. She managed a reply. Should I be flattered?

Three dots danced before his words appeared. Are you?

So you kept my number.

She nodded approvingly at her nonanswer. It made her appear indifferent to him and his little display—okay, *big* display. Maybe she even came off as tough, too. Probably tougher than she'd looked in her green avocado mask last night. Considering what she'd found out about this man when she had done her digging today, she didn't want to appear a pushover. Her text also implied that she thought him rude and inconsiderate. He'd ignored her attempts to have a conversation up until now. She gave herself a mental pat on the back.

His reply finally came. Yes.

So he got her notes and thought it was okay to just blow her off. Fuming, her fingers flew. And were you ever planning to respond? Before now?

Before he decided to give her a peep show?

He texted back. Been busy.

Not too busy for other things. After hitting send on that, she stared at her words, regretting them almost immediately. So much for appearing indifferent. She sounded angry.

Dancing dots appeared. He was texting her back. She held her breath and waited. Listening at walls again?

Heat flared in her cheeks. She fired off another text. I believe your bedroom wall borders mine. Please have a little common courtesy. Some of us have to get up early in the morning for work.

How old are you?

She blinked at the out-of-nowhere question.

What does that matter?

Trying to get a visual. Couldn't tell underneath that junk on your face yesterday. You sound like you're seventy.

Seventy! Was he serious? She replied: I'm twenty-six. Wouldn't have thought it. Why am I not hearing your bed frame knocking the wall? Her mouth dropped. He followed that up with a single word: Prude.

She shook her head. He was baiting her by calling her a prude? Was this junior high? She was too mature for this. It wouldn't work on her. It *shouldn't*.

She texted back: Let's try to be civil. I would appreciate it if you keep the noise down.

She would also appreciate it if he wore some clothes. If he kept his penis under wraps so she didn't salivate like some horny stranded-on-island woman.

To be fair, it's not me doing all the shouting.

She snorted. The ego on this man. Sadly, from what she'd seen of him, she knew it wasn't undeserved though. Really?? I am sure you can control yourself.

The giving of orgasms? I'm sure I can't.

Oh. My God. Just the mention of orgasm made her stomach muscles flutter. She rolled onto her back on the couch, the TV long forgotten. She splayed her hand over her abdomen to try to quell the flutters there.

Dancing dots appeared again. Her pulse hummed faster in her veins as she waited for his reply.

Not every woman is open to wearing a ball gag. I can try . . .

Oh. My. God. He was the devil.

She slammed the phone down on the couch beside her and stared up at the ceiling. Why was she even trying to talk to him? She swung a glance at her nearly empty wine glass. Drinking and texting. Definitely bad idea.

She snatched up her phone and went to his name in her contacts, changing it from **Cock of Wonder** to **Orgasm Giver**. Then, shaking her head, she dropped her phone back down on the couch and released a forlorn sigh.

Deliberately not looking at her phone again, she headed upstairs to take a shower. Turning it on, she tested the water until it was the desired warmth. Stripping off her clothes, she stepped under the spray. Her body throbbed in places that had felt numb for the last few years, as stunted and forgotten as shriveled-up weeds alongside the highway. Now those places stirred with life.

She flattened her palms against the shower wall and let the water beat down on her. She blew out a breath against the downpour.

Her head still felt delightfully woozy. That sensation combined with the tingle at her core had her lifting a hand from the wall. She slid her fingers down her stomach and between her legs to one of those places that suddenly shouted with life and need. At the first brush of her fingers, she shuddered.

She parted her slick folds, unerringly making her way to that little nub of pleasure. Her breathing hitched and she swallowed water. She was merely wet from her shower. That's what she told herself as she stroked and rubbed her clit until her legs felt like rubber, ready to give out under her. It wasn't as though texting the hot felon who lived next door had anything to do with that. He wasn't why she was suddenly masturbating in the shower. Her orgasm, usually so elusive even when self-delivered (not that she had them any other way), swelled up on her. Her fingers worked faster and she bowed her head under the spray of water until she was gasping. So close. Almost . . . there . . .

She latched onto the memory of North Callaghan with his ridiculous body standing in front of her.

BAM! She was there, crying out and shuddering, her thighs clamping together on her hand.

Several moments passed before she lifted her head. Water sluiced over her face, trailing down her overheated cheeks. That was incredible. And awful. She'd gotten off to the thought of her next-door neighbor . . . the very guy she had just learned was an ex-con. He was not fantasy material! Her date with Brendan couldn't come soon enough. He was the stuff of fantasy. A man worth dreaming about because he could become her reality. Maybe. That's what dating would find out anyway.

She turned off the shower, then grabbed a towel hanging off the rack and pulled it around herself tightly. She stopped in front of the sink and stared at herself in the mirror, hardly recognizing the woman gazing back at her. She was bright-eyed and flushed. Like a woman well pleasured. God. What might it be like to actually have a real man between her legs? A man like the one next door? *The man next door?*

Shaking her head, she turned away from her reflection. Clearly she needed to get that thought out of her mind.

TEN

*H*E WAS TEXTING her.

And rather shockingly, she was texting him back.

Maybe texting her wasn't the smartest move after giving her a peep show, but she had left him her number. Two times. And he had memorized it. Numbers stuck in his head that way. Math had always been his subject. In college, he probably would have chosen a major with a strong math emphasis. He'd just been starting to think about that, about his future in college, when everything came to a grinding halt.

She was feisty. He'd give her that. Instead of calling the cops on him for indecent exposure or whatever appropriate charge, she was talking to him. Because she wasn't as indifferent to him as she would like to think.

He didn't know what to think about that. She

was more than a faceless prude with killer legs and a stick up her ass. It all seemed contrary to the ideas he had formed about her, but he had actually enjoyed himself during that text exchange. It had been . . . fun.

An uncomfortable tightness wrapped around his chest and propelled him outside into his shop. This time he wore clothes. Even so, he forced himself not to glance, not even once, at her bedroom window.

He slid his helmet on and picked up his cutting torch. He didn't know what he was creating, but that was usually his process. Equipment in hand, he simply went to work. Welding emptied his mind in a way that he so desperately needed. He felt clear-headed and free of all the usual shit weighing him down. He found a stillness in those moments that eluded him the rest of the time.

Sparks flew as he cut, bent, burned and manipulated the metal until it became something that resembled art. At least he hoped so. He hoped that when he was done, it would be fashioned into something someone would pay good money for.

An hour later he surfaced from the stillness to call it quits. He closed up his shop, locking it with a chain, and then walked across his yard, his gaze unavoidably drifting to her upstairs window. It was impossible not to look up on the walk back. She was still awake. Light bled out through her closed blinds.

Entering his house, he went for his phone to see if she had texted him any more.

Nothing. Not surprising.

Before he could consider it, he started typing.

> So you only wanted to talk to me to complain about the volume?

He set his phone down and stared at it for a long moment. Waiting.

"Shit." Shaking his head, he turned away with a grunt of disgust. He couldn't leave well enough alone. The question was a lame excuse to keep engaging with her, to reach for the pleasure he had found texting her earlier.

For all he knew, she wasn't anywhere near her phone. He wasn't going to stand staring at his screen like some idiot pining for a girl to text him back. He moved into his kitchen to get a drink, but the sound of his phone buzzing had him turning back. He snatched it up.

> I actually had a list of complaints.

He snorted and felt himself smile. Of course she did. He replied: What else?

Three dancing dots appeared as she started typing. Could you please refrain from parking your bike on my side of the driveway?

Huh. Yeah. He did do that. Just habit, he supposed. The place had been vacant for a while and he was used to hogging both driveways. He texted: Nothing else?

The three little dots appeared and then went away as though she changed her mind about commenting. He grinned and typed. Don't be shy now. You've come this far.

Maybe wear more clothes . . .

He laughed and then glanced at their shared wall, wondering if she could hear him. So you were looking.

Just for a second.

Liar.

You'd like to think I stood there spying on you.

I saw your shadow.

You're wrong.

Chuckling, he decided to let her cling to the lie. He next texted: Summers are hot in Texas.

Another text popped up. I'm perfectly aware of that. But I don't walk around naked. He could practically hear the indignation in her words.

Maybe you should. I wouldn't mind.

More dots appeared and then disappeared.

"Come on, sweetheart," he said under his breath, his thumb stroking the side of his phone. "Don't go all shy."

She took the bait. One naked neighbor is enough.

Two naked neighbors would be better.

Yeah, he was flirting. Only her next text proved that she was resistant to his efforts.

We don't know each other. You haven't even seen my face.

Easy to rectify. Open your door. Show me your face.

She took her time replying and he wondered if she was actually giving the proposition some thought. Something that felt like hope swelled in his chest. Finally, her reply popped up on his phone: I don't think so.

Why? You got something better to do?

I've got a bottle of wine and a *Cupcake Wars* marathon.

Sounds boring.

You're clearly not a fan of wine. Or cupcakes.

Oh I like cupcakes. I eat them all the time. He was not talking about cupcakes and she was smart enough to realize that.

I bet.

He couldn't help himself. What are your cupcakes like?

Rest assured. You'll never know what they're like.

He was grinning now. In fact, he had been grinning this entire text conversation. He didn't know the last time he had smiled for this long. He squashed his smile, but texted back: Now you have me intrigued. Is that your game?

I don't play games.

Good to hear. Neither do I.

Dots appeared and then vanished. He must have thrown her a little with that bit of honesty. And it was honesty. He was always direct with his women. Not that she was his woman. The dots reappeared signaling she was replying back.

It seems like you play lots of games.

What do you mean?

I can hear you remember? Through the walls. Often.

Oh. That? That's called fucking.

Do you just say whatever pops in your head?

Like I said. I don't play games.

So you just say whatever you want?

He sank down on his couch and adjusted his hardened cock inside his jeans. Hell, just texting with this woman got him turned on. He needed to get laid. Someone other than Serena apparently. He'd burned that bridge.

He continued texting. I thought we were being direct. You were the one to point out that you can hear me fucking.

Actually I can't hear you. Only the women.

Wow. You really are listening.

It's hard not to . . .

I make sounds. You just got to be closer to hear them. I say all kinds of things. Would you like to hear me? Yeah. He just went there. And he kept going. Why stop now? After what he'd already done tonight this was the least outrageous thing. He added: You like dirty talk Faith?

That's none of your business.

His thumb again stroked the side of his phone. He was going to take that as a no. She had never dirty-talked before. Somehow that didn't surprise him. The things to come out of his mouth would probably horrify her. His fingers hovered over the keys, tempted to type more, to keep flirting, to keep doing whatever it was he was doing with her.

No. Shaking his head, he set his phone down on the counter and slid it firmly away. It might start out fun and good but it would turn messy. With a good woman like her that was inevitable. He had a flash of himself standing naked in his backyard, one hand on himself as he gazed up at her window. Messier than it already was. She lived next door to him. It would be hard to avoid her when things went south—and things inevitably would. Because nothing fun or good ever lasted.

ELEVEN

IT WAS SATURDAY night and North was going to get laid. He was done talking about it. Finished thinking about it. Since he'd been paroled a week hadn't passed without some action. It was time to make it happen.

He decided he would pay a visit to Joe's Cabaret—even if it meant he might have to run into Serena again. The place was easy if he was looking for a quick fix. He could also check in on Piper again while he was there. Two birds, one stone.

He'd worked later than usual at the garage finishing up a frame for a custom chopper his boss needed yesterday. He parked his truck in the driveway beside his bike. Faith's car was already there . . . probably where it would sit all night. She didn't have much of a social life as far as he could tell.

He'd just reached his front door when a gleaming black Audi pulled into Faith's driveway. He hesitated, watching as a guy got out from behind the wheel. A loafers, chinos and polo shirt kind of guy. He wore a blazer over the polo shirt. Even at dusk, it was hot as hell to be wearing a blazer when you didn't have to. He held a bouquet of flowers in his hand. Yellow roses. If that didn't scream first date he wasn't sure what did. Not that North brought flowers to any doors these days. He might not date, but he'd bought wrist corsages before—his junior and senior year. One might have even been yellow.

Fancy Pants spotted him and nodded a greeting in his direction, smiling politely even as his gaze skimmed and assessed North in his work clothes. Clothes that consisted of well-worn jeans and a grease-stained T-shirt with the garage's logo on his chest. It was a cursory inspection, but one that seemed to say *beneath me*. Or maybe North was projecting because he felt that way? *Because you are*. He was good for fucking a woman and getting her off . . . but not dating. Not marrying. Not being the kind of man a girl took home to Mom and Dad.

North nodded back at him, jerking his chin up once in stiff acknowledgment. He shut the door but didn't move away from it. He didn't walk into his house and do his normal things like a normal human being. No, he turned around and peered through the living room blinds, straining to see as much as he could of the man walking up to Faith's front door.

The guy moved out of sight, but that didn't prompt North to move away. No, he waited. He heard the knock at her door. He heard the door opening. He heard the low rumble of voices. A man's deeper voice followed by a softer female voice. His body tensed, leaning toward that sound—Faith's voice. It was her.

And still he waited. Listening. He heard the door shut. Keys jangled in the lock.

Fancy Pants came into view, walking back down the driveway (minus the flowers) with Faith following him. North gazed at the back of her head. At the sleek fall of brown hair that fell a little past her shoulders. Still no view of her face. Damn it. How hard could it be to see what she looked like? The irony wasn't lost on him that she had seen him. *All* of him.

She was wearing a dress. A little black number that looked like definite evening attire. *Date* attire. Not something she would wear to the office doing whatever it was that she did. Except those shoes. She still had on sexy shoes. Black heels with laces that wrapped around her ankles and tied off in a little neat bow. Her legs were still endless, still perfect, in his mind, for wrapping around a man.

Fancy Pants opened the passenger side door for her like a gentleman. Because he was a gentleman. That was the kind of man she would date because that was the kind of man she deserved.

She slid into the car with her face averted, impossible to see in the fading dusk. He still had no view of her face. Still.

NORTH CHANGED HIS mind. Instead of Joe's Cabaret, he decided to go to Roscoe's, his family's bar, which Knox ran. Knox had offered him a job there when he got out, but he'd declined, feeling the need to distance himself from his brother and the rest of the family.

Two years ago, he had been angry at the world when he was paroled. And wrong or right, a lot of that anger had been directed at Knox. He'd needed time and space from his brother, who had somehow managed to build a pretty nice life for himself. Maybe he still needed that space. Maybe he always would. It was for the best. North had found his own path. He liked his work at the garage and the freelance projects he did on the side. He was his own man. No longer Knox Callaghan's kid brother. He faced the world alone and stood on his own two feet. Just as he'd had to do in those last four years at the Rock.

He didn't mind visiting Roscoe's now and then though. His drinks were on the house. Knox, Aunt Alice and any of the other servers on shift never charged him. Saturday nights were always hopping. Plenty of pretty barflies for him to hook up with for the night.

He was eyeing his choices when Knox started in on him. "Hey, man, what about dinner. Tomorrow night? Briar will cook up something good."

Of course she would. His brother's wife was Betty effing Crocker. North was on his second beer, eyeing a petite blonde dressed in a micromini denim skirt that alerted the world she was wearing a pink G-string—the polar opposite of his uptight neighbor, and that was a good thing. He didn't need to think about Faith Walters with her nice clothes out on her date. Maybe Fancy Pants would take her back to his place and they would have polite, nice-people sex. Lights off, missionary-style, quiet and civilized, those long legs of hers probably flat on the bed, neglected and unappreciated.

"Hey. Earth to North?"

North grunted, watching as the blonde lifted the bottle to her lips. Instead of drinking from it like a normal person, she played with the mouth of the bottle, circling it with her tongue as she stared at North. It didn't particularly do anything for him except convey that she was DTF.

"Oh. I see you've spotted Mindy. She's been a regular here since her divorce last year. She's steadily working her way through the regulars. Loves the hardcore bikers. Looks like she's taken a shine to you tonight, brother."

North took a deep swig of his beer, staring at the girl on the other side of the bar who was nothing like Faith. Faith, who was on a date. He wondered where Fancy Pants took her. He snorted. Why should he care how his stick-up-her-ass neighbor spent her nights? He was spending his exactly how he preferred.

The blonde made eye contact with him and nodded for the door. Invitation sent. He nodded back. Invitation accepted.

He started to get up, but Knox stalled him, dropping a hand on his arm. "You can do better than this."

And by *this*, he knew his brother wasn't simply talking about the girl. She was just part of it. Another anonymous woman for him to lose himself in for a night.

Knox continued into the silence, "When is it going to stop, North? You're thirty-two. You gonna be one of those tired old men who comes to the bar and drinks himself past pain every night? You won't be young forever. There will come a time when hooking up won't be so easy and you'll really be alone."

"I'm alone now," he returned, his voice empty, without inflection, as he held his brother's gaze across the bar top. A bright Budweiser light from behind the bar haloed his brother in red.

"By choice," Knox shot back. "You don't have to be."

"Don't try to make me into something I'm not. I'm not you. I'm not going to find some nice girl that's gonna make me forget everything. I can't do that." Couldn't forget even if he wanted to.

Knox stared at him a long moment, looking helpless and not a little guilty, and North regretted that. He didn't want his brother to feel guilty. North wasn't his brother's responsibility.

He shrugged his arm out from beneath his brother's hand. He jerked his head toward the door. "She's waiting."

"We'll see you for dinner tomorrow?" he called, the hope still there, hanging in his voice.

North looked back. His brother's gaze searched his own, looking for something. Something that wasn't there. Not anymore.

"Sure," he agreed, not sure if he meant it or not, but it was easier to agree at the moment.

He stepped outside of Roscoe's into the warm night and inhaled. He glanced left and right, looking for the blonde. The blonde who was nothing like Faith.

He walked down the wooden porch steps leading to the bar and caught sight of her. She stood in the parking lot, leaning against the hood of a truck, her elbows propped behind her so that her chest was thrust out.

He moved toward her, burying one hand in his back jeans pocket. "Hey," he greeted.

"Hi there, sexy. Thought you changed your mind about joining me."

She wasn't as young as he first thought in the dim confines of the bar. She was at least his age. Maybe older. Out here with Roscoe's perimeter lights and the sporadically situated parking lot lights, he could see the heavy application of makeup on her skin. It was like a layer of beige primer that failed to hide the drawn and tired flesh of her face. No amount of makeup could disguise the lines and heavy shadows that resembled bruises under her bloodshot eyes.

"C'mere," she slurred, her hands reaching for him. She grabbed his shirt with two hands, twisting the fabric in her balled-up fists. "Wanna go back to my place?"

He opened his mouth to say yes. Yes. That's what he wanted. That's what going out tonight had been about. Find a willing partner. Down a few beers. Fuck like rabbits and then pass out. Sleep a dreamless sleep. The offer was here for the taking. It shouldn't be so very difficult to find the words to accept.

He closed his hands over hers where they clutched at his shirt. "I . . ." The single syllable stretched long and then faded away.

Apparently it was difficult because staring down at her the only thing he could see was the defeat in her stare. It was a familiar sight. He'd seen it enough times in himself over the years.

He wouldn't be one more thing, one more reason, chipping away at what remained of her soul.

She read his hesitation. "What?" she asked in her hoarse smoker's voice. "You want to go to your place? Or we can do it right here in my car?"

He lifted her hands from his chest and dropped

them away from him. "Sorry. I'm gonna call it quits for the night."

"What?" Her face twisted with angry emotion, which only seemed to highlight the broken spirit within. "It's not even that late yet. What did you follow me out here for if you weren't up for it?"

"My mistake."

She shoved off the truck and lurched past him. "Asshole." Mindy jabbed a thumb at the building. "Plenty of guys inside there will be happy to tap my ass." To emphasize her point, she twisted around and slapped her backside.

She walked away, her strides choppy with the frenzy of her temper, her shoes crunching over loose gravel.

"Hey," he called. She stopped and glanced back. "You can do better than this." He motioned to himself and Roscoe's with one sweep of his hand.

Even as he uttered the words, he cringed inside to hear himself use his brother's own words on someone else. And he didn't know why he even bothered. He wasn't anyone's savior.

Red splotches broke out across her face. "What are you, a missionary? Fuck off." She slammed back inside the bar.

He stood alone in the parking lot for a few moments before managing a laugh. A missionary was the last thing he was. He was not in a position to save anyone.

He couldn't even save himself.

He moved to his bike. Straddling it, he felt especially grim. This was not the way he'd planned to spend the night. Heading home alone and it wasn't even 10 P.M. yet. He bet his neighbor was having a better time than he was.

And that thought was the cherry on his already shit night.

THE DATE WAS going well.

The encouraging thought ran through her mind on repeat. Almost like she was trying to convince herself of that fact, but it was true. Brendan Cooper was a gentleman. He never made a misstep.

She had liked him in all their previous interactions, but still, with her track record, buried deep inside, she had been braced for disappointment.

Over an appetizer of fried calamari he asked about her job. Over their entrées of lasagna and chicken parmesan, he asked about her family, voicing his respect and admiration for her father and brothers. All checks in the respect-for-family column. It was companionable and intimate and comfortable.

When he offered Faith a portion of his chicken parm, she offered him some of her lasagna.

"I'll never say no to food." He smiled as he handed her his small bread plate and she gave him a portion of her entrée.

He cut into her lasagna and closed his eyes as he brought it to his mouth. After he swallowed his bite, he pronounced, "Wow. Don't tell my mother, but that puts her lasagna to shame. She's half Italian and would take great offense."

Faith smiled, certain those were just words. "I won't say anything." He surely didn't mean that she would meet his mother. They weren't talking that far ahead yet.

"Do you like to cook?" he asked.

She nodded. "Yes. I love to bake actually."

His eyes widened. "Uh-oh. We could have a problem . . . because I love to eat sweets."

For a moment, she had a flash of North Callaghan texting her that he liked cupcakes. She knew he had not been talking about true cupcakes. In this case, she knew Brendan was talking about eating sweets. For some reason her chest sank a little. What was wrong with her? She *wanted* Brendan to be a little dirty? This was a first date. He was appropriate and respectful and she should appreciate that and not long for something else.

She fiddled with her lasagna. "Oh, do you? Then you might like my cheesecake." Okay, so she was attempting to flirt a little. Not to the level of last night's flirting with North Callaghan, but definitely flirting.

"I hope dating you doesn't make me gain too much weight." He patted what she could see of his flat stomach. Clearly he took care of himself.

They were dating now? A slow ribbon of pleasure curled around her.

"Weight gain," she mused. "A natural side effect of being in a relationship."

"True, but there are worse things than turning into a plump contented man in a relationship."

"Such as?"

"Being single and skinny." He mock shuddered and she laughed. "I mean, if you're happy, that's what's important, right?" His hazel eyes held hers. They were nice eyes. Not probing or intense.

"Yes," she agreed. "I suppose that's true."

For some reason a vision of North Callaghan's hard body flashed across her mind. She couldn't picture him ever being soft. Or being in a relationship, for that matter.

She mentally kicked herself. She did not want to be thinking about him right now when she was having a lovely dinner with a lovely man. He'd already intruded far too much in the course of the evening.

They shared an order of tiramisu and finished their bottle of wine. It wasn't hurried. After wine, they ordered coffee and chatted. Still, mostly about work. There was a lot of intersection in their careers. He'd represented the city of Sweet Hill in several of her cases. Things in common. She should have loved that.

But after working all week, she almost wished they could talk about something else. Anything.

She brought up some of her favorite shows, but he didn't watch much television.

"I know I shouldn't, but I bring home a lot of my work with me at night."

"That's . . . admirable." And a little disappointing, but maybe that would change if he had a girlfriend. Certainly, he wouldn't do that if he had a wife and family. He would have other things, more important things, to occupy him. She stared at him across the table as though she could see into the future to whether or not he would be one of those men obsessed with his job to the point that he neglected his family.

It was close to ten by the time he drove her home.

She couldn't stop herself from looking to see if her neighbor was home. North's truck and bike were present when Brendan pulled his car in behind hers. He'd been home when Brendan picked her up earlier. It was a Saturday night. Surely he had things to do. *Women* to do . . .

Brendan walked around to get her door.

"Thank you," she murmured.

He smiled and gestured for her to proceed ahead of him. Her heels clicked softly as she made her way to the front porch. At her door, she stopped. This was always the awkward part.

She motioned behind her. "Would you like a tour?" They had talked about her new house over dinner. He was aware that she was a first-time homeowner and she was excited about it.

Anyone else might read the invitation to come inside as an *invitation*, but she had been working with Brendan for a while now, and it felt more awkward *not* to make the offer. They were already friends and she would have issued the invitation to any friend.

"Sure. I'd love to." He stepped inside behind her.

She dropped her purse on the kitchen table and led him through the house, relieved that she'd tidied up the place—not that she was much for clutter. He remarked kindly about her attempts at decorating. She thought her place looked nice and homey, with copper pots hanging in her kitchen, and an array of pillows on the couches and her bed. Still, she knew it wasn't like something out of a magazine. She didn't really have an eye for that kind of thing.

"Thanks. Decorating is not really my thing. I've started watching HGTV though. Trying to pick up some tips."

It didn't take long to show him around. They quickly covered the downstairs: living room, kitchen, office/guest bedroom. She showed him her yard, mentioning she wanted to plant a garden in the spring. Her mother had loved to garden and it was something she wanted to try her hand at.

Next, she showed him the upstairs: the master bedroom and bathroom. The bathroom was her favorite with both a shower and a large spa tub.

Fifteen minutes later they stood in her kitchen again. The first-date-saying-goodnight awkwardness she had been hoping to avoid crept in then.

Thankfully he took it as his cue to leave. "I guess I'll get going."

She nodded and released a breathy sigh of relief, moving to open the door for him.

"Would you like to have dinner again? I'm really swamped this upcoming week with a trial. I'll have several late nights. How about the week after? Actually I'll cook and bring you dinner."

She blinked. He would cook her dinner? "You

cook?" He hadn't mentioned that talent in their dinner conversation.

He shrugged. "I can make a decent pasta, bake some garlic bread and open a bottle of wine. Maybe you can make that cheesecake you bragged about." He winked at her.

"That sounds great."

He nodded. "Good. Six? It's a work night."

A work night. *Because work is his priority. Where's the passion? The spontaneity?* She pushed aside the niggling little voice that wanted to be annoyed over this. "Sounds perfect."

What do you want, Faith? Impractical and wild? Dirty-talking and irresponsible? A guy with a revolving bedroom door who has sex whenever he feels like it—any time, any day of the week.

She winced. No. She didn't want that. *That* lived next door and she found him objectionable on every level. His body and face flashed across her mind. Well, almost every level.

Before departing, Brendan stepped in to give her a hug. She patted his shoulder and told herself that none of this was awkward at all.

Closing the door, she kicked off her shoes and moved upstairs, struggling with the zipper at the back of her dress. Finally able to grab it, she stepped out of the dress and tossed it in her laundry hamper.

She slid on a pair of pajama bottoms and a soft camisole. Making her way back downstairs, she spotted a text from Wendy demanding to know all the details of her date.

Laughing lightly, she moved into the kitchen. Opening the dishwasher, she started unloading it. She'd wait to reply to that one. There would be a lot of back and forth. Wendy was demanding that way.

Moments later, the phone buzzed again. She sent it a glance, assuming it was more from Wendy.

Date wasn't that great?

Speak of the devil. A smile tugged at her mouth. She snatched the phone up and stared at it one long moment before lifting her gaze to stare at her wall as though she could see through to the other side.

It appeared she wasn't the only one listening at walls and staring out between blinds. North Callaghan was monitoring her comings and goings. He'd seen Brendan bring her home and come inside her house. He'd accurately surmised she was on a date. He knew. It should be creepy, especially considering what she knew about his background, but she couldn't feel creeped out. She'd done her share of spying on him, after all.

Huffing out a breath, she succumbed and texted back. No. It was great.

> Not that great. I don't hear your headboard knocking.

Oh! Heat clawed her face. Not every date ends in sex. It doesn't mean it was a bad date.

> Definitely doesn't mean it was great.

> You have messed-up dating standards.

> Just saying. If you can't help tearing each other's clothes off and going at it like rabbits the chemistry must be off.

That was his definition of good chemistry? She lifted her gaze to the wall again and bit her lip. Was he right? The impulse to do *that* hadn't even been there. Should it have been? She wasn't saying she *should* have jumped into bed with Brendan, but shouldn't there have been the desire? The chemistry? She hadn't even thought about sex once when she looked at Brendan tonight. She dropped her gaze back down to her phone and typed. I hate you.

Very faint, laughter drifted through the walls. He was over there *laughing* at her.

She stomped her foot and resisted the urge to storm next door. Her phone buzzed in her hand. She glanced down.

> Don't get mad at me just because I pointed
> out some truths.

Her fingers flew back with a response. I'm not angry. I just don't like you very much Mr. Callaghan. Lust after him? Fine. There was that. But he didn't need to know it. And fortunately (unfortunately?) Faith wasn't the type of person who could go to bed with a person she didn't at least like. She was attracted to him because he looked the way he did. Because he filled out a T-shirt with a body that looked like it could break granite. Clearly. No other reason.

Brendan Cooper was good-looking, too. An insidious little voice reminded her of that fact. Over half the women at the courthouse salivated over him. Wendy wasn't the only one.

Her phone buzzed with another text. Back to being formal? A little late for that isn't it?

Please stop texting me.

Women who've seen my dick usually just call me North.

Her heart pounded faster, harder as the memory of a naked North Callaghan flooded over her—not that the sight of him naked was ever far from her thoughts.

Sorry. Did I see it? I can't remember.

Liar. You saw it. I bet you're still seeing it.

Your arrogance is amazing. Goodnight Mr. Callaghan.

Goodnight Ms. Walters.

She stood there for a few moments, staring at her phone and wondering if he would decide to text her back despite his goodnight. She vowed not to reply if he did. She'd just had a date with a handsome, decent guy. Exactly the kind of guy she had been looking for. And, most importantly, there would be a second date. She needed to stop whatever it was she was doing here.

I bet you're still seeing it.

The muscles low in her belly quivered as she stared at his previous text message. The words were branded on her. She closed her eyes and released a hissing breath. After a moment, she closed out the screen and moved into her contacts so that she could edit his name again.

She changed him from **Giver of Orgasms** to **Arrogant Cock**. She told herself he would be less appealing that way.

TWELVE

Sunday dinner with her father and brother wasn't quite everything she had expected it would be. There was no sweet nostalgia about coming home and cooking in the same kitchen she had been cooking in for the few years since she'd returned home.

Maybe it was too soon. She hadn't moved out and been in her own place for very long and it felt almost like she had never moved out at all as she opened familiar drawers and cupboards. As she refreshed Dad's and Hale's drinks. As she brought them crudités and dip where they lounged in the living room watching a game on TV. She turned the mixer on high so that it whipped the potatoes to a nice, airy consistency, frowning at the explosion of shouts carrying from the living room.

It felt as though she had slipped through a

wormhole. Like she hadn't broken free at all. Like she was still in the same rut she was desperately trying to escape.

Except there was North Callaghan in her life now. He was very un-rut-like.

She scowled. *He's not in your life. He's the opposite of in your life.*

She finished preparing the rest of dinner over Dad's and Hale's exclamations at the TV. She had always marveled at them when they shouted and addressed the players. Did they think the players on TV could hear them?

When she called them to the table, it didn't take long for them to start grilling her about work—apparently they had heard about the outburst at the courthouse the other day.

"I don't understand why you can't pick a different career, Faithy." Hale smeared butter onto his bread as he offered this to the conversation.

Her father followed the observation with "Why can't you just get married? Settle down and have a couple kids?"

"Woah, let's not go that far." Hale held up a hand and pulled a face that seemed to indicate how repellent that idea was to him. Probably because it meant that his sister would have sex. Her father might as well have suggested she start hooking.

She resisted snapping at her father. In his world, marriage and kids meant she wouldn't work anymore. Her dad was very old-school in that capacity. It would never cross his mind she might want to continue working after starting a family.

Also, in his mind, Faith's mom had loved staying home and being a wife and mother. Dying young and leaving all that behind had not been her choice. It had been her greatest regret. For Faith to protest this seemed like an insult to her mother.

She tore off a hunk of bread and liberally lathered it with butter. She deserved carbs right now. Dad kept talking and she endured it, opting not to tell them about her date with Brendan. It might lift their hopes too much.

And then there was the matter of her neighbor. She didn't expect to have to *avoid* the subject of him. Her family knew nothing about him. Her anonymous neighbor would not cross their minds. They would never bring him up. She had Doris's word that she wouldn't say anything to Hale about him. But Callaghan had been on her mind so much lately that it felt as though he were another thing she was hiding.

Then her brother went ahead and surprised her. As though he could read her mind, he asked, "Meet your neighbor yet?"

Hale poured a generous amount of gravy over his mashed potatoes. It rolled close to the edge of his plate, threatening to spill over onto her mother's plaid green place mats. That much gravy would leave her bloated for a week, but not Hale. Her brother was six feet five inches of honed muscle. Her mother had always pointed to their Viking ancestry as the culprit for their great size.

"No," she said. Too quickly.

"No?" He looked up. "You been in your place over a week now and you haven't met your neighbor."

Yeah, that sounded odd. "I've been working late." She shrugged, then felt relief as that led her father into a diatribe about her working too long and not getting out there and meeting her future husband.

Suffice to say she was relieved when the meal ended. Dad and Hale chipped in and helped with the dishes, so cleanup went fast and she ducked out with an excuse about being tired.

She pulled up in her driveway and sat there for a moment, clenching her steering wheel and staring at her humble abode. She needed to get some potted plants or flowers for her front porch.

He gaze drifted to the emptiness that stretched along her neighboring porch. Not a potted plant

or flower in sight. North's bike was gone and she
wondered where he could be. She supposed booty
calls happened any night of the week . . . even on
Sundays. He was probably out banging some girl
with a name like Bambi.

That kind of thinking, of course, made her mentally slap herself. She needed to get accustomed to
pulling into her driveway without thinking about
her sexy neighbor.

Hard to do, especially considering last night.
Their texting had taken another level. It went
beyond dirty talk to *I'm up for it if you are.*

Of course, in no way could she entertain the
idea of sleeping with her neighbor. That just had
Bad Idea written all over it. And that wasn't even
touching on the fact that he was an ex-con. Even if
she could see herself having a fling . . . she couldn't
have a fling with a guy like him.

She could almost hear Wendy's voice in her
head. *That's precisely the kind of guy you have a
fling with.*

She sighed, internally chatting back as though
Wendy were in front of her. Fine. Maybe. Okay.
But then she was left with the not-so-minor issue
of living next door to the guy. If things took a turn
for the bad, she couldn't exactly avoid him.

After stepping inside her house, she locked the

door behind her and rolled her neck, stretching out the tense muscles. She knew what she needed. A long bubble bath with a book. Something smutty. No, eighty-six that. A suspense novel. That sounded perfect.

Nodding, she pushed off her door and headed upstairs.

"WE'RE SO GLAD you joined us for dinner." Briar looked at him with her heart in her eyes. As though it was such a big fucking deal that he came out to visit them at the old farmhouse.

And he supposed it was. He hadn't done it in a while. He'd caved when she had texted him directly this morning, sending a picture of the chocolate cake she had made. A man couldn't very well resist chocolate cake, could he?

Besides. Just because he didn't have much in common with Knox anymore didn't mean he didn't care about his brother. He loved him. He just couldn't *be* him—or anything like him. No matter how much Knox wanted that for him.

Still. He felt like a fraud sitting at Briar's cloth-covered table, a spread before them bountiful enough to rival a Thanksgiving feast. Unbidden, he wondered if she knew Faith Walters. They were two of a kind. Good girls who liked to cook.

He forked another mouthful of mashed potatoes, saving himself from having to reply to Briar. He wasn't sure what he was supposed to say anyway. He nodded, telling himself he just had to act the part of contented and well-adjusted for another hour and then he could go home. It's what he did day to day. At his job. When he met with people who bought and commissioned his work. When he met with his PO. The only problem was that his brother was more observant than most people.

"How's work?"

"Good." He stabbed a bite of green beans. "Busy."

"Still working on the custom bikes?"

"Yes."

"Glad that you were able to learn a trade," Knox said, referring to North's welding. "At least something good came . . ." Knox's voice faded at North's swift look.

He wasn't about to say anything good came out of his stint in Devil's Rock. So he'd learned to weld while locked up. Big deal. If they hadn't fucked up and gotten sentenced to prison, he would have gone to college. He was good at math back then. He might have made something of himself. If his life hadn't wildly swerved off course.

"If things slow down or work becomes thin at

the garage, you know we could use help at Roscoe's," Knox reminded him. Roscoe had been their great-grandfather's name. He'd opened the bar right after prohibition ended. The place went way back. It was an institution in these parts, and the reins had fallen to Knox to run it. Knox was good at it. It was like the place was in Knox's blood. Even if Knox hadn't gone to prison and he had finished college, North could see him doing just what he was doing right now. Running Roscoe's. Married to a nice girl and living at the farmhouse. He grimaced. He guessed for some people shit was able to just roll off them.

Briar closed her fingers around Knox's forearm. "We hope you'll come more often for Sunday dinner. It's been a while since your last visit."

He glanced around the place he'd grown up in with Uncle Mac and Aunt Sissy. It looked different. More light and airy. The furniture updated. His uncle had moved into town with his sister, Alice. It was closer to the hospital and all his doctor's appointments. Uncle Mac had had to start dialysis a few months back and he had regular appointments to keep. In addition, he'd insisted the house was too big for him, and Knox and Briar needed their own space as a married couple.

"Especially now," Knox added, his voice taking on a strange quality.

North was in the process of stirring his mashed potatoes and gravy together. He paused and looked up, his gaze drifting back and forth between his brother and sister-in-law. "Why especially now?"

Knox glanced at his wife, lacing his fingers over hers. He then looked back to North. "We're having a baby."

The meatloaf and mashed potatoes in his stomach suddenly turned to lead.

"I'm due in October," Briar volunteered, looking giddy with excitement, her eyes shining.

"That's great," he said numbly. "Congratulations." Did his voice sound as tinny to them as it did to him? His brother was going to have a baby. He was going to be a dad.

Knox stared at him intently, his eyes piercing. "We want you around, North. Around *more*. You're going to be an uncle, and we want you to be the baby's godfather—"

"I don't think that's a good idea, do you?" he blurted before he had time to think how harsh that sounded. He usually tried to pretend. He tried to hide the empty shell that he'd become from his brother and sister-in-law because he didn't want them worried and all over his case. When he first got out of prison, Knox was on him to meet with a counselor. Apparently after meeting Briar, he'd started seeing someone himself. The church they got married in required counseling for their wedding, and he'd continued to go even after the wedding, claiming it was helpful to talk about his problems. *Problems*. Like years at the Rock with men reduced to animals was a problem. Like a clogged-up sink or busted radiator hose.

"What do you mean?" Knox demanded, looking affronted. "It's a fine idea. Who else would—"

"I can't, Knox. I'm not at ease with . . ." People, life, the world. *Everything*. That pressure was back in his chest again, a hot knife digging deep. "You don't want me around your kid. I mean, can you see me at his school functions and shit?"

"North, you're family." Briar leaned forward, still clinging to her husband's hand.

He pushed back from the table. "I appreciate the sentiment, but you're a family." He motioned to both Knox and Briar and the house in which they sat. "You've built a home here. It's the two of you . . . three of you, now. You're all the family you need." He stood and looked down at them sitting close together on the other side of the table.

He knew without looking that their hands were laced together underneath the table. "You don't need me. I know you think you do . . . the idea of including me makes you feel better, but it's not necessary."

"North," Knox tried again.

North held up a hand. "I'll be around. Thanks for dinner." Turning, he exited the house, grateful his brother didn't chase after him.

He walked out into the familiar yard. It was green and well maintained, potted flowers everywhere like when Aunt Sissy had been alive.

The last four years he had been in prison without Knox had been the hardest of his life. Even harder than when he first entered prison. Because Knox had been with him then. He'd never known what it truly felt like to be alone until then. To have to watch his own back. Sometimes he'd succeeded. He reached up a hand and stroked the scar bisecting his face. And other times he'd failed.

His brother had visited every other week, but that hadn't helped. Seeing his brother out, free, had only made being inside, the suffering, all the worse.

Unfailingly though, Knox always came. He never gave up on him. Even when the COs would call his name out at visitation hours and North stayed in his cell, refusing to come out to see him.

He couldn't face his brother and let him see what he'd become. He hadn't wanted to be around his brother then, and he didn't want to be around him now.

THIRTEEN

*S*HE STAYED IN her bathtub until her skin shriveled up like a prune and the water went cold. Setting down her novel, she climbed from the tub and wrapped herself in a towel.

Despite having eaten a serving of cobbler at her father's, she felt like she needed a brownie or something else that could bring on a sugar coma. The evening at her dad's had been distracting and she had not eaten her usual Sunday dinner portion, which could pretty much feed the Green Giant.

Patting herself dry, she wrapped herself in her thick terrycloth robe and padded barefoot downstairs. She opened her pantry and fridge, discovering she had everything she needed except for eggs. Stepping back, she considered if she actually wanted to get dressed, leave the house and go to the store. While she internally debated whether she wanted brownies *that* much, she heard the growl of a bike outside.

She moved to the window and peered out through the blinds, watching as North climbed off his bike. A bike that he parked *behind* her car.

Was he serious?

How was she supposed to go anywhere?

Before she could even think about it, she marched toward her door and yanked it open. Stalking outside into the night, her bare feet slapping over concrete, her robe whipping at her calves, she huffed furiously, knowing she must look like some kind of cartoon character with steam coming out of her ears. But for the love of God she didn't care. It was the height of ridiculousness for him to think that was okay.

She was too annoyed to stop and think. Too annoyed to consider what she was wearing—or rather, what she wasn't wearing. Too annoyed to think that this would be the first time (discounting the green-avocado-mask encounter) that she would be face-to-face with North Callaghan.

The evening air slid over her wet hair and inside the opening of her robe to her naked skin, but she did not care. She'd had it. Grabbing the belt at her waist, she cinched the robe tighter with resolve.

Dinner with Dad and Hale had been agonizing.

Her date last night had been . . . nice . . . and that somehow rubbed her wrong, too. Nice was her grandmother's banana bread. Damn it, she didn't want banana bread.

And then there was this joker with a penchant for having loud sex at all hours, strutting around naked and sending her rated-R texts.

He refused to take her seriously.

She scanned the area for him. He was no longer in their driveway. She spotted him at his door. He looked up at the sound of her approach, turning to face her. Her feet charged toward him over the still-warm concrete.

His face was expressionless, his gaze hooded as it moved up and down her advancing form.

She stopped a couple feet in front of him and stabbed the air, coming close to touching his chest but not actually making contact. She wasn't that bold. Even as pissed off as she was, she wasn't about to get physical with the likes of this man. He had a criminal record.

Keeping her distance, she propped her hands on her hips. "You're trying to provoke me, aren't you?"

He angled his head. "What are you talking about?" Despite the spark in his brown gaze, his voice sounded bored, and that only pissed her off more.

She motioned to the bike. "You're blocking my car."

He sent a slow glance over his shoulder. "You going somewhere? It's late. And a Sunday night. I figured you'd be inside baking muffins or scones or whatever."

She ignored his jabs. "Is it so hard to park in the street?"

He shrugged, but the casual gesture seemed at odds with the intensity of his gaze. "I don't want my bike to get sideswiped."

Of course he had to sound reasonable. But he wasn't. He was a jerk.

"So you just think it's okay to park behind me. I might not have anywhere to go, right?"

He crossed his arms over his chest. "Were you waiting for me to come home to bawl me out?"

"No. I heard you drive up."

His top lip curled in a sneer and she was torn between two overwhelming urges: either to stroke that well-sculpted mouth with her fingertips or smack him.

"Sure you did," he drawled, taking a step closer that made her pulse jump at her neck. "You know, you could have just texted me and asked me nicely to move my bike. Instead you came out here half-cocked—" His gaze dropped. "Half dressed."

She gaped. "Are you insinuating I'm looking for a fight?"

"I think you're looking for something."

There was no mistaking the sexual nature of that statement. Heat flushed through her. That heat sank deep and took up residence in all her girl parts.

"I don't sit around staring out my blinds hoping to get a glimpse of you." She managed not to wince. Okay, yeah, sometimes she did do that, but it would be the last thing she'd admit to.

He smirked and she knew he was remembering when she had watched him in the backyard—when he had been naked and touched himself.

She swallowed and took a few steps back.

He followed with a few steps forward.

"You got somewhere to be?" he asked.

After his jab about her baking scones, she wasn't about to admit she wanted to make herself some brownies. "Yes." Her chin went up.

"Yeah. Where?"

"None of your business." She bumped into the wall of her house. "Just move your bike," she bit out and turned.

He grabbed her wrist and pulled her around to face him. Her hand went to the front of her robe, making sure it wasn't gaping open.

He looked her up and down again. "The truth

is I've had a shitty night, Faith Walters, and I don't feel like having you read me the riot act."

"Yeah? Well, I haven't had the best night either."

"No?" He seized her other hand then, the one gripping the front of her robe. Holding both hands in his, he tugged her toward him.

"You know I've been wondering what your face looked like."

"Yeah?" she bit out, her voice hard with challenge even if she felt shaky and uncertain inside.

"Yeah," he repeated with a nod.

She swallowed, fighting against the sudden lump in her throat. Her porch light glowed strong, bathing her in its yellow glow. There was no hiding her makeup-free features from him. Her wet hair fell around her face in a curtain. "Disappointed?"

He stepped closer and picked up a lock of hair off her shoulder. "Is this your way of fishing for compliments? You want me to tell you that you're pretty? That I'd fuck you."

She snorted. "We know you'd do that with anyone."

"Yeah, well, I'll say it." His gaze dropped to her mouth. "You're pretty." Her breath seized in her chest at the simple declaration. She didn't realize until that moment how badly she wanted him to find her attractive. "I'd fuck you."

"Yeah." Her voice escaped in a whispery rasp. "Well. Not happening. I'm not going to be another notch on your bedpost. I'm certain you can find someone else to fuck."

She closed her hands over his and lifted them off her, desperation hammering inside her. She had to flee. Coming out here, talking to him, letting him touch her . . . it had all been a mistake.

He angled his head and rubbed at the back of his neck with an idleness she didn't feel. "Yeah, that's gonna be a problem."

"Why's that?"

"You see . . . ever since you moved in, I've kind of wanted to fuck you." He shrugged like he was just commenting on the weather.

She laughed weakly even as her heart knocked like a battering ram against her chest. "This is the first time you've even seen my face."

"I know. It's crazy." He nodded his dark head. "I never wanted a woman without knowing what she looked like."

"Bullshit," she snapped, certain that he was lying. Mocking her. As always.

She spun around and charged toward her door. Maybe she did need to rethink staying here. Maybe she did need to move because—

A hand on her shoulder had her whirling around.

She caught a flash of dark eyes before his mouth slammed over hers.

She inhaled through her nose as his mouth slanted over hers. His lips were soft. She didn't know what she'd expected. He was so hard. His eyes. His body. Everything about him, but his mouth was gentle and coaxing on hers.

He spoke against her mouth. "Does this feel like bullshit? I wanted you before I could see you. And now that I've seen you . . . I want you even more."

His words sapped her lingering willpower. She couldn't stop herself. She lifted her hands and grabbed his neck, her fingers curling through the strands of hair at his nape, pulling him closer, drawing him in. And still it was not enough. Still not close enough. She wouldn't be close enough until she had managed to crawl inside him.

There were distant sounds. A dog barking. A car starting somewhere down the street. The sudden burst of wind stirring the heated air and wrestling with dry leaves in trees. All this was muted background to the roar of blood in her veins for this man. For his mouth on hers. His tongue sliding past her lips. For the hard plane of his chest mashing into her.

He made a growling sound of approval. His

hands, contrary to his mouth, felt firm and hard, controlling as they grabbed her waist and turned her, guiding her backward while never breaking their kiss until he hefted her up and plopped her down on the hood of her car—as though she weighed nothing at all. And that was saying something.

She was no small package. At five feet ten inches she could seriously throw out a man's back. A normal man. Just not this one. He would have been a warrior in another time. A warrior with a marauding mouth. Her hands pulled and tugged at him, desperate for more. She ached and wanted with every burning fiber of her being. A terrifying realization. Faith had never wanted anyone like this. It was scary. A person did not just enter into a fling with their next-door neighbor and not suffer consequences. Especially not with a man like this. He was complicated. Dark and edgy.

And yet here she was, panting and kissing him as though a gun were pointed at her skull demanding she do so.

She shoved her body back against him, pressing breasts that suddenly felt tight and aching into his chest. Her robe was thick and fluffy. He couldn't possibly feel her hardened nipples, but she did. She felt the prodding tips chafing against the terrycloth of her robe, dying to be acknowledged . . . touched, *anything* . . .

"I knew you wanted to be bad." His deep voice rumbled against her mouth.

Those words jarred her.

She broke her lips free of his, opening her eyes to a blurred world. She blinked off her daze, focusing on his looming face.

He sucked in a breath and looked down at her. His skin was flushed, the scar standing out starkly, a white tear against the heated color of his skin.

"Wait, wait, wait . . ." she gasped.

He waited. Staring down at her in a way that made her feel like cornered prey . . . moments before the wolf decided to pounce and feast.

Looking up at him, she noted the various golden-brown flecks in his deep brown eyes. Who knew brown eyes could have so many colors? Who knew *any* man's eyes could make her feel so warm and melty inside? Her hand shook between them, pressing against the hard wall of his chest. Not so much to ward him off as to keep herself from diving back in.

He really was a beautiful man. The scar only seemed to highlight the near-perfect symmetry of his face. She itched to touch that face, test its texture, feel the scratch of a day's growth of beard. He was this close. She could.

"What?" The gravelly pitch to his voice made her shiver. The sound of his voice told her everything. He might be waiting, but it cost him. He wanted her. A lot. It seemed impossible.

Wait? Why did you tell him to wait? She couldn't even remember what she had wanted to say. All she could do was stare at his face, his eyes, the mad tic pulsing in his cheek, and think how much she wanted all of that—*him*—to unleash on her.

Even with a foot between them, she felt the heat radiating from him. His body was a pulsing rod of electricity. And she wanted that rod. Her lips felt bruised and tingly and aching. Aching for the return of his mouth. Aching for the rest of him.

She didn't want to stop. She shook her head and leaned forward. "Never mind," she muttered.

"Thank God." His head swooped back down. His hands moved from her waist to her hips and yanked her closer, forcing her thighs to open and accept him more fully. "You taste so good. Like you smell. Fresh and clean like rainwater."

Her robe parted below the waist, falling open to the point where she had belted it tightly. Otherwise she would be sitting spread-eagled and bare from stem to stern. Balanced on the hood of a car with him wedged between her thighs, his hardness positioned directly where she most needed it.

She wasn't wearing any underwear and the rough hard scratch of denim abraded her tender parts and shot bolts of sensation into her sex. Her eyes flew open even as his mouth continued its assault on her lips.

She cried out, her fingers digging into the hard wall of his chest. She couldn't even properly kiss him as he ground his cock against her.

He didn't seem to care. His mouth moved down her jaw to her neck. Her head fell back. He kissed her neck, laved it with his tongue and then bit down on the stretched cord of her throat. A strangled sob broke from her. Wetness rushed between her legs. She inched down and tilted her hips, angling herself, searching, trying to find what it was she needed. *OhMyGod. OhMyGod. OhMyGod.* A wave welled up on her. Big and frightening in its intensity. Like nothing she had ever felt and yet she knew what it was. She knew what was coming, as unbelievable as it seemed, and she swam hard for the crest of it.

"Please, please," she begged, tears pricking at the corners of her eyes.

He seemed to know. He understood. His hands slid under her, cupping the bare rounds of her ass inside her robe. She didn't even jerk at this first touch on her naked flesh. It felt right. The most natural thing in the world.

He groaned. "You have a tight ass, Faith." Squeezing the mounds, he lifted her, brought her closer, harder against him, digging his denim-covered cock into her weeping sex.

She moaned, her hands dropping to clutch at his biceps. Just a little more, a few more scrapes of denim against her clit and she would be done. Finished.

"Please," she choked again.

It was like he knew exactly what she needed. He slid one hand deftly between them, testing. His fingers found her core, wet and soaking for him. It was shameful how wet she was, but she was too gone to care. He stroked her folds, parting them slightly to test her opening, tracing it in a slow teasing circle.

It was too much. She was shaking now, crying out against his lips, needing him firmer, harder, driving into her, filling up the unbearable hollowness.

"That's it, baby. Come for me."

She bit her lip until she tasted the coppery wash of blood. She didn't care. She welcomed the pain. She had to treat herself so cruelly to stop herself from begging. She craved him inside her. Now. Hard and fast, she needed him to put out the fire he had started in her.

She arched her throat and lifted up, toward him, toward that hand. She was close.

He pulled back from her mouth with a ragged gasp. "Let's go inside your house."

She stared at him, unable to speak. Unable to think. That battering ram inside her chest was working overtime now. "Wh-what?" she managed to get out, speaking amid the maelstrom of sensations bombarding her.

"Let's go inside your house," he repeated. The words shuddered out of him, a spaced breath between each one. She felt them reverberate into her. Through her. His eyes were dark mirrors reflecting her own torment. "I need to be inside you bad, Faith."

She blinked and gave her head a small shake, coming to as if breaking free of a fog. "No."

"No?" he echoed, his voice and face strained.

She nodded, regaining her composure—and good sense.

She wiggled enough to dislodge his hand from between her legs. She brought her thighs back together, locking her quaking knees tight and hastily covering them up with her robe.

Unfortunately, she could not hop down from the hood of the car without touching him. Without bringing her body flush with him, which was the last thing she wanted to do right now with all of her still burning and aching.

He was in the way, staring at her with flaring nostrils and dark, hooded eyes. Part of him looked ready to ignore her and that should have frightened her. But somehow she knew he wouldn't do that. This killer . . . this criminal . . . he wouldn't force her.

He wouldn't have to. She shook off that insidious whisper. Sure. He could probably persuade her. Kiss her a little more, touch her. Bring her to a screaming climax. But he wouldn't because she told him to stop.

Her voice emerged much firmer. "No. We can't. *I* can't."

Because this was insane. And she was not. She was sane. She was Faith Walters. A sensible woman. A woman who lived a safe life without risk. And face it. North Callaghan was a risk.

His eyes narrowed to slits. "What's the matter? I'm not good enough for you? I don't drive an Audi and wear slacks and have a membership to the local country club?"

His words struck like a well-aimed arrow.

She knew he knew about her date, but she had no idea he had been watching *that* closely. It didn't make sense that he should be so very interested in who she was dating. That he gave a damn about *her* at all. That she was anything beyond a potential roll in the sack. It went against everything she thought she knew about him.

"That's not it at all," she denied, wanting to believe that she wasn't that superficial. She wasn't after the things he'd just accused her of wanting. She was a social worker. She could have gone to college to be anything else, but she spent her days working with the less fortunate and it definitely wasn't because it paid the big bucks.

He nodded and smirked slightly. "It is. A little. Come on, admit it."

She stubbornly shook her head. She wasn't interested in Brendan Cooper for those reasons.

He continued, "I bet if your Fancy Pants boyfriend could get you this hot and bothered you'd be inviting him inside your house . . . inside your bed right this second."

"I would not," she insisted. Although she wasn't so certain. She thought back to their date. Their very *nice* date. As far as first dates went, it barely registered on the Richter scale. If Brendan had entered her house and started making out with her with half the skill that North Callaghan just exhibited, would she have hesitated to jump his bones?

At his dubious look, she insisted, "I'm sure he can get me hot and bothered! We just haven't tried yet . . ."

He laughed once, a hard bark that made her skin jump. "Sometimes it's not a choice, you know. The chemistry is just there and you have to have each other." His dark eyes heated and that battering ram was back again, beating against her chest so hard it hurt to breathe.

Oh, this guy was good. Every time he opened his mouth he affected her. She guessed that was the gift of bad boys. The thing that gave them the advantage over all the good boys of the world.

She shook her head, feeling confused. "Brendan and I just started dating. He's a gentleman. If things continue to go well, then, yeah, our relationship will progress to that level." She shook her head, suddenly angry with herself for feeling so defensive. She didn't need to justify anything to North.

"*That* level?" He laughed harshly. "You mean *our* level?"

"The last time I checked you and I were not dating," she snapped. "You are not Brendan."

"In that we are both in agreement." He looked

smug as he flung that out at her. Then he shrugged, adding, "With enough time, maybe you and Fancy Pants will reach third base?"

Fury flashed through her. With both hands she gave his chest a mighty shove and hopped down off the car hood. Her hands flew to her robe, straightening it and making sure it was still in place, covering all her girl parts. She backed up, her feet sliding over the concrete as she closed the distance to her door.

"You're a jerk!"

"You weren't saying that a few minutes ago."

She raked him coolly for good measure, doing her best to convey her utter contempt.

His deep brown eyes squinted at her. If possible his smirk went deeper. "Things would go much smoother if you just went ahead and let this happen between us."

"You arrogant—"

"Not arrogant." His smirk vanished as he closed the distance between them, stopping directly in front of her. "You and I are going to collide." He allowed a fraction of space between them. "That's where this train has been headed since the moment you moved in here."

His face was so close. She could easily mark the light brown striations in his eyes. The dark fan of his lashes. The thick slash of his eyebrows. She thought for certain he was going to kiss her again. And contrary her . . . she leaned forward incrementally. "Don't kiss me," she pleaded in a whisper.

He chuckled lightly. "I won't do that. You've drawn your line in the sand, Faith Walters. I'll sit back and wait for you to step over it." That said, he moved away, walking backward slowly, his gaze devouring her. When he reached his door he turned. Keys already in his hand, he unlocked his door and moved inside. Disappearing from her sight, though not disappearing from her thoughts.

She reentered her house, thoughts of him chasing after her, the sensation of him trailing her like a ghost.

It would be a long sleepless night.

FOURTEEN

*T*HAT MONDAY FAITH left work early for a dentist appointment. She'd gone to the same family dentist since high school. She had attended Sweet Hill High School with Dr. Brown's goddaughter, Teeny Roberts. Contrary to what her name might indicate, Teeny Roberts wasn't teeny. Considering Faith's own impressive size, she was not one to cast aspersions either. Teeny was a member of the high school wrestling team and the biggest bully to come out of the Sweet Hill public school system since ever. Truly, training her in wrestling might have been an irresponsible move on behalf of the coaching staff as far as Faith was concerned.

Teeny had been an equal-opportunity bully. All kids, boys and girls alike since kindergarten, had been subject to her wrath at one time or another. Still, Faith smiled as Dr. Brown shared the fact that

Teeny had just had her fifth baby. She had married Bobby Landers right out of high school and it appeared they had spent the next seven years steadily procreating.

The irony, of course, was that Teeny had used Bobby Landers as a punching bag all through elementary school. Apparently she had been harboring a secret crush on him all these years. One could assume she'd found a healthier way to convey her ardent love, since the two of them were married now and working toward populating the world. Figured. Even Teeny Roberts had found the love of her life.

Faith talked around his hands in her mouth as he asked about her family and work and dating life (because everyone seemed to think that was ripe ground for conversation). In the universal way of all dentists, he seemed to understand all her answers.

Her mouth felt clean and new again as she drove across town to her house, making one stop along the way to pick up her dry cleaning. "Is it true you're dating that nice Brendan Cooper?" Mrs. Smitty, the owner of the dry cleaner, asked as she handed over Faith's clothes.

Faith winced. Mrs. Smitty happened to be sisters with Nora Blattenberg, who owned the *Sweet*

Hill Recorder and, naturally, spent a lot of time at the courthouse. Of course, as a reporter, Nora would be privy to all of the gossip that went on in that building.

"We did have a date a week ago." She nodded politely, remembering that Mrs. Smitty had been a friend of her mother's and had brought over dinners for months after her mother passed away— long after everyone else had moved on with their own lives and forgotten about the grieving Walters family.

"Ah, I reckon he took you someplace nice. Such a gentleman that man! And so handsome! Where did you two go?" She leaned forward expectantly, her eyes bright as she waited for Faith to spill all the details, and Faith dutifully answered, including what they ordered and how much the restaurant charged for iced tea. As far as Mrs. Smitty was concerned, a three-dollar iced tea was criminal.

Half an hour later, Faith extricated herself, promising to attend the annual boosterthon spaghetti dinner. Mrs. Smitty's nephew played football and they had dreams of making it to state this year.

North wasn't in the backyard. His bike was gone. As she pulled into her driveway (thankfully vacant), she noticed North's side gate was wide open. She'd never noticed it open before. North was always mindful about that. Maybe the meter reader had come by and left it open.

Emerging from her car, she hesitated. She looked left and right up the quiet street. No one was outside. Only a few cars were even parked in driveways. Everyone was either at work or school this time of day. The neighborly thing to do, the right thing to do, would be to close the gate for him. He surely had all kinds of valuable things in his backyard shop.

Slamming her door shut, she crossed his side of the driveway and walked into the yard, her heels sinking into the soft grass. She grasped the edge of his open gate door. Instead of shutting it, however, and sliding the bolt into place, she hovered there thinking, biting her lip in contemplation.

She sent a glance over her shoulder as though she expected him to appear. Which was unnecessary. She would hear the motor of his bike pulling into their street. He would not magically manifest out of thin air.

Maybe it was the fact that she was home by 2 P.M. and she knew he wouldn't be home anytime soon.

Maybe it was because he spent hours working in that shed and she simply felt compelled to make sure her neighbor wasn't running a meth lab next door.

Hey, it could happen. If a well-respected chemistry teacher could turn into a meth cooker, then anyone could.

She snorted and stifled a laugh. Obviously last summer's marathon of *Breaking Bad* still left its mark on her.

She tried to tell herself it was just about self-preservation. She was a lawman's daughter, after all. And she was a social worker. Investigative instinct ran in her blood. The more she knew about him the better. The more she knew about him, the more at ease she would feel. And contrary to what her brothers and dad wanted, she was not selling her house and moving, so she needed to do whatever she could to feel more at ease.

The reality was . . . she just wanted to know what kept him so occupied in the backyard. She wanted to know what made him tick. She wanted to know *him*.

All that considered, she really didn't intend to go fully into his yard.

She just wanted a closer glimpse of his workshop. But then she saw that the door to the shop was wide open. Wide open and beckoning to her. An invitation she couldn't refuse.

With one last glimpse over her shoulder, she scurried across his freshly mowed yard. She noticed he was good about that. His grass never got overgrown and there wasn't a weed in sight. He took care of his yard and home.

She stopped at the threshold of his shed and peered inside. Something large sat in the middle of the space. She angled her head, trying to make sense of the object in the midst of various machinery and equipment—all things she couldn't even identify by name. She wasn't good with knowing about tools and mechanical things.

It was large and made of different-colored metals. She stepped inside and walked around it. It was art. Very modern in sensibility. The central focus was a dog in midleap. There was a striped cat, too, swatting at the dog's tail. He had used different shades of metal to create the striped effect. It was incredible. Curled at the base was another dog with sleepy, soulful eyes. The legs supporting the piece were several large copper goldfish. It was detailed and amazing. Even abstract, one got a sense of emotion from the expressions on the animals' faces.

She reached out a hand and brushed it against the warm metal, a breath of awe escaping her.

"What are you doing in here?"

She whirled around with a yelp. North stood there, his big body framed in the hot afternoon sunlight. And speaking of hot . . .

Her face burned at being caught on his property. She felt cornered. The only way out was through him—this big, sexy man who filled her with far too many naughty thoughts.

"I—I—"

"Did you just walk into my backyard?" he asked evenly, that deep voice of his reverberating in the hot, still air of the shed.

She stammered some more. "N-no. The gate was open and then I saw that the shed door was open—"

"So you decided to trespass?" He stepped closer and the air just felt thicker, the space tight, his body bigger.

"I decided to be neighborly and—"

"And take the opportunity to snoop around?"

"No!" *Yes.* That was it exactly.

They stood there, neither budging. Silence stretched. She gazed uncomfortably into the dark brown pools of his eyes and shifted on her feet. She motioned lamely to the metal sculpture. "You built this."

He didn't respond to her noncomment, and that only made her feel all the more lame. Although, he wasn't indifferent. A muscle feathered along the cheek of his strong jaw.

"It's amazing," she added. "Beautiful."

He turned to stare at what he had created and some of the tension ebbed from his shoulders. "Yeah?"

"Yes. It really is. Is it for . . . you?"

"A veterinary clinic commissioned me to do it."

He got paid for creating sculptures? For his welding? How many people could say that? And this guy had spent almost half his life in prison, no less.

She shook her head, marveling. He was more . . . so much more than she realized, and then she felt slightly ashamed. She didn't really know anything about him. That being the case, she shouldn't have such preconceived notions of who he was. She prided herself on being open-minded. On her job, she'd seen people with all odds stacked against them turn their lives around. Of course, she'd also seen the dregs of humanity just slide lower.

"That's really . . . impressive," she said.

He looked back at her, his gaze sharp. "You sound surprised," he said flatly.

She winced. "No," she started to say. "It's only—"

"I can count, too. All the way to one hundred," he continued, his voice cutting. "I know my letters and everything."

"Look, we don't really know each other, do we?" she snapped. "Why shouldn't I be surprised?" She motioned to the sculpture. "I can't do anything like this. I don't know anyone who can. It's a surprise because it's incredible. Maybe you shouldn't be so defensive," she accused.

His lips pressed into a flat line, apparently digesting this.

"It's a compliment," she added. "That's all I was trying to do. The gracious thing to do is to accept it."

After a long moment, he nodded. "All right. Thanks."

"You're welcome."

He was slow to move, but he finally did, stepping closer to her, a great wall of living heat coming at her. "That doesn't erase the fact that you trespassed."

She swallowed. "Er, yes. Sorry."

"It's just there's lots of dangerous equipment in here." His eyes rested on her face even as he motioned around him with one hand. "And the space is . . . tight. And filthy."

She stared at his mouth, hearing those last words and suspecting he wasn't talking about his workshop anymore. He reached a hand between them and touched the thick silk ribbon dangling from the collar of her blouse. Her breath caught at the proximity of his fingers to her breast. "A nice clean thing like you could get dirty."

She swallowed again. "I won't come on your property again."

"Oh, you can come over any time. I just want you to know what you're getting into when you do." Okay, he definitely was talking about more than her stepping foot into his shop.

Her face warmed and she remembered his earlier words. He'd charged her with drawing a line in the sand. It was up to her to cross it.

He dropped the ribbon and stepped to the side, suddenly all brisk business as he waved her to pass. "Thanks for closing my gate . . . even though you have yet to do that."

She sniffed and smoothed a hand down her skirt. "I would have."

"Right." He grinned and her stomach did that heady flip-flop.

She stepped past him quickly, making sure they didn't brush each other. Not touching North would be the smartest thing she had done all day. Far smarter than snooping around his backyard and discovering there was, in fact, much more to North Callaghan than she could ever have imagined.

FIFTEEN

$\mathcal{F}$AITH MANAGED TO avoid North Callaghan over the next few days. She actually didn't even have to try very much. They simply didn't bump into each other. She was starting to wonder if maybe *he* was avoiding *her*. For some reason that stung. Was he trying to make a point? Did he really expect her to come after him? To cross that proverbial line in the sand? Not. Happening. She went about her life and tried not to glance next door every time she emerged from her house or pulled into her driveway.

She spent Tuesday and Wednesday conducting interviews around Sweet Hill. She visited the elementary and the middle schools, responding to concerned calls placed by staff members regarding specific students. She completed a few home visits as well. She thought she was done for the day at five but just before leaving the office, she received a call from the local police department requiring a social worker present as they executed an arrest at a home with a child in residence. Faith took the four-year-old and stayed with her in one of the back rooms at the police station. One of the officers ran out and bought the little girl a Happy Meal, which she happily munched on as she and Faith drew together in a Dora the Explorer coloring book until the grandmother was able to come and collect her.

It was after nine by the time she arrived home. North's bike was missing from the driveway. She told herself she didn't care as she stumbled through her house to her bathroom. After a quick shower, she made her way down to her kitchen. Opting for easy, she pulled a frozen pizza out of the freezer and stuck it in her oven.

Leaning against her stove, she sighed as she waited, rolling out her neck. Truthfully, it wasn't the day that had her tense. Her gaze drifted to the kitchen window and the shut blinds. Call it pent-up sexual frustration.

She released a gust of breath. Things were gonna get a whole lot more pent up because trains would *not* be colliding and she would *not* be crossing that line in the sand.

When her pizza was ready, she took it upstairs with her diet soda and ate in bed while watching TV. She rarely ate in bed, but she did it now so that she would not hear when North pulled into the driveway. It would keep her from rushing to the blinds to score a glimpse of him. She didn't need that temptation.

Her plan worked. Only she was more tired than she realized.

She didn't hear North come home. Nor did she hear her alarm go off. Probably because she forgot to set it. She fell asleep with the TV on. She opened her eyes to the sounds of a morning talk show and sunlight streaming through her blinds. Her heart lurched to her throat. She'd overslept. She bounded from bed with a yelp, her plate flying to the carpet with a thud.

She dressed quickly, wildly shoving a blouse into a skirt. She cast a quick glance down to make sure her top half matched her bottom half at least moderately well. Satisfied, she raced downstairs, skipping applying even the minimal makeup she used for work. She could put it on at stoplights.

She forwent breakfast and flew out the front door, hopping as she stuck first one foot inside a heel and then the other. She wasn't looking where she was going. Head down, hunkered halfway over, she caught herself just seconds before colliding into North.

"Faith Walters," he greeted with exaggeration. North looked rested and shower-fresh. Yes, that was annoying. Especially considering she looked like a train wreck. His dark damp hair brushed the collar of a shirt that bore the logo for Sammy's Garage in the corner and his jaw was clean-shaven. "Late night? Looks like you went on a bender."

"Charming as usual," she grumbled, straightening her spine and adjusting her briefcase bag over her shoulder.

His gaze flicked over her. "Your shirt isn't tucked."

She glanced down with a huff of indignation. Half her blouse dangled out. "It's called a blouse. You're wearing a shirt."

"Ah." He rolled his eyes. As though to clarify, he pointed at his chest. "Shirt." He pointed to her. "Blouse. I'll be sure not to make that mistake again."

She stalked past him.

"What? Good girls don't go on benders?" he called behind her back.

"Don't confuse your behavior for mine," she tossed over her shoulder, punching the unlock button on her keys.

She yanked open her car door and tossed her bags inside.

"Faith," he called.

She stopped and looked back at him. "What?"

"I've missed you." His tone was mocking, the glint in his dark eyes taunting. Even if he was teasing, just hearing those words out of his mouth made something flutter inside her.

Just like that, some of her bluster faded. He grinned, his flashing smile transforming his face, softening his usually severe features.

"Say what you will. I'm still not crossing that line in the sand."

"Not yet," he countered. Without another word, he moved down his driveway and climbed into his truck.

Shaking her head, she sank down behind her steering wheel. He backed out and turned down the street. She stayed where she was, suddenly forgetting that she was late. Or not caring. *I've missed you.*

She wondered if he really meant it.

HER PHONE RANG all day. From the moment she arrived (one hour late), it was nonstop. While it was a great way to keep her mind off North, it was not very conducive to keeping headaches at bay. Everyone wanted to complain about something . . . or wanted to make their jobs easier by inconveniencing her. Or they simply wanted her to perform a miracle.

She managed to escape for a brief lunch break. When she returned it was only to find her phone ringing—again. Sighing, she lifted it to her ear, ready to resume the marathon. "Faith Walters here, how can I help you?"

"Do you sleep well at night, Miss Walters?"

Faith stopped midaction as she was tearing a sticky note off the pad to remind herself to check on a case before leaving the office today. "I beg your pardon?"

"Stealing people's children? You sleep well, you cunt?"

She jerked at the words. "Who is this?" Her voice came out a breathy demand, but at least she wasn't stammering. She'd dealt with disgruntled parents before. She'd been called ugly things before. She didn't take it personally. The rewards of her job made this occasional verbal attack worthwhile. In moments like this, she just had to remember that.

"What? You steal so many kids from their parents, you can't guess who this is?" the voice demanded.

"If you would like to lodge a formal complaint—"

"I'm complaining to you, bitch. You're the kidnapper who took my kids." She thought back to the last child she had placed in foster care just yesterday. A little girl. Faith didn't recall any men in the picture when she had searched Hannah Moriarty's background for relatives to take her. The mother had been MIA for days. The little girl had gone to a neighbor when her mother had left her alone.

"You belong in jail," he continued. "Or worse."

Or worse. It didn't take much imagination to realize what he meant by that. Still, his words made her shiver a little. She'd dealt with unhappy people before. They only needed to blow off steam and she was a good target for that. Even so, that didn't mean she didn't have her moments where she wondered if maybe she should have been a music teacher. Or an architect. Something with a little less day-to-day drama.

His words flayed her like bullets. "Enjoy your sleep, bitch. While you can."

The phone went dead. She pulled it back and stared at it for a moment before setting it back down.

"Who was that?" Wendy asked from her desk across the way, looking at Faith curiously.

Faith shook her head. "Just someone that wanted to nominate me for Social Worker of the Year."

"Riiiight." Wendy snorted as she lifted her coffee cup and took another sip. "So you never answered my text. I want the scoop on your date."

"It was nice."

"Uh-oh."

She angled her head. "What?"

"Nice. That's the kiss of death."

She stifled her wince. "What are you talking about? That's not true."

Wendy lifted her eyebrows in disbelief. "I'm just saying I've been on a lot of *nice* first dates. Sometimes they make it to a second date . . . even a third. But notice, I'm still single?" She wiggled her fingers, pointing to her ring finger for emphasis.

Faith shook her head. "Well, I want a *nice* guy so a *nice* date is just fine with me."

"Oh, Faith." Wendy tsked, moving her head in a reproving motion. "Don't you want passion? A guy that can drop your panties with one look? Chemistry is an important foundation."

Chemistry! She sounded like North. Faith would bet that Wendy would tell her to go for it—to go for him.

"I thought friendship was the most important foundation," she countered.

Wendy made a *pfft* sound and waved her hand in dismissal. "What will keep you warm at night? Friendship or a sexy beast of a man, ready for a romp—"

"Okay, okay, Wendy." Faith cut her off as their supervisor walked between their offices, sending them both speculative glances.

Faith swung back around and returned her attention to her laptop. Unfortunately Wendy's words replayed through her head and made her think. And wonder. She already knew North could make her panties drop.

But Wendy was wrong. It wasn't enough. Not long-term. Passion wasn't everything. It wasn't enough. She needed friendship. She needed *nice*, too.

If that meant she had to leave dirty, gritty passion for others, then so be it. It wasn't for her. Not for Faith Walters.

She'd have to learn to let that go.

SIXTEEN

FAITH HAD JUST arrived home from work when her doorbell rang. She opened it to find her brother standing there. The fading sunlight limned his powerful figure. He held up a bag with a giant grease stain on the bottom of it. The delicious aroma of savory smoked meats drifted toward her.

"Bob's BBQ?" he offered, waggling the bag.

She clapped her hands together in delight. "You're a saint."

"Remember that the next time you're mad at me."

Hale entered her house and dropped the bag on her kitchen table, doubtlessly leaving a giant grease stain on her place mat. He started pulling out foil-wrapped ribs, sausage and brisket from the bag and setting them on the table.

"God. There's enough for an army here."

"Leftovers," he explained. "Dig in."

She grabbed two plates. They loaded them and ate with gusto. She licked the barbecue sauce from her fingers and talked about work—failing to mention the phone call from earlier today. That would only set him off and she didn't want to ruin their dinner.

"Still dating Cooper?" he asked before taking a thick bite of brisket and then chasing it down with a bite of pickled jalapeño.

She froze over the rib she was about to bite into. "You heard about that?"

"Small town," he replied, taking a sip from his glass of tea.

"Didn't know you listened to gossip." Wendy alone was probably responsible for spreading that bit of information.

"I'm a small-town sheriff. I listen to everything. Even old Mrs. Carnahan's complaints that an alien terrorizes her the second Wednesday of every month."

"Oh my God."

"That's right. It's happens after bingo at her church. The little bastard climbs into her bed and sucks the polish off her toes."

She held her side, laughing so hard. "Oh my God, that's disgusting!"

"And a real problem." Hale looked at her solemnly. "Apparently she's had to stop getting her usual pedicures."

Her fit of laughter eventually subsided. "Nothing stays a secret," she grumbled.

"Was it a secret?" he countered.

"Well, I didn't see any point on advertising it to the world. It's still early stages." She shrugged and sank her teeth into her waiting juicy rib. Chewing, she wiped her mouth with a napkin. She toyed with a slice of pickle and eventually clarified, "We had one date."

"And? How'd it go?"

"We're supposed to have a second date next week."

He nodded as he spooned a pile of creamy coleslaw onto his plate. "Good. He's a good guy. You could do worse."

She snorted. "Glad I have your approval."

"You're welcome," he said evenly. He knew her well enough to pick up on her sarcasm, but he clearly didn't care. As far as he was concerned, his approval was a priority. At least to him.

"What about you?" Faith asked, turning the tables. "Dating anyone?"

"Me?" He looked at her like she had lost her mind. "You think I want to go down that road again? No, thank you. I'm quite content—"

"With your occasional one-night stand?"

He froze, and then frowned. "Now who's listening to gossip?"

She laughed and shook her head. "Just because you don't diddle anyone here in Sweet Hill, doesn't mean I don't know about your visits to that CPA in Alpine. Or the financial planner in Fort Stockton."

"Diddle?" he echoed.

She lifted her eyebrows. "You know what I'm talking about."

He cleared his throat and finished off the rest of his brisket. Watching him, waiting for him to say something, she finished her last rib and then wiped her sticky fingers with her napkin.

"I know better than to get involved with anyone here in town. Too many busybodies ready to get in my business."

"But Alpine and Fort Stockton are fair game?" She smirked.

"Never claimed I was a monk. I gotta go somewhere if I want . . ." He paused, looking uncomfortable. He shifted his big body in her kitchen-table chair. Her brothers were old-school in that they thought certain subjects were taboo to talk about around their sister. Subjects like sex.

She watched him thoughtfully as he stood and started to clear the table. Her brother was a good guy and deserved more than empty flings in neighboring towns. Unfortunately, she was afraid he had been burned too badly in the past to ever want another relationship again.

He helped her rinse dishes and load them into the dishwasher. She lifted an eyebrow as he started packing up all the food and stowing it in her fridge. "I won't finish all that—"

"It will be gone in two days," he assured her with a wink. "I've seen you stress eat."

"Ha."

He winked at her.

"Well, thanks for dinner," she said, stepping in to give him a hug.

"Hey, gotta keep my eye out for my lil' sis."

"Naturally." Opening the door, she walked him out. That was when she noticed the sound of a lawnmower. Somehow she hadn't paid any attention to it before . . . or at least she hadn't realized how close it was to her house. She had failed to notice the lawnmower was actually mowing right *next* to her house.

It was North.

"Your neighbor?" Hale asked as he stepped out on her porch. She followed his gaze to a shirtless North pushing his lawnmower. Hale sent a nod of greeting toward him.

She flinched. A normal reaction, she supposed,

when her brother came face-to-face with anyone she had made out with. At least that's what she told herself. It was reason enough. It was the whole they'd-kissed-and-touched thing. *Touched.* She snorted. There was an understatement.

It wasn't because this guy had a criminal record that she was desperate to hide from her family. No, not that at all.

She murmured some vague agreement, trying to sound casual.

Hale turned to watch him, following the movement of North as he worked the lawnmower across his front yard in steady rows.

She knew her brother was assessing him, doing that cop thing where he didn't miss the fact that this guy was young and virile and wore tattoos as naturally as the skin on his body.

Hale shot her an equally assessing glance, no doubt trying to gauge her reaction to this very male, *very* virile guy living right next door to her. Even a hetero male would know most females' ovaries would be going into hyperdrive at the sight of him—Faith no exception.

Hopefully he couldn't detect her sudden increased breathing.

She pasted a bland smile on her face and tried to appear as though she wasn't like most females.

Okay, so she wasn't immune to the display of virility, but she wanted her brother to think she was. She really wasn't in the mood to endure the big-brother routine and be forced into denying her interest in her neighbor.

"He looks . . ."

She held her breath, waiting for her brother to say something condemning about him. *Criminal. Dangerous.*

Working in law enforcement, Hale did have those opinions, after all. He'd seen it all. Sweet Hill might not be the largest community, but it had its share of degenerates. And it would be just her luck for him to make that assessment.

North turned and started mowing another row, facing them now. She felt his brown-black gaze on her—on them. It wasn't friendly and she felt her brother tense beside her as he recognized this, too.

"Familiar," Hale finally finished saying. "He looks familiar."

Familiar? Uh-oh. Whatever she had thought he meant to say hadn't been *that*. Had he seen mug shots of North?

"Maybe he's just got one of those faces," she said offhandedly and tried to move inside her house, ready to say goodnight and watch Hale drive off in his Bronco.

Hale didn't take the bait. He shot her a skeptical look, his feet staying firmly planted in place. "I'm going to introduce myself."

"Hale, no," she snapped, grabbing his arm as he moved to step forward.

And that, she knew, was her mistake.

Her brother looked down at her hand on his arm, then back to her face, frowning slightly, his gray eyes narrowing.

So much for acting casual.

She dropped her hand, but it was too late. She had overreacted. Being a people person was part of his job—talking to people was no big deal. Her brother introduced himself to people every day in an effort to assess, disarm and acquaint himself with the community. She knew that. Her dad had been the same way. It was no big deal.

Hale squared his shoulders and stepped forward, walking down the driveway at an easy amble that she knew was in direct opposition to his investigative mood.

North saw him coming and shut off the lawnmower. The late-evening sun kissed his glistening skin and made her stomach twist. Would there ever be a time when the sight of him did not hit her hard? A day when she could walk up her driveway after work and not glance to his front door with hope for a glimpse of him humming through her?

He wiped at his brow, revealing the paler, muscled underside of his arm. Her stomach quivered. No, she realized with a flash of anger. That day would never come. A sense of hopelessness swept over her. Was she destined to be one of those women that fell for the wrong kind of man? She'd never thought that of herself. She thought she had more self-respect than that.

North schooled his expression to reveal nothing as her brother approached. Only she sensed the edge to him, the wariness as he assessed her brother back, his brown gaze skimming over her brother's uniform. Of course he hadn't missed the fact that her brother was law enforcement.

She followed a few feet behind Hale, dread curling through her as he stuck out his hand.

"Hey, there. Hale Walters." He inclined his head in her direction. "Faith's brother."

Something flashed in his eyes. Relief? Surprise? Whatever she thought she saw vanished almost as instantly as it appeared.

North nodded as he finished shaking Hale's hand. Dropping his hand back at his side, he stood back.

"I was just telling Faith that you look familiar."

Hale gestured aimlessly in a way that made him appear nonchalant. Except she knew Hale wasn't nonchalant. He missed nothing.

Hale continued, "I like to think I'm good with names and faces, but I encounter lots of people on the job." He angled his head, his sharp gray eyes speculative. "For the life of me, I can't place you."

"I'm sure my name will ring a bell," North said in that rumbly voice of his.

She started a little in bewilderment. Had North just confirmed that they did in fact know one another?

"I was a year ahead of you in high school," North added.

Hale laughed, his body instantly relaxing. "That so?"

Oh. No. *No no no.* The dread thickened in her veins.

"Yeah." North looked at her, his grim gaze seeming to convey that there was no avoiding the truth now. "I remember you and your brother . . . he was a year ahead of me."

Tucker? He knew him, too?

"Didn't realize you had a sister though." North looked at her and no mistake about it. There was something accusatory in his stare. As though he should have somehow known this about her. It was unlikely for him to have made the connection on his own. They hadn't exactly gotten around to swapping family histories.

She lifted her chin in defiance. Why would it have come up? Walters was a common enough name.

"Faithy was a freshman my senior year, so you would have graduated by then," Hale volunteered. "What was your name again?"

He still hadn't said his name. Once he did Hale was bound to know . . . bound to remember who he was and what he had done. There weren't too many murders committed in Sweet Hill. And even less of them committed by guys that attended high school with her brother. North must just look that different . . . that much harder than the teenage boy he once was.

"North Callaghan."

Hale went still.

She held her breath. Her brother didn't speak, but she knew he was remembering, putting together all the pieces.

It seemed forever before he said anything at all. "You and your brother killed Mason Leary," he finally said, his voice flat.

North said nothing, merely held her brother's unflinching gaze. It was the only agreement needed.

"When did you get out?" Hale continued, all friendliness gone from his voice. Her brother was gone. There was no sight of the mischievous boy who used to leave garden snakes in her backpack or the big brother who popped in with barbecue. Now the steely-eyed sheriff of Sweet Hill stood in his place.

"Two years ago."

Again, her brother lapsed into silence. The quiet was excruciating. She hoped he was processing what North said and realizing that two years was a positive. He was two years out and leading a clean life. No criminal activity. Two years as a good citizen. That had to mean something. That had to matter.

She shifted uneasily on her feet. He stared at North for so long it was beyond uncomfortable, and she knew. Two years didn't mean squat to Hale.

Her brother wasn't looking at North Callaghan and applauding him for turning things around and honoring the terms of his parole. He was looking at him and thinking how much he disliked her living next door to him.

North stared at her then, his gaze probing as though trying to assess her reaction to the news that he was a former convict. She swallowed thickly and lifted her shoulders in a fraction of a shrug. Because she already knew. Only he didn't know that. He didn't know she already knew the ugly truth about him.

He probably expected her to be horrified. Maybe even disgusted as any good woman would be when she learned a guy she had made out with had been to prison for murder.

North was waiting, his jaw locked. Watching her for some such reasonable reaction. She couldn't even pretend. Couldn't fake it. She had known about his sordid past. She knew he was a murderer.

In her own mind, she had come to terms with his criminal history. Did that mean she wanted to know more about what happened? Naturally she wanted to hear about his past. What he had felt then, when it happened, and how he felt about it all now. But she had already made up her mind that it was not her place to judge North Callaghan.

Her brother, however, was of a different opinion.

Hale snapped his gaze back to her. "You knew about this?"

Looking at North, she nodded slowly, never breaking eye contact, speaking to him even though she was answering her brother. "Yeah. I knew."

North's nostrils flared with a sharp breath and she felt that breath like the cut of a strong wind.

This was a problem for him. Faith knowing . . . and not letting him know she knew.

"Does Dad know?" Hale asked.

She stared at him. Was he serious? If she hadn't told him, she sure as hell wasn't going to tell her father.

"I didn't think so." He shook his head at her again and then looked back at North.

"I'm sure you remember our father. He was the sheriff before me. He just retired a couple years back."

There was the barest flicker of something in North's eyes that indicated yes. He remembered her father.

Hale continued, "I believe he was the one that made your arrest. Yours and your brother."

No. Oh no no no. *Please don't let that be true.* Her father had not arrested this man.

"Yes," North said quietly. "He came out to the farmhouse and arrested us both."

Hale nodded and looked at her, his expression saying it all—saying everything. *See? This is fucked up. You're living next door to a guy our dad locked away for a seriously long time.*

And it was fucked up.

"How long?" North bit out, not even looking at her brother anymore. It was like Hale wasn't even there to him. It was just the two of them. "How long have you known about me, Faith?"

She shrugged uneasily. "A while."

She didn't say the rest . . . she didn't voice the words, but she told him with her eyes.

Since we started texting. Since before I saw you naked outside the house. Before I touched myself in the shower with your image burning a fire through me.

Since you kissed me.

Since I kissed you back.

His chocolate eyes went dark, the pupils almost indistinguishable from the irises. He was not happy. She thought she had seen him unhappy before, but this was true misery. It might even go deeper than that. It was something else . . .

"Guess you weren't going to mention that to me?" Hale inserted, his entire body one rigid line. She knew this sight of him. She had seen it before in many a childhood squabble when he lost his temper and tried to bulldoze over her.

"Why should I, Hale?" She set her hands on her hips. "It had nothing to do with you."

He looked at her like he didn't even know her. "When my sister lives next door to a parolee, I should know about it. Damn straight that's my business."

"Hale!" Angry heat flushed over her face, she shot a quick glance at North.

"It's the truth." Hale swung around to glare at North again, speaking *of* him, *about* him as though he were not even present. "This guy went to prison for murder, Faith."

"If you know who he is, then you know *why*," she hissed. "You know the circumstances." She wasn't pretending North didn't do the crime, but she wasn't going to pretend either that he was just any criminal. He wasn't a heartless killer. She knew that. Even as much as they bickered, as much as he drove her crazy, as much as she both longed for and regretted kissing him, she knew he was not without decency.

"And you do," North interjected quietly. "You know the circumstances." He waited a beat before adding, "You've done your research on me, Faith. Well done."

That said, North turned and started away from both of them, his long legs eating up the distance separating him from his front door.

"Hey, where are you going?" Hale called. "We're talking here."

"I'm certain he did not appreciate the two of us arguing about him as though he wasn't even standing here." She punched his arm. "You're so rude, Hale!"

North turned slightly to call back at them. "I'm going inside my house. I served my time. I'm living my life . . . not hurting anyone. I don't have to answer to anyone about the past." It wasn't in Faith's imagination that he stared at her as he uttered this.

A horrible hollowness filled her as she looked at him. He only stood across the yard from her, but he felt a million miles away.

He waited a beat, letting both Faith and Hale absorb his words before turning around again and disappearing inside his house.

As soon as the door slammed behind him, she whirled around on her brother. She slapped him on the arm. "Way to go! That was mortifying!"

"Mortifying? What did you expect me to do?" He gestured toward North's house. "You're living next door to a killer! And you knew it! You. Knew!" He shook his head and looked at her like she had lost her mind.

With a growl of frustration, she stalked inside her house, knowing he would follow. And that was fine. She wasn't going to have this argument with him in the driveway.

He was fast on her heels, slamming the door to her house after him. "You're moving."

She crossed her arms over her chest and whirled to face him. "No. I'm not."

"Faith," he started in.

"No. I'm a grown woman. I'm not in danger."

He raised an eyebrow as though that were debatable.

She continued, "Now I love you, Hale, and I appreciate your concern, but I'm an adult. I bought this house and I'm not selling it. I put money down. Besides. I like it here. I'm not moving. Weren't you going home?"

"This conversation isn't over."

"I'm not changing my mind." She opened the front door for him and waved him out. "See you Sunday. I'm making chicken-fried steak."

"Don't think you can soften me up by making my favorite dinner."

"I was planning to make it before you turned into a lunatic on my driveway."

"I'm the lunatic?" He flattened a hand to his chest, his gray eyes wide with incredulity. "You're the one living next door to a convicted murderer."

"Perfectly sane," she replied easily.

Hale rested his hand against the edge of the door before passing through it. "This isn't because he's easy on the eyes, is it? I always thought you were smart when it came to men."

Because her love life was nonexistent? He thought she was smart because of that?

She pressed her palm against brother's chest and pushed him out. "Good-bye, Hale. Thanks for stopping by and thanks for dinner." She meant it . . . even if she was annoyed with him right now.

He turned and walked down her driveway, his gaze turning to stare in the direction of North's yard.

North hadn't returned yet to finish his mowing. They had chased him off. She felt bad about that. About all of it.

She imagined he would return once her brother's vehicle left the driveway.

As she heard her brother's Bronco start up and drive away, she reached for her phone. She pulled up North and fired him a text.

I'm sorry about that.

She stood there, staring at the phone, waiting for him to reply, but somehow knowing deep in her gut.

He wouldn't.

SEVENTEEN

$\mathcal{T}$HE NEXT FEW days Dad and Hale used every opportunity to let her know just how unreasonable she was being. Even Tucker FaceTimed her from some undisclosed location halfway around the world. Haggard and bearded, his gray eyes had stared accusingly at her through her computer screen and wanted to know if she had lost her mind. Hale had apprised him of the situation and, of course, he had to weigh in on Faith's poor judgment.

Throughout it all, she couldn't help marveling at what any of them would think if they knew the *extent* of her involvement with North Callaghan. She shuddered to think of their reaction if they were privy to their text messages . . . if they had witnessed her the other day propped on the hood of her car with North between her thighs. The memory sent her face flaming . . . along with other parts of her body.

Dad stopped by the day after Hale's visit, stone-faced as he explained that he wanted her to move back home with him. She'd been firm but kind with him as she explained that that was not an option.

Thankfully, North Callaghan wasn't home during that visit. She hadn't missed her father's razor-sharp gaze eyeing North's house. Had he been home, she knew Dad would have marched over there to throw his weight around. He would have grilled North and then probably ended the conversation by warning him off from even looking cross-eyed at her.

So North not home then had been a blessing.

In fact, North hadn't been home a lot. At least not when she might have bumped into him. His bike or truck was gone when she woke up every morning, and he was never around when she got home in the evenings. He never did reply to her apology text. It seemed like he had stopped caring about her. He certainly didn't miss her anymore. Or if he did he had a funny way of showing it.

She was brushing her teeth and getting ready for bed when her phone rang from where it was charging on her nightstand. A quick glance revealed that it was Hale again. She sighed through the bubbly froth of her toothpaste.

Turning away, she let it go to voicemail. It was late. He'd just think she was already asleep. Or that she was ignoring him. Either way was fine.

She finished brushing her teeth, rinsed her mouth and headed downstairs to shut off all the lights. It was Friday night. She was going to bed by 10 P.M. This was her life. Brendan had texted her sporadically throughout the week. Nice texts telling her he was looking forward to their date next week. *Nice*. There was that word again.

North Callaghan was probably just getting started on his night. She imagined him with Serena or someone else and an uncomfortable knot formed in her throat.

She poured herself a glass of water. Standing in her darkened kitchen, she couldn't help drifting over to the large window that faced the driveway.

So much for waiting for her to step across that proverbial line in the sand.

She guessed he was finished with her. Understandable, she supposed.

She knew all the dirt on him and he probably felt weird about it now. Through all their interactions, she had known he was a convicted murderer.

And she was the sheriff's sister.

As an ex-con, he'd probably decided he didn't need that aggravation. That certainly made sense. She should forget about him. She *should*. But she wanted to talk to him. Although when she imagined what she would say nothing came to her mind. She couldn't tell him his past didn't matter. That would be a lie. It would always matter. It mattered to him, clearly, but it was as he said. He didn't owe her any explanation or defense. If he wanted an explanation as to why she had investigated his background, then she could offer none other than that she was nosy. A busybody just like her brother described half of the women of Sweet Hill.

She peered out between her blinds.

It shouldn't bother her so much that he was not at home. She shouldn't be peeking out the window like a stalker. She winced. That ship had already sailed. By definition, that's what she was. Ugh. This was what she had become, how far she had descended.

She should not be wondering so much about where he was . . . what he was doing. *Who he was doing.*

Grimacing, she let the blinds snap back into place and forced herself away from the window and the hope of seeing him.

It was for the best.

SHE WAS THE sheriff's sister. For days this reeled through his mind. She was also the daughter of the man who'd come out to the farmhouse and cuffed him and Knox in front of their aunt and uncle. In front of Katie. Already traumatized Katie. Already broken. Sure, he was just doing his job, but Faith's father was a part of that past North worked so hard to forget.

Now Faith was a part of it, too.

The past was like that. Never really gone. Always there to sneak up on you and tap you on the shoulder just when you thought you were getting over it.

North put in a lot of overtime at the shop for the rest of the week. His boss was only too happy to pay him. They had more work than they could handle as it was these days. He might have gotten some funny looks showing up Saturday, but the few guys working didn't say anything.

Home was the last place he wanted to be, which actually infuriated him. Getting his own place had been a huge thing for him upon getting paroled. It had been his number one goal. A place where he could be by himself and have the privacy he never had at the Rock. Something that belonged to him. A refuge for him alone. Now that was wrecked because he was avoiding the woman living next door to him.

North usually protected his weekends. It was his time. He worked in his shop, fished, took runs out along forgotten paths where birds sang in the trees, indifferent to his intrusion. Sometimes he just drove out to the desert mountains to stare at the expanse of wilderness. Because he could. Because he wasn't locked up in a cage anymore.

The nights were his, too. Those he spent in typical fashion. Exorcising his ghosts by pumping into some willing female body. Only lately, getting laid did not seem nearly so important. At least random hookups weren't. His sex drive hadn't diminished. No, he hadn't lost interest in sex. He'd lost interest in indiscriminate sex.

Now, however, he had to ignore her. She was an itch he would have to leave unscratched. Knowing who she was had changed everything. Fucking her was out of the question. She was trouble. For two years he had managed to avoid trouble. He wouldn't start looking for it now.

Hale Walters's hard-eyed face flashed across his mind. *This guy went to prison for murder, Faith.*

The words were true—and accompanied with such a contemptuous look. It still stung . . . the way her brother had looked at him. The look, however, said it all. He thought North was a worthless piece of shit and he didn't want such shit anywhere near his sister.

Her father had actually arrested him. He didn't have a hell of a lot of scruples left, but he figured that made Faith Walters a bad choice as a potential fuck buddy.

North pulled over at the grocery store. With all the overtime this week, he didn't have anything in his refrigerator to eat and he was sick of takeout.

He grabbed a cart at the front of the store and headed for the produce section, which took him through the deli and bakery. They already had some deli meat sliced in a cooler. He snagged a couple packages of ham and turkey, nodding politely to the girl staring at him from behind the counter. He'd noticed her before. They'd chatted once or twice. Open interest gleamed in her eyes. Clearly she was willing to strike up a conversation with him again. Too bad he wasn't in the mood.

Scowling, he wondered when he would be in the mood again. He should go over there and flirt with her, find out when she got off work and invite her back to his place. He *should* do that. It had been a while for him. Too long.

He pushed his cart through the bakery section and tossed some bread into his basket.

By the time he got to the produce, he was almost done. Lettuce and tomatoes went in the cart. It wasn't fancy, but he could make a decent sandwich. He picked out a watermelon and threw some oranges in the cart. He'd missed fresh fruit in prison. All the fruit they had was usually canned. He hadn't had fresh watermelon while he was at the Rock. Twelve years without fresh watermelon. Kind of like sex. When he'd gotten out he'd been starving. Fresh fruit and pussy.

Except the desperate hunger he had felt when he was first paroled was worse now. Because he felt it for one woman. A woman he couldn't have.

Deciding to grab a gallon of milk, he headed for the dairy department.

That's where he saw her.

Looking very un-Faith-like in a pair of black yoga pants and T-shirt, she was standing in front of the milk section, the door to the refrigeration unit open as she studied the selection. His eyes dropped to her flip-flops. Pink toenails.

With the exception of when he saw her in her robe, she was always polished and put together in her work attire.

Un-Faith-like or not, he was still hit hard with a wave of lust.

Hell, he had already accepted how much he

liked the look of her, but this Faith looked young and fresh and far too clean for the likes of him. He wanted this. He wanted to dive into her. He wanted to take her and claim her and mark her as his.

His flight instinct kicked in and he whirled his cart around.

She must have caught the movement. He heard her voice behind him. "North! North, wait up."

Her cart rolled behind him, wheels whirring over the linoleum. Christ. She was chasing him.

He kept going, fighting the totally irrational urge to run. He turned down the toilet-paper-and-tissue aisle.

"North!" Her hand grabbed his arm, fingers pressing into his skin, and that was a mistake. Touching him was a mistake. It was hard enough forgetting her taste or the sensation of her soft skin, too soft for the rough scrape of his palms. Hard enough not to remember the wet silk of her sex against his fingers.

He didn't need her touching him.

"What?" he growled.

"I texted you."

"Yeah." He'd seen it. He hadn't replied to the apology. What should he have said? "I know."

She pulled back, dropping her hand, looking

hurt and so young right then. She blinked rapidly and looked down, as though fighting tears. Finding her composure, she looked back up at him.

He sighed and glanced left and right, dragging a hand through his hair. He swallowed back an expletive. The store wasn't crowded. No one seemed to notice or care about them standing in the aisle. Christ. He couldn't do this. Not here.

Even in public, it was a battle not to touch her, not to pick right up where they left off the other night . . . even knowing who she was now made no difference to his dick.

"What do you want from me?" He tossed a hand up in the air.

She blinked as though the question caught her off guard. "We're neighbors. I want everything to be all right between us. I want us to be—"

"Don't say *friends*," he snarled, everything in him seizing tight, wanting to lash out at her—pull her to him so he could let her know just what he thought of that idea . . . and what it was he really wanted to be to her. "That's not happening. You and I were never going to be friends."

She stared at him, looking hurt all over again. He took a step toward her. She backed up, stopping when she bumped into a wall of paper towels. "The only thing that was ever going to happen between us was sex." He propped one hand against a shelf right over her shoulder.

Fire lit her eyes. "Oh, really?"

"Yeah. And that's *not* happening now."

"Oh? Because you decided?" Her face screwed tight with irritation. "Hate to tell you, but that wasn't *ever* going to happen because I wasn't going to let—"

He shut her up by kissing her. Hard. Her mouth parted on a cry and he slid his tongue inside, tasting her, groaning when her tongue thrust out to meet his. He pressed his body into hers, sinking into her shape. He grabbed her hip, pulling her to him, angling her so that he could settle his cock against the soft juncture between her thighs. Her hands went for his shoulders, her fingers curling into him.

He angled his head, deepening the kiss, drinking long and hard from her like a starving man. They pushed against one another, desperate, yearning. He gripped the shelf as though he could use it to leverage them closer.

It wasn't enough. It wouldn't be enough until they were melding into one. Until he was in her so deep—

Paper towels started to fall around them. He broke away, coming up for air.

She stared at him with wide, glazed eyes, her mouth inching back toward him, after more.

He reached out to stroke her pretty bottom lip, swollen and damp. "You still lying to yourself now?"

She blinked, the glazed look leaving her eyes like clearing smoke. Her hands worked, shoving between them, red splotches breaking out all over her face as she launched him away from her like he was some kind of poison and not the man she had been kissing for all she was worth moments ago.

Her eyes shone wetly, brimming with angry emotion as she sputtered, "Don't touch—"

"I won't. Never again." His voice was hard with finality as he looked at her, standing before him, her face flushed, her lips still mocking him, begging for him to pick right back up where they'd just ended. "Forget I live next door. Forget you even have a neighbor."

He stood back and looked at her solemnly, letting his words sink in. For her. For him. She appeared a little shell-shocked as she held his gaze. But still mad. Still furious. Angry fire shot from her eyes. Good. Better this than her looking at him like he was something worthwhile. In the back of his mind, he had started to feel almost normal; he'd started to think he could have a normal life.

It was a necessary wake-up call. There was no normal for him.

Turning away, he grasped the bar of his cart in a white-knuckled grip and left her standing in the aisle.

HOME WAS STILL the last place he wanted to be. Bumping into Faith at the store only reaffirmed that.

He stayed only long enough to drop off his groceries. Sticking the cold stuff in the fridge, he exchanged glares with his empty walls before pushing off the counter. "Forget this," he muttered to himself.

Grabbing his keys, he hopped back in his truck. Without thinking about it, he found himself pulling into the gravel parking lot surrounding Joe's Cabaret.

For midweek the place was hopping. He stepped inside the smoke-laden space to the raucous cheers of patrons waving money for a pair of dancers dressed like pink bunnies.

He assessed the crowd in one sweep. He spotted Piper weaving through tables. She looked harried even with a smile etched onto her face. Her big doe eyes looked tired with shadows underneath them. He knew Cruz hated that she had to work so hard, but there was little else she could do with no parents around, a brother in prison and a fourteen-year-old sister to raise. With her day job and picking up shifts here at night, she was burning the candle at both ends.

Her face lit up when she spotted him. She waved him toward a vacant table near the back. Naturally, all the tables near the stage were occupied. Fine by him. He wasn't here to stuff money in G-strings.

He seated himself with his back to the wall, settling in until Piper could get to him.

He was still waiting when the main door opened again and an officer stepped inside, the dark blue of his uniform with its glinting brass bits unmistakable. There was a noticeable shift in the air as everyone became aware of the new arrival. He stepped deeper into the room. The red stage lights cast him in a glow and revealed his face. North released a low, mirthless chuckle.

Why the hell not? He'd already run into one Walters sibling tonight. Why not toss in another one? Maybe Tucker Walters would show up, too.

Sheriff Hale Walters slowly navigated the room. Several of the waitresses and dancers eyed him and it wasn't out of trepidation. North guessed it didn't hurt that the guy had the kind of face women liked. Not that he was any judge, but if the girls who worked at Joe's—the girls who saw men all day long in every shape, size and flavor—were eyeing him, then he was better than average. He was impressive. Taller than North at several inches over six feet and built like a tank. North recalled that when he was in high school Hale Walters basically was the Sweet Hill football team's defensive line.

As it became clear that he wasn't there to break up the fun, the customers relaxed and resumed their catcalls. North kept his gaze fixed on Walters.

Eventually, the sheriff came to stand before him. "Callaghan," he greeted.

He dropped his head back. Damn, Faith's brother was a big bastard. "Looking for me?"

"How'd you guess?"

"Well, you found me." He didn't even want to consider how the guy tracked him down. He'd either followed him or had an APB out for him. He wouldn't put such things past him. The man had power and influence. Enough to make North's life very complicated. He wouldn't forget that. "Surprised it took you this long. You could have just knocked on my door."

"I thought it was a good idea for us to have a little talk someplace . . . neutral." And by *neutral* he meant someplace where his sister wouldn't see him hounding North. "I would have come sooner, but I was hoping to convince my sister that she needed to move." He shrugged one shoulder. "Faith is headstrong. She believes in second chances." He lowered himself into the chair across from North. "But you and I have been around. We've seen the worst that life has to offer. We aren't so optimistic. Are we?"

North stared long and hard at the man across from him. "You and I have nothing in common. *Sheriff.*" This last he added with a touch of force, spitting the word off his tongue as though he didn't like the taste of it. He'd had enough exposure to lawmen to last him the rest of his life. The fact that he now lived next door to the sheriff's sister was a major point of discontent. He was leading a law-abiding life. He shouldn't have to deal with the man.

Hale Walters glanced to the stage, where a patron was making an ass of himself attempting to climb the stage to reach one of the dancers. A bouncer emerged to grab him and cart him away.

"We both know men don't change," he murmured idly in a voice that belied the tension lining his shoulders. "Not really." His steely gaze drifted back to North as though waiting for him to reply.

There was no point. For the most part, North didn't disagree with him.

"Sorry for the wait," Piper's sweet feminine voice

said breathlessly as she arrived at their table. "We're slammed. What can I get you, North?" Her dark gaze slid to the sheriff. "And your *friend* here?" She uttered the word *friend* in a skeptical manner. She might walk the straight and narrow, but she was a Walsh. North doubted there was a family member of hers that had not seen the inside of a jail.

"Ice water is fine," Walters said.

Her lips thinned and he could imagine she was calculating a zero tip from him on that order.

"I'll take a beer. The usual," North supplied.

Nodding, she gave his shoulder a friendly pat before moving on.

Walters's gaze didn't miss the touch. His eyes followed Piper as she moved away. "Cute girl," he murmured.

North followed the direction of the sheriff's stare, noticing it followed Piper's ass until she disappeared behind the bar.

"She's a good girl."

"You know her well then."

North heard the judgment in his voice. "Well enough."

The sheriff grunted. "Right. Seems like if you have that tasty piece on the line, you can leave my sister alone."

He smiled without bothering to correct Walters's assumption that he was banging Piper. This man was determined to think the worst of him and nothing he said would convince him otherwise.

"So we've reached the part when you warn me off your sister?" He crossed his arms across his chest. "Does it even matter if I tell you that your concerns are misplaced?"

"No. It wouldn't matter. I saw the way you looked at her."

"And how's that?"

"Like a wolf ready to eat its next meal." He leaned back in his chair, the wood creaking under his weight. "Only you can forget about that. There are hundreds of girls for you to fuck with." He stabbed a finger in North's direction. "So hands off her."

North shook his head and laughed. The sad thing was . . . he couldn't even deny wanting her. He did. He *had*.

"Yeah," Walters said smugly. "Thought so."

"We're just neighbors. That's all we'll ever be." That much was true.

"She's too good for you." He gestured around the room. "Why don't you stick with your strippers and bimbo waitresses and steer clear of her."

A bottle of beer clunked down in front of North. He looked up, startled. He hadn't even noticed

Piper's return. "Oh, and here's your ice water." She plopped the glass down clumsily in front of the sheriff, close to the edge. Too close apparently. The glass toppled over and spilled all over Walters.

"Shit!" He erupted from his chair, wincing at the icy deluge soaking the front of his pants.

"Oh, my goodness!" Piper grabbed a napkin and patted savagely at his crotch, making him yelp. North covered up his smile with his hand.

"Stop! I'm okay! Really." Walters dodged her hand, backing away.

"I'm so sorry, Deputy. I didn't—"

"Sheriff," he ground out, snatching the napkin from her hand when she came at him again. "Sheriff Walters."

"Oh!" Piper's enormous, Disney-princess eyes rounded in her face with exaggerated zeal. "Sheriff Walters. I'm so, so sorry!"

"It's quite all right—"

"I'm so glad you can forgive me." She hopped a little in place, sending her rack bouncing as she grabbed a lock of her dark hair, curling it around her finger. Her bottom lip stuck out in a pout. "But gosh . . . what can you expect from a bimbo waitress?"

Hale's eyes narrowed. He flung the napkin down

on the table. He clearly understood then that the drink in his lap had been deliberate. She had overheard his remark and was having a little fun at his expense.

"Exactly," he retorted.

Piper squared her shoulders and stared him head-on, not the least bit intimidated. In that moment she reminded North of her brother. That mean bastard fought like a rattlesnake. Multiple men. Bigger men. Cruz would take on anyone. Reid always said it would be a miracle if the guy ever made it to thirty.

Walters wrenched his gaze back to North. "Remember what I said." His gaze returned then, lingering for a long heated moment on Piper. Then he was gone, stalking from the table.

"Piper," North said warningly. "You don't need to go making enemies with men like that."

She snorted in disgust. "I'm not afraid of him."

"Maybe you should be. Your family doesn't exactly have a good track record when it comes to the law."

Piper sobered and looked at him somberly. "I'm nothing like my family. Me and my sister . . . we're different."

"I know that." And she was. She might work

at this unsavory establishment, but she wasn't like the rest of her clan. She worked two jobs and took night courses and raised her little sister. "But Sheriff Walters is a powerful man—"

"Him? He looks like he has a stick up his ass."

North released a hard laugh. Hadn't he had a similar thought about the man's sister?

"I appreciate you looking out for me—"

"It wasn't just you, my friend. He insulted me. I heard that man call me a bimbo."

"He said bimbo waitresses. That doesn't necessarily mean you specifically—"

"Oh, he meant me." She rolled her eyes.

North shrugged, watching the fiery bloom of color in her cheeks and knew there was no talking her down.

"Men like him are used to getting whatever they want and *saying* whatever they want because they think they're superior." She sniffed and picked up his empty water glass. Frowning down at the table, she said, "And he didn't leave a tip."

North chuckled. "Big shock."

Shrugging, she strolled away.

North's laughter faded. He picked up his beer and took a long pull. Now that Piper had left, he was alone with the echo of the sheriff's words. *I saw the way you looked at her. Like a wolf ready to eat its next meal.*

If that was true, then he needed to stop looking at Faith Walters, because there would be no feasting on her. He finished his beer and lifted his gaze. Spying Piper, he signaled for another one.

EIGHTEEN

SHUTTING OFF ALL the downstairs lights, Faith moved upstairs and went about her bedtime routine. Washed her face. Brushed her teeth. Pulled her still-damp hair into a bun. She hooked her phone to the charger beside her bed and got under the covers. Sighing, she folded her hands across her stomach. This was the same routine she'd had most of her life. It hadn't changed. Despite the fact that three nights ago she had bumped into North at the store. Her attempt to clear the air between them had gone abysmally wrong. He didn't want to be friends. Or even friendly.

He had kissed her right there in the paper-towel aisle. To punish her. To prove the point that she wanted him. Then he had told her she couldn't have him. He'd made a fool of her. It was like he held out a cookie jar for her to take a cookie and slammed the lid on her fingers when she reached inside. Jerk.

Forget I live next door. Forget you even have a neighbor.

Fine. She would do just that. Difficult as it might be, she would forget all about him. Brendan had called and they'd finally nailed down the day for their next date. She would focus on that. And forget all about North Callaghan.

Despite her turbulent thoughts, her lids grew heavy.

Outside, she heard the distant rattle of wheels on a garbage can as it rolled toward the curb, and it jarred her from her state of semiconsciousness. Damn.

Tomorrow was garbage day. They wouldn't pick up again for another two days. Unless she wanted her trash overflowing onto her kitchen floor by tomorrow evening, she needed to take it outside now. She doubted she would be awake at five in the morning for pickup. Definitely not. Tomorrow she was sleeping late.

Flinging back the covers, she hurried downstairs and pulled the garbage bag out of the can.

Opening her front door, she was careful not to drag the bag over the concrete. The last thing she wanted to be doing at midnight was picking up smelly garbage.

The rest of her neighbors had remembered to set out their trash, including North. Garbage lined the curb up and down the length of her street. The night was quiet. Various porch lights glowed in the darkness. Two houses down, the little boy had forgotten to bring in his bike. It lay on its side in the driveway. Hopefully it would still be there in the morning. Or maybe his mother would remember to bring it in.

She deposited her trash at the curb and then turned to go back inside. Yawning, she scratched her elbow as she shuffled back to her house. A car door slammed shut. She glanced over her shoulder, noticing a man getting out of a truck parked across the street from her house. There wasn't usually a truck parked there. The house had a garage and the lady who lived there always parked inside it.

The driver of the truck started walking toward her house. It almost looked like he was walking toward her. She hesitated, her feet dragging to a halt. He was walking toward her.

She squinted, trying to get a better look at him. His face was in shadow, but she didn't think she'd ever seen him before. His lanky form ate up the distance between them with purposeful strides.

She backed up several steps, unease filling her. "Hello?" Sweet Hill wasn't exactly a mecca of crime, but it was late and a man she didn't know was coming at her in the middle of the night.

"Hello, bitch," he greeted in turn.

The profanity, the slur, wasn't actually the thing that panicked her. It was the way he said it. The way he spoke . . . the absolute rage shaking his voice that clued her in to his identity. She knew his voice. This was the same guy that called her on the phone at work the other day.

Whirling around, she sprinted for her door.

She wasn't quick enough. She had her hand on the doorknob and was pulling it open when he came behind her. He grabbed her shoulder, forcing her around.

In the glow of her porch light, his features were no longer hidden. His narrow face was in perfect view. She didn't only know his voice. She knew *him*. She'd seen this man before. He was Noah Grimes's father. This was the man that went crazy in the courthouse the other week.

She opened her mouth to speak, but his hand shot out to wrap around her throat and she gasped. It was the last bit of air she was able to draw through her lips as hard fingers dug like knives into her.

"You're up late. Having trouble sleeping, you child-stealing bitch?" His eyes were like ice. Cold and furious.

Her lips worked, trying to form words. Speech was impossible. Choked, gurgling sounds spilled from her lips. She brought her hands up to claw at his hand around her throat. It did no good. She used her nails, scratching and digging at his flesh.

Oh my God. This wasn't happening. She was becoming a *Dateline* episode. She could imagine it now. The headline flashed through her mind.

Woman Strangled to Death on Her Front Porch.

No. It would not happen. Her life would not end like that.

She let go of his hands on her throat. Giving up that battle, she attacked his face, sinking her nails deep into his gaunt cheeks.

Grimes released her throat with a curse. She fell back, colliding with her door and sliding down. She struggled to rise to her feet, but he was back on her, his hands grabbing, bruising.

"Mr. Grimes! Stop! Please!"

"You didn't think I would forget you, did you? You stole my boy!"

"I understand your distress, but the court—"

"Distress? You understand my distress?" Spit flew from his lips. He hauled her closer, his hard hands digging into her arms, crushing and painful. "You can't talk your way out of this. I see what you really are. A cold vicious bitch who likes to destroy happy families."

All attempts at diplomacy flew out the window. He was delusional. "Happy families? Your family was not happy or even a family."

His eyes flared. He slapped her and gave her a shake.

She kicked and struggled and screamed. Someone had to hear. Someone would come.

She managed to wrest one arm free and land a blow to his face. He staggered and shook his head. When he fixed his gaze on her again his expression mirrored the same astonishment she felt. She had never struck another person in her life. Even with two older brothers, they had always been mindful never to be overly physical with her. As children, they never so much as shoved at her. She had never been forced to defend herself.

Shaking off his shock, he came at her with a roar. She braced herself for further pain, turning her face sideways and jamming her eyes tightly shut.

The pain never came.

Suddenly she was free. Released.

She fell back a step, falling against the door, her hand flying to her throat. Her eyes opened, searching wildly.

Grimes was gone. A shirtless North filled her

vision. He moved like a panther, all fluid muscle. Speed and force and fury.

She hadn't heard his approach. Not that she had seen much beyond the man attempting to steal the life from her.

Pressed against the expanse of her door, she could only watch. Stare and marvel at the fury of North Callaghan. She had never seen the like. The man was a firestorm, a hurricane of rage. Bone smacked bone as he hammered blow after blow.

In this moment, this man appeared capable of murder. His face was twisted into an expression of rage, so unlike the impassive expression he usually wore. She shuddered and brought her arms around herself, hugging tightly.

Grimes was under him now and North kept hitting him and hitting him, breathing hard, angry pants as he swung his fists over and over.

She heard her voice emerge. It sounded tinny and far away even to her ears. "North! Stop! You'll kill him!"

Other voices arrived then, too. Down the street people surfaced, coming out of their houses to investigate the commotion.

"North! North!" Fear for him fueled her. She stepped forward to seize his arm, her voice urgent and desperate. "You need to stop."

He did not even seem to hear her. He was a man possessed. He shook off her grip, so she added a second hand clutching him harder, shaking him harder, not to be deterred.

He straightened suddenly and turned on her, swinging around, a savage light in his eyes, as though he meant to strike her next. She lunged back a step with a gasp, her hand flying to her face as though to shield herself.

North stopped and shook himself. Blinking, he stared at her as though coming out of a daze. "Faith," he whispered and his voice sounded broken. It took everything in her not to go to him then. Not to wrap her arms around him.

"What's happening here?" a neighbor walking up her driveway called.

She held North's stare. "North . . . are you okay?"

He looked down at his hands. She followed his gaze, noting his cracked knuckles. She made a small sound of distress at the apparent damage.

He looked back up at her, his eyes ravaged. He moved forward in a few jerking steps. She didn't shrink away as he came at her with his wrecked hands.

He said her name again. "Faith?" He took her face in his hands, angling her chin higher so that the porch light hid nothing. His breath escaped him in a hiss at whatever he saw. His hands slid lower, his fingers grazing her tender neck and making her wince.

"He did this to you." He made a growling sound and made a move toward Grimes as though he intended to finish his beating.

She snatched hold of him and tugged him back to her, her hands tight on his waist. "North, no. Leave it be." She glanced around uneasily at the gathering of neighbors.

Grimes lay on the ground, moaning and writhing. He would not be getting up without assistance. She sighed. There was nothing to be done for it. They would have to call the police and an ambulance. She stifled a groan. The city police department worked closely with the sheriff's office. Once her name was given, the SHPD would immediately notify her brother. She would have to file a report. Press charges.

Almost as though she'd summoned them, sirens started wailing in the distance. Apparently someone had already called the authorities.

North turned his head in the direction of the sound, too. "It's about to get real now," he muttered.

Dread pooled in her stomach and bottomed out when she recognized her brother's Bronco swerving onto her street. Of course he would get here first, even before the SHPD.

He came to a stop with a hard push on the brakes. He was probably alerted once he heard her address on dispatch. Or maybe someone heard about it on the police scanner and notified him. Or maybe Doris called him. Whatever the case, he was here and things were about to get a whole lot more complicated.

Her brother was walking up her driveway with murder in his eyes as two SHPD cruisers pulled onto the street. She spotted Ford Willis through the windshield of one of the cars. He had gone to high school with Faith and also happened to be their minister's kid. You couldn't meet a nicer person than Ford. He couldn't even bring himself to give out speeding tickets.

She sighed and then winced because the action of exhaling that hard actually hurt her throat. North was watching her closely. He did not miss her reaction. He tilted her chin up and his thumb lightly brushed the raw skin of her throat, his expression tightening with concern.

Suddenly her brother was there, shouldering his way through neighbors. He took one glance at North and looked ready to start a beat down of his own. "Callaghan!" he roared.

Naturally, he would think this was somehow the *felon's* fault. She shook her head and stepped in front of North, holding up her hands. "Hale, stop! He didn't do anything!"

Her brother's bigger body collided with her hands, but he didn't seem inclined to stop and listen to her. He kept walking forward, pushing against her hands, ready to plow through her to get to North. "No! Stop! It wasn't him. He didn't do anything."

Except save her life. He did do that.

She turned, still keeping one hand on her brother's chest to ward him off. She looked up at North. "He saved my life."

North didn't even glance at her brother. His eyes were glued to her face, as though she were the only person in the world . . . the only one who mattered in this scene of chaos.

"What the hell happened?" Hale demanded, not one to waste time getting to the point.

She shook her head and quickly realized that was a mistake. Dizziness swamped her and she staggered to the side. North let loose a curse beside her. Before she knew what was happening he swept her up into his arms. Closing her eyes against the spinning world, she pressed a hand to her forehead.

Dimly she heard her brother exclaim something. She wasn't sure what he said, but there may have been a curse word or two trickled in there. North carried her a short distance. And then she was no longer moving. She sank down onto something soft and yielding.

She opened her eyes slowly. All she could see, the only thing she could even look at in that moment, was North's face hovering so close to her own.

"North," she breathed.

"I'm here, Faith."

NINETEEN

*T*HE SON OF a bitch tried to kill her. There was no mistake about it. If North had been two minutes, even one minute later, Faith could be dead.

He could have been too late. Too late again. The story of his life.

He took a peek through the blinds, sending a glance to where the bastard was writhing on the ground. His hands curled into fists at his side. The urge to continue beating the shit out of the guy was overwhelming. One of the officers that had just arrived was cuffing him even as a medic attended him.

He looked back down to where Faith sat on the couch. Another medic was examining her. He forced himself to stand back. It wasn't easy. He longed to touch her. Feel her. Know that she was okay. He didn't even care that her brother was there. Her brother. The sheriff. The one guy with enough power to ruin his life. To take away his freedom. And he didn't give a shit.

"I'm fine," Faith insisted, not for the first time, to the medic. Her imploring gaze lifted over the woman's head to her brother.

"Let her finish looking you over," Hale Walters commanded, his thumb hooked inside his gun belt. He must have felt North's stare. He cast him a quick look. The wariness was still in his eyes. North might have saved Faith's life tonight, but her brother still didn't fully trust him.

"I'm fine. I just want to go to bed and forget this night ever happened."

"You can't do that yet," her brother commanded. "We need a statement from you about what—"

"Maybe you can do that later," North suggested. "I'm sure it won't hurt to wait until tomorrow morning."

The sheriff stared at him with hard eyes as though he wanted nothing more than to slap some cuffs on him and throw him in a cell. "That's not protocol—"

"She's your sister," he bit out. "I'm sure you can be flexible for her."

Walters's gray eyes shot to flint. "I know who

she is, asshole. I don't need the reminder." He stabbed a finger in North's direction. "This doesn't concern you . . . *she* doesn't concern you and you don't forget that—"

"Hale," Faith interrupted. "He saved my life." She motioned to her door where somewhere beyond her attacker was being hauled away. "That guy was choking me. He would've finished me if North hadn't been here."

The medic stood then. She closed up her kit and lifted it off the floor beside the couch. "She looks all right." Her glance slid over each of them uncertainly. "I'll go now."

She stepped out and the door snicked shut after her.

Walters opened his mouth, clearly wanting to argue with Faith, wanting to reject that he owed North any thanks at all, but then his gaze swung to his sister and something softened in his eyes. Clearly he loved his sister and didn't want to add misery to her already shitty night.

She lifted her ravaged eyes to her brother. "Can I just give my statement in the morning?"

She trembled slightly. Walters must've noticed it, too. He nodded jerkily. "Sure, Faithy. You get some rest tonight. It can wait."

Walters left them alone in the living room, walking down the hall and disappearing into her bathroom.

North looked down at Faith to find her already watching him. "You should get your hands checked out," she said.

He flexed his sore knuckles. "I'll be fine. Had worse."

She studied him, her gaze unreadable.

"Who was that guy? Did you know him?"

"Just a lost soul . . . angry at the world." She sighed and moved her hands to her throat. She gently rubbed the skin there. His gaze followed the movement, his stomach knotting. The red smudges were already starting to bruise in the definite shape of fingers. "And angry at me. I'm a social worker. Sometimes that means I piss people off. Goes with the territory."

"Oh. This happens a lot then?" He didn't like that. He didn't like knowing there were people out there who wanted to hurt her. Scum who could get it into their heads that they could put their hands on her.

She shook her head. "Nope. This was the first time."

"Maybe you should consider a change of careers."

"I like my job. Tonight doesn't change that. One bad day—"

"He tried to kill you," he snapped. "That's more than a bad day."

Her brother returned then with two Tylenol in his hand and a glass of water. "Take these."

She obeyed, downing the pills with a swallow of water. "Thanks," she whispered.

"Why don't I stay for—"

"No. I'm fine."

"You sure?"

"I'm just going to bed. It's not like that guy is going to come back. And besides . . ." Her gaze drifted to North. She was going to say he lived next door, but decided against it. That still might not be a good thing in her brother's mind.

Hale's lips tightened, compressing into a hard line. Yeah. He knew what she was going to say and he didn't like it. With a reluctant sigh, he turned to face North. "Appears I was wrong about you. I owe you my thanks." He gave a single nod.

"I didn't do it for you or for your thanks," North said. He sent one more look at Faith. Her lips parted and she inhaled. He watched the rise of her chest. She seemed to be holding her breath as he looked down at her. "You take care, Faith. I'm next door if you need anything."

That said, he turned and left her house.

SHE HAD ALREADY showered for the evening, but that seemed a long time ago. Before Grimes showed up in her driveway. Before he tried to kill her. Before North saved her life. How was she supposed to forget him now when he had gone ahead and done that?

That was damn confusing.

After stepping out of the shower for a second time tonight, she slipped inside her robe hanging on the back of the bathroom door. Pulling the collar close, she inhaled the laundry-fresh scent, taking comfort in it. She was still here. Still alive.

She picked up her hairbrush and moved into her bedroom. Sitting at the end of her bed, she started brushing out her hair in slow strokes. She'd left her bathroom light on, so a soft glow carried into her bedroom. Even in the dim glow she could see the skin of her throat already bruising.

She pulled her brush through her hair and stopped. Staring at her neck, she touched it lightly with a hand that still trembled with the aftereffects of her attack. She supposed it was an adrenaline crash. Or shock maybe.

She would have to wear a turtleneck or a scarf. In summer. That wouldn't make her look weird or anything. She shivered where she sat on the edge of her bed, and that didn't compute. Her thermostat was set to seventy-six. Maybe she wasn't ready to be alone, after all. Maybe she should have let her brother stay. She winced. Except she didn't want her brother to spend the night. She didn't want to endure his hovering . . . his questions. Well-meaning as he was, he could be overbearing.

She stood abruptly, then moved to her phone on her nightstand. She snatched it up and opened her messages. She scrolled to the person she was looking for and started typing. She wasn't sure what she wanted from him. It was impossible to articulate.

But she seemed to know the one word to type.

* * *

Please.

HE STARED DOWN at the single word on his phone. Worry punched him in the chest. It was a single, ambiguous word, but it had him flinging off the covers on his bed and vaulting out of his room. It might as well have been *Help*!

He jumped down his stairs and was out his front door, slamming it after him. He didn't worry about locking it. Faith could be in trouble.

He pounded on her door. "Faith! Faith!"

She opened quickly enough, but it felt like forever. Forever standing there and worrying that she wasn't okay on the other side of that door. Worrying that leaving her alone after her attack had been a mistake. He should have stayed longer and made sure she was okay.

It was a terrible feeling—one he had vowed never to feel again. He'd cared and worried for Katie and look where that had gotten him. Look where it had gotten her.

"North." She breathed his name, her eyes wide and haunted in her face. She had showered. Her hair was wet and she was wearing her robe again. That damn robe.

"Are you all right?" He looked her up and down as though checking for injuries. Bare skin peeked out at him between the open lapels of her robe, the V of skin distracting him.

He swallowed, gave a single, hard shake, commanding himself not to think about what was under that robe—or rather what was *not* under it. "Do you need something?"

"I—I can't—" She stopped and looked down for a moment, inhaling a shuddery breath. Composed again, she lifted her gaze back up. "I don't want to be alone."

He nodded with a swift inhalation. "Sure. I get that. Do you want me to call—"

"Can you stay with me the night?"

"Me?" She wanted him to sleep over?

"I just can't be alone." She quickly went on to say, "I'm not asking for you to *sleep* with me . . . just *sleep* with me."

"Of course." The last thing she was looking for was a roll in the sack. She'd just been through a traumatic event. She wasn't here asking for him to rock her world.

"Would you mind?" She looked up at him, her wide eyes so guileless and unaware of what she was asking. *Would you mind?* Would he *mind* spending the night with her? Sleep next to her and not touch her?

He nodded and entered her house, stepping past her. She closed and locked the door behind her.

She smiled tentatively and stood before him for a moment, her hands worrying the lapels of her robe. She looked so small and vulnerable, two words he would have never used to describe her before. He didn't like it. He wanted the fiery Faith back, but he knew that was about him and this wasn't about what he wanted or needed right now. She'd been through hell tonight and he would be there for her because she asked for it.

"You sure you don't want to call your father or brother?"

She let go of her robe and hugged herself, shaking her head firmly. "Oh, hell no." She released a choked laugh. "They'd come over with a U-Haul. You know this is my first home. They were never keen on me living alone, and tonight doesn't do much to help my case."

"I understand." And he did. He would have been the same way with Katie.

Faith inclined her head toward the stairs, and then led the way. He followed, realizing belatedly as he ascended that he was only wearing his briefs. He hadn't taken the time to throw on jeans. At least it was something though. Half the time he slept naked.

She moved ahead of him to turn off her bathroom light, plunging the room into darkness. It took his eyes a moment to acclimate to the dark and make out the outline of her in the gloom. She dropped her robe, so he guessed she wasn't totally naked underneath it. She pulled back the covers on the right side of the bed, nearest to the bathroom.

He rounded the bed, tugging down the covers on that side.

Springs squeaked softly and sheets whispered as she slid into bed. He hesitated and took a bracing breath. He knew this was just for comfort, so she wouldn't be alone, but it still felt awkward. He couldn't recall ever sleeping with a woman and not having sex with her.

"North?"

The soft utterance scratched the space between them. She might as well have said *please* again. That's what his name sounded like in her voice. A plea.

"Yeah?" He slid into bed beside her, not touching, keeping as much space between them as possible. He was determined to hold himself back and not take advantage of her. Not like this. Not when she was vulnerable and shaken. He held himself still. Rigid. Probably too rigid. It was going to be a long night.

"Thank you," she whispered into the quiet of her room.

"No problem." He slept with plenty of women. So what if this time he would actually *sleep* with one? It was late. He was tired. He could do this.

There was a rustle of movement and he felt fingers brush his arm. He jerked slightly.

"Sorry," she murmured. "C-could I maybe hold your hand? Just until I fall asleep?"

He lifted her hand from his arm and laced his fingers through hers. "Of course." Their arms stretched between them, not touching except for where their fingers were linked, the only point of contact. Her hand felt small and slim clasped in his. Their palms were flush and he could feel the steady pulse of her heartbeat, fusing with his own.

His chest swelled with something he had never felt. Something that made him want to do more than hold her hand. It made him want to pull her against him and fold her into his arms. It also, ironically, made him want to bolt out the door.

Hopefully she would fall asleep soon and he could let go of her hand and scoot to the edge of the bed until he fell asleep. Hopefully.

TWENTY

SHE WOKE TO darkness.

She inhaled and then winced. Her throat hurt. She lifted her fingers to her neck. Frowning, she swam through the fog of her thoughts, trying to make sense, trying to remember and piece everything together.

She shifted slightly, and then noticed that the bed felt different. The mattress felt different. More solid somehow. And then it . . . moved. The mattress lifted underneath her cheek. She brought fingers to rest near her cheek. And then she realized her head did not rest on the mattress. She rested her head on a person. A chest. Her neighbor's chest. North Callaghan's chest. They shared a bed.

Because she had asked North to spend the night with her. At the time it had seemed like a good idea. At the time it seemed like the only option considering how unbearably agitated she felt. Aloneness had never bothered her before. *That was before someone tried to kill you.*

Tonight she had allowed herself the weakness. She allowed herself to make the request. Just once she would let herself be vulnerable.

But now she was faced with the consequence of that weakness. She was in bed with North Callaghan. Plastered over his chest.

Isn't this what you wanted? All along? Tonight's events, as terrible as they were, had given her a reason to make it happen.

She lifted her head up slightly from his chest.

"Can't sleep?" His voice grumbled deliciously across her skin in the darkness.

She glanced over his body to the clock. It read 3:51 A.M. "I was sleeping soundly. I don't know why I woke."

Only she did know why. It was the strangeness of sleeping with someone, of being wrapped up in someone so closely and so tightly that it was impossible to know where she began and he ended. "Sorry," she mumbled as she extricated herself from his arms and settled back on her side of the bed. "Thank you for being here for me."

"No problem." He waited a beat before asking, "You didn't want your brother to stay?"

She thought about that for a minute. "I love him. He's great . . . but a little overbearing. It's hard for him to just be around me without telling me what to do . . . how to live. Tonight, I didn't want that."

She thought she sensed him nod. "Older brothers can be like that."

"They excel at it," she agreed. "What about your brother? He's around still, I presume. Doing . . . okay?"

"Yeah. He's doing great. Married and happy. His life is . . . His life is great."

She imagined that she heard something in his voice besides happiness or even neutrality. There was something there. Something he felt toward his brother and his brother's state of "greatness" that he wasn't okay with.

"When it comes to overbearing brothers, I totally get it." He shifted on the bed. She turned and studied his profile, noting the arm he tucked behind his head. She caught a whiff of him. Warm male. "The guy gives me a hard time. Calls and texts. Pops in. He always wants me over for dinner."

"I don't know. Sounds kind of . . . nice."

"They're going to have a baby."

She watched his chest rise and fall on a great, silent breath.

"You're going to be an uncle."

"Yeah. They want me to be the godfather."

"Wow. That's great." She'd hoped she would be an aunt by now. She was the youngest.

"Not really. What can I do? What can I show this kid?"

She moistened her lips. "You can love him. Be there. That's all anyone can really do."

"You make it sound easy."

She nodded in the dark and then realized he probably couldn't see the motion. "You can do it. You were here for me when I asked . . . and this after you told me to forget you existed. You don't even like me." She laughed lightly and the sound fell flat.

"Is that what you think, Walters?" he asked, his disembodied voice floating between them. "That I don't like you?"

She released a gust of breath, regretting her words. She had meant to make a joke but now things were awkward. "I just think you're a better person than you think."

Her whispered reply didn't improve the awkwardness. Silence swelled between them. Moments passed and slid into minutes. Her thoughts drifted. She swallowed and felt the rawness of her throat muscles. Grimes's face flashed across her mind, his feral expression as he tried to choke the life out of her.

"I took his son away." Her quiet voice sounded distant and far away in the darkness.

He didn't say anything for a long while. She started to wonder if he would speak at all. Maybe he had fallen asleep.

"He didn't deserve to be a father," he finally replied, obviously understanding her reference.

"How do you know that's true? Maybe I—"

"Because you took his kid away. You wouldn't have done that if he deserved to keep him."

"How do you know that?" Her voice sounded strained even to her ears. And not because of her bruised throat. "You don't know me."

"I know you enough to know that. Some people are messed up. Sick. They don't deserve to be a parent . . . they don't even deserve their freedom."

"I guess you would know about that."

"Yeah. I do."

"Did you deserve to be put away?"

"Yeah. I got what I deserved. And this guy who hurt you . . . he needs to get what he deserves, too. For being a shitty parent, you lose your kid. For attacking you . . ." His voice faded for a moment. She knew what he was thinking right then. She knew he was remembering what he did to Mason Leary.

"I'm sure there will be a restraining order on him come morning. My brother will see to it. Not that he'll be out of jail yet. Knowing my brother, he'll be in there for a while."

"Handy having law enforcement on your side."

"Not as handy as having you next door, it would seem."

He released a breath that sounded suspiciously like a laugh. "You moving in next door has been interesting, too."

She sensed that he had turned his head on the pillow and was looking at her. Not seeing her, but looking at her.

He continued, "I haven't texted this much since I got my phone two years ago."

She snorted. "I'm sure that's not true. You with the endless booty calls." Even as she said this, she realized she hadn't heard him with anyone in a while.

"Yeah, been kind of in a drought since you moved in though."

Ha. So what . . . almost two weeks? "What's going on with the lovely Serena?"

The bed shifted as he rolled onto his side. "I wouldn't know."

Pleasure suffused her at this admission—even though she knew she shouldn't care. It didn't matter. It didn't mean anything.

She rolled onto her side, too. She felt the soft fan of his breath on her face. She tucked her hands under her cheek. "You stopped holding my hand," she murmured and even to her own ears her voice sounded almost coy.

His eyes gleamed like black pennies in the dark. "What are you doing, Faith?"

Her heart thundered against her ribs. "Just . . . talking."

"I'm not going to touch you again."

"Why not?" she shot back.

"Because that would lead to other things and tonight isn't the night for that."

"Why not? Tonight feels like the perfect night for that. I almost died." She propped herself up on her elbow. "Maybe I need you to remind me that I'm alive."

He didn't respond and she knew she'd made a valid point. He was thinking. She decided to push her advantage. She leaned forward, unsure exactly where she was headed until she felt her nose brush his jaw. She dove in closer, ducking into the crook of his neck. She pressed her open mouth to his throat, letting her teeth scrape the salty-clean flesh. Her tongue laved the velvet of his skin, tasting, exploring the texture with undulating licks of her tongue that would probably leave a mark.

She inched up to his ear, breathing into the whorls, "I want to taste you everywhere."

He growled and before she realized his intent, he flipped her on her back. Then he was over her. "Be careful what you wish for, Faith."

Her hands grasped him by his sides, tugging him toward her.

"No," he bit. "I'll give you what you want. I'll remind you that you're alive, but it's happening my way."

She nodded hastily. Whatever that meant, whatever he had to give, she would gladly take. Just the sensation of him over her, his big body wedged between her thighs, set her afire. He pulled back slightly, knocking their blankets aside. Snatching the waistband of her shorts he slid them down her legs in one smooth motion.

"I dreamed of these," he growled, his hands skimming up the outside of her calves and then roaming over her thighs. He slid down between her knees, pushing her thighs wide to make room for his head and shoulders.

"Let me taste you," he murmured, seduction dripping in every word. His fingers grazed the outside of her knees in teasing circles that made her limbs shake. He turned his face to trail kisses along the inside of her thighs, his tongue darting out to lick. His teeth occasionally biting and nipping.

Her hands lifted above her head and grabbed fistfuls of pillow. She arched, noisy pants escaping her, broken by the occasional yip.

With a groan, he crawled above her and latched onto a nipple through the thin cotton of her tank. She felt the perfect prod of his cock through his briefs, poking and thrusting into her bare sex, only a barrier of cotton separating them and saving her from direct penetration.

"North, please," she begged.

"Please, what?" he asked, his mouth talking around the aching nipple he was working with his tongue, lips and teeth.

"Fuck me!"

He bucked harder against her and ground his erection against her weeping sex. "Oh, you're soaking for me, baby."

He moved to her other breast, sucking the nipple deep into his mouth as his hand came up to squeeze the other one roughly, his finger and thumb clamping down on the distended peak. She screamed, coming up off the bed as her orgasm washed over her.

He moved then, sliding down her body and

dropping between her splayed legs. His mouth claimed her, drinking her climax deep. She jerked, startled at the sensation of his mouth down there. No one had ever—

He sucked her clit deep into his mouth and she forgot everything. She cried out, her fingers clawing through his hair as his hands slid under her bare bottom, pulling her closer to his face. He pulled her clit between his lips, savoring it with hard licks.

He continued to taste her, drowning his face in her. She should be mortified . . . if it didn't feel so amazingly good. She started to shake and rock against his questing tongue. He settled deeper between her thighs, adjusting his hands under her ass and lifting her higher for him.

It was wicked the way he feasted on her. She screamed and cried out . . . and now she understood what he meant about making women scream. He hadn't been lying. No woman could hold silent while he did this to her.

Her fingers tightened in his hair as he increased his mouth's pressure, his tongue playing with her until she was senseless, tears leaking from her eyes as he launched her into another orgasm. She cried out, pushing into his mouth wantonly.

Then he added his hand to the mix. As he

thrummed his tongue over her clit, he slid a finger inside her wet channel, pushing deep and hard, curling inward. He started a rhythm, pushing and pulling in and out of her body. She released a muffled shriek, convulsing all around him, coming apart yet again, her channel tightening around his finger.

He lifted himself up. She still shook in the aftereffects, clinging to his head. His gleaming eyes locked onto hers in the darkness.

She wasn't the only one shaking. His hands trembled where they clutched her hips. And there was still his erection, hard as a rock against her sex. She shifted, bumping her swollen sex against him.

"North," she pleaded. Her hand trailed down his chest, searching for him. He stopped her from touching him, hopping off her and landing on his feet outside of the bed.

"I told you this would happen my way. I'm not fucking you."

She stiffened. "What about you?" Was it so easy for him to turn away from her? She'd felt his erection. She knew he wanted her.

"I'll survive." Turning, he headed into her bathroom and shut the door behind him. Soon she heard water running.

She dropped back on the bed, tugging her tank

down to her waist. She needed to find her shorts but her limbs felt like jelly.

He'd pleasured her, but a part of her still felt empty and dissatisfied . . . and hurt. It was that same part that wanted to follow him into the bathroom and tempt him into finishing this the way she wanted it to end. He gave it to every other girl. Why not her?

Was he not tempted? Was his control so great, so unbreakable? She wanted to please him *and* herself. She wanted to feel him thrusting inside of her. It was more than a physical ache. She frowned. And that, she realized, was the most dangerous thing of all.

TWENTY-ONE

*T*HIS WAS NOT good.

He took the coldest shower he could tolerate. He didn't shut off the water until his dick had gone limp. By the time he emerged she was asleep again. She hadn't bothered to put her shorts back on and he got an unfettered view of her beautiful ass (which woke his dick back up) before he turned the bathroom light off.

He dared to get back in bed with her. He had promised to stay the night, after all.

North shifted uneasily as Faith slept beside him, her breathing slow and even. She rolled close and flung an arm over him. Fucking misery. He could feel the hammer of her heart against his side and all of him pulled tight as a wire about to pop free.

Not good. How he came to be in this position,

this role of comfort giver, he couldn't fathom. He didn't do this.

In prison, after Knox and Reid left, he kept his head down. He never played hero. A guy would get himself killed at the Rock trying to be a hero. He'd learned to turn a blind eye. To look away and ignore the cries for help. He'd gotten really good at that—he'd killed his humanity to survive. And yet now here he was . . . rescuing women and giving comfort and solace. Pleasuring her but taking none for himself.

Oh, he'd enjoyed it. He could still taste her sweetness on his tongue. But his cock ached. His balls burned from lack of release.

What he should do was roll her over and do what he'd been fantasizing about since he first spotted her getting out of her car.

She wouldn't resist. She was too vulnerable right now. And the way she had screamed and responded to him, he knew he aroused her. Traumatized or not, he could have her climaxing and clawing his back in no time.

Dawn tinged the sky, lightening the room as his conscience (what was left of it) battled against his willpower. He closed his eyes tightly, forcing himself not to look at that ass, at the pussy his mouth knew so well now. His cock wanted to know it, too.

He couldn't take her. Not like this. There was some humanity left to him, after all, he supposed.

With a muffled curse, he climbed out of the bed, moving stealthily, careful not to look at her, not to wake her as he slipped from her bed.

"North?" Her voice sounded fuzzy and still half asleep.

He hesitated at her door before turning to face her.

She sat up, rubbing at one eye. He wished it was still dark so that he didn't have to see her like this. "Where are you going?" she asked.

"It's morning now."

"Barely."

"You asked me to stay the night. I did."

She stiffened, dropping her hand. "I'm sorry it was such a *chore* for you."

"That's okay. You had a rough night. You needed someone with you."

She nodded stiffly. He knew he'd made it sound like he didn't want to be here with her, but that was for the best.

"Thanks," she said, her voice cold, distant. As though she were totally unaffected by him. "I appreciate you taking such good care of me. It must have been torture."

She would never know the extent of his torment.

Touching her, tasting her and then turning away practically killed him.

"No problem," he reassured her as though he hadn't caught her sarcasm.

"Don't worry. I won't trouble you again."

He hesitated. She hardly seemed like a traumatized victim this morning. Even with the bruises marring her throat, she looked strong. Composed as she sat in the bed staring at him coolly.

He wanted to crawl between those sheets with her and finish what they started, wrecking that perfect composure. Except she was *still* the sheriff's sister and a white-picket-fence kind of girl—exactly the type of trouble he had vowed to avoid—and he was still North Callaghan.

He would never say the right thing. Never do the right thing.

Never be the kind of guy she deserved.

Without a word, he turned and walked out of her house.

THREE DAYS LATER, Faith was finally having that second date with Brendan. She'd seen North once in the few days. Only from afar. When she'd been checking her mail, she watched him pull into the driveway and go inside the house.

So the sudden text from him caught her off

guard. Why was he reaching out to her? Was he feeling guilty about the way he'd walked out on her?

Hey . . .

She stared down at that text on her phone. Just seeing that single word, knowing he was texting her, thinking about her, made her stomach pitch.

Sucking in a bracing breath, she replied. Hey. How are you?

Keeping busy. How are you? Everything ok?

Was this his way of alleviating his conscience and verifying that she was okay after Grimes's attack? Or was he concerned that making out with her and then walking out on her had devastated her?

Honestly, he'd flipped a switch inside her, waking a part of her that had been long dormant. She dreamed of him, waking up panting, her sex aching and clenching.

Last night she had actually resorted to taking Mister Right out from her drawer. He'd gotten the job done, but just barely. Her O had been elusive. She'd finally gotten herself off by visualizing North. By remembering his mouth and hands on her. She channeled that memory and that had done it, brought her to shattering release.

Shaking off the thought, her fingers flew. I'm doing really well. Getting ready for a date.

With Fancy Pants?

His name is Brendan and he's coming over to cook me dinner.

Wasting your time. You don't want him.

Rage burned through her. Who was he to make that judgment? You don't know that.

Faith didn't even know that. Not yet. Maybe tonight would be the night that *nice* grew into stupendous.

I do. What happened between us wouldn't have happened if you were hot for this guy.

We'll see . . .

Try it. I dare you. See if he can get your rocks off.

He was daring her? She narrowed her gaze and marched upstairs. At her dresser, she opened the drawer and riffled through it until she found her matching black bra and panties. Not the most comfortable lingerie she owned but definitely the sexiest—and the most color coordinated.

She snatched up her phone again and typed: Challenge accepted. Happily.

Have fun.

She attacked the keys on her phone, stabbing them with her fingers. I will. I'm picking out my sexiest underwear now.

He didn't reply to her goad.

She stared down at her phone for several moments, her temples pounding.

Her doorbell rang. She glanced at the clock. Two minutes before the hour. Brendan was punctual, of course. She hurriedly stripped out of her clothes and swapped lingerie.

Dressed again, she smoothed a hand down the sleeveless blouse she wore, willing her stomach flutters into submission. Flutters, sadly, that were not a result of her impending date despite the avowal she had just made to see if Brendan could get her rocks off.

Touching up her lipstick, she nodded at her reflection one final time before heading downstairs.

Let the night begin.

NORTH DIDN'T KNOW what was worse. Faith being on a date with Fancy Pants or Faith entertaining him privately at her house.

Okay, at her house where they were alone with a bed in proximity was definitely the worse-case scenario. No doubt about it. And daring her to get intimate with the guy was about the dumbest thing he had ever done short of landing himself in prison.

He stared down at her texts, rereading the messages.

I'm picking out my sexiest underwear.

Fuck that.

He charged to the door and yanked it open, only to see the Audi already parked neatly in the driveway directly behind Faith's car.

He was already here.

North shut his door. Hard.

He paced his living room, thinking about her next door with some guy that North had all but told her to go ahead and fuck. What if she thought he didn't care what she did? What if that made a difference for her?

What then?

TWENTY-TWO

"I **DON'T THINK ANYONE** has ever cooked for me," Faith ventured to say as Brendan sat across from her at her kitchen table. It was strange seeing him here. A man at her table. He wore a polo shirt tucked into starched slacks. She wondered what he looked like in a T-shirt and jeans—and then gave herself a mental shake. Who cared what he looked like in a T-shirt and jeans? She should be more interested in what he looked like naked. She sat there for a moment, letting herself think about that. Nope. The idea wasn't very intriguing to her either. Damn.

"Never?" Brendan grinned as he lifted the glass of wine to his lips.

"Well, definitely not my dad or brothers. I might have starved if I had to rely on them. My life would have consisted of eating out and grilled cheese sandwiches." She used the side of her fork to cut into her lasagna. "Now I love a grilled cheese, just not five times a week."

She bit into the lasagna, ignoring that the noodle sheets were a little too al dente. It could have used another twenty minutes in the oven.

He was right. He was a passable cook, but hey. He had cooked. No man had ever done that for her before. That was saying something.

Al dente noodles or not, he had made a pretty good lasagna. Definite bonus points for that even if he had apologized for the fact that the sauce wasn't homemade. She figured most of the world bought tomato sauce in a jar. She always made sauce the way her mother did. From scratch. It was a tradition. A way to keep her mom alive.

"You get major props," she complimented.

"I can't lie though. I bought the tiramisu from Angelo's."

Her smile deepened. He really was nice—that he had even cared to do this . . . to order a tiramisu and pick it up for their date. *It only took him practically two weeks to follow up with the second date.*

She shoved that negative little voice aside. He had an important and demanding job. She could appreciate that.

"Well, I'm having a nice time." And she meant it. She was having a nice time. *Nice*. Argh! There was that word again. It was as though something was wrong with it. Damn North and damn Wendy for putting it into her head that *nice* wasn't good enough.

She stood to gather their plates.

"Let me help," he said, rising to his feet.

They cleared the table together and he pulled the tiramisu out of her fridge.

"Hm?" She cocked her head. "Wine and tiramisu . . . or should I make coffee?" They stood in the cramped space between her island and the refrigerator. She held up the bottle of wine thoughtfully while he held the cake.

His gentle eyes looked down at her and suddenly she didn't think he was thinking about cake. His Adam's apple bobbed and his eyes glanced to her mouth before looking away.

He suddenly cleared his throat. "I don't think wine can ever be a mistake . . ."

He'd changed his mind. For whatever reason. Shyness. He thought it was too soon. North's texts flashed across her mind. *Have fun*. He was so smug he thought she was wasting her time with Brendan.

Resolve steeling her spine, she set the wine bottle down. He watched her movements, his head moving almost owl-like as she plucked the cake from his hands and set that on the island behind him.

"What are—" he started to say, but she cut him off. Leaning forward, she grasped his shirt and tugged him closer. His eyes widened, darting from her eyes to her lips. She inched closer. Close enough for her to press her mouth to his. To kiss him.

He responded readily enough after a fraction of hesitation. It was a good kiss. Proficient, she thought as his lips moved against hers. She'd had worse.

She winced inside. *She'd had worse?* Not the best method of measurement. She willed the heat, the sparks to race along her nerves. She deepened the kiss, tracing his lips with her tongue. His breathing picked up, hot air rushing from his nose to moisten her face.

His hands shifted from her back to her shoulders, as though he wasn't sure where to put them. She grasped them herself, put his hands on the small of her back and leaned her body against the long line of his, pressing her breasts into his chest.

He worked out. There was that. Nothing soft about him and yet . . .

Sudden music blared on the air, making them jump apart. Her hands flew to her ears as Guns N' Roses welcomed them to the jungle.

Her wild eyes went to her kitchen wall. Her framed picture of coffee mugs rattled against the wall—the shared wall.

Brendan shouted unnecessarily, with one hand over his ear and the other hand pointing to North's place. "Your neighbor is playing music really loud!!"

North! That jerk! He was trying to ruin her date.

She nodded, murder pumping fast in her heart. "Do you want to move into the living room?" she shouted.

He nodded.

She took his hand and led him to her couch, determined that North would not wreck this night for her.

Unfortunately, the music followed them. She forced a smile. "Who doesn't like Guns N' Roses?" she yelled.

"What?" He held a hand up to his ears.

She tried a second time as she sank down on the couch. "Who doesn't like Guns N' Roses?"

"*What!?*" He shook his head and pointed to his ears like some elderly man trying to convey that he was hard of hearing.

Oh, never mind. She grabbed him by the shirt and leaned over him again, intent on continuing. North would not be right about this.

Suddenly a loud motor revved to life directly in front of her house.

"What the—"

The loud spray of water hit her living room with hurricane force. She squeaked and lunged off her couch. Brendan stood beside her. "Sounds like a power washer," he shouted. "You hire someone to do your windows tonight?"

"No," she fumed. "I did not."

She marched to her front door over the loud screeching of Axl Rose, the roar of a power washer and water blasting her living room window. She wrenched open her door and marched outside, managing to get caught directly in the water hose's line of fire.

She hopped and yelped, flailing her hands as if that might ward off the stinging spray. It was strong enough to peel the skin back from her bones. "Stop!" Her gaze found North. North looking casual, his expression mild as he directed the hose at her house. As if it was the kind of thing he did all the time. "Turn it off!" She pointed to the motor parked behind him.

He obliged, moving to the motor and flipping it off. He turned a polite smile back on her. Half the volume decreased but there was still the music blasting from his house.

"What are you doing?" she shouted, blood rushing to her head.

"Just being neighborly. Was gonna power wash the driveway and house this evening like we talked about, remember?"

"Liar," she hissed, her fingers flexing wide at her side, itching to take a swipe at his face. They had discussed no such thing!

She spotted Brendan, watching them uncertainly from inside her door. She must look like a woman about to come unglued—which would be an accurate assessment. She took a bracing breath, trying to compose herself.

"Would you mind doing it another time?" she asked between clenched teeth.

"Aw, won't take but a little while to finish, and I've already started. You said tonight would be okay, remember?"

Her composure snapped. She stomped her foot. "No! I said no such thing! Stop lying! You're doing this on purpose!"

"Doing what?" His eyes glinted. He was enjoying himself.

She marched closer and stabbed a finger in his chest. "Don't act all innocent. *You* know what you're doing! *I* know what you're doing!"

"Uh, Faith?" Brendan stepped fully outside. "I

think I'm going to go. It's getting late and we have work tomorrow."

Oh God. She must look deranged to him. She moved away from North and hurriedly blocked Brendan, waving her hands. "No. Don't leave yet!"

Okay. That didn't sound desperate.

She shot a look over her shoulder, catching North's smug expression before it was masked again by a look of innocence. This was all his fault, damn him!

Brendan was talking now, but she barely heard a word over the roar in her ears. She only caught the gist of what he was saying. He had a good time, thank you, blah blah blah. He pressed a kiss to her cheek. "I'll text you later. Enjoy that tiramisu."

Then she watched helplessly as he walked down her driveway and got in his car. She stood there for a moment, her frustration and anger bubbling over.

Inhaling through her nostrils, she turned and leveled a glare on the man waiting behind her.

North stood there, arms crossed over his broad chest, looking calm and satisfied. Ready for her.

"You," she growled.

He held up the hose. "So . . . you want me to finish the windows?"

She jabbed a finger at him. "Keep that hose away from my house. As a matter of fact, you stay away from my house." He turned and glanced at the duplex, his sweeping gaze seeming to convey how hard that would be to manage when their homes were conjoined. She accused, "You ruined my date!"

"Did I?" he asked mildly.

"Don't look at me like you don't know." She dropped her fists to her hips. "Don't act like you didn't do this on purpose."

North scratched his jaw and glanced out at the street where Brendan had just beat a hasty retreat. A wave of defeat swelled over her. She followed his gaze. Fabulous. Maybe he wasn't meant to be, but North had no business interfering.

He made a tsking sound. "I didn't expect him to turn tail so easily. Honestly, Faith. You could do better."

She saw red. "I agree." Stepping forward, she shoved him in the chest. "So do me a favor. Stop interfering and let me find him." For good measure, and because she was *that* mad, she shoved him again.

His features turned stony. "Don't do that."

"What? This?" She did it again, hoping to annoy him as much as he annoyed her.

He growled, "I said stop—"

"What are you going to do about it?" She stepped nearer, thrusting her face closer.

"You don't know who you're tangling with—"

"Oh, yeah? Show me," she challenged.

He laughed roughly. "You're a fool. It's like you want to get hurt. Is that it?"

For a moment she actually considered what he was saying, but despite how mad she was at him right now, she had never been afraid of him. "I'm not an idiot. You won't hurt me."

He sobered. "Oh, baby. That's what I do to people."

She felt his voice like a feather stroking down her body. Crazy considering the words he was saying were not the least bit seductive. Shaking her head, her voice shuddered past her lips. "I don't believe that."

"No?" His hand shot out to circle the back of her neck, hauling her flush against him. "You're fucking wrong." His thumb stroked her throat in tantalizing brushes. "That's all I know . . . how to ruin things."

She wet her lips. Glancing down, she stared at

where their bodies were mashed together tightly. Close. Still not close enough. She wanted . . . she *wanted*.

His heart beat hard against her. She moistened her lips and before she could consider what she was doing, she said the words that popped in her head. "Then ruin me."

TWENTY-THREE

*T*HE OFFER HOVERED between them like a great big swelling balloon.

His eyes dilated, the deep brown darkening nearly as black as his irises. Not a sound passed between them. The air in her lungs froze, trapped.

Did she really just say that?

She opened her mouth to retract the words, to pop that balloon, to say anything to take them away or erase what she had just said. But no sound escaped.

His big hands dropped to span her waist. "You want me to ruin you?" His gravelly voice rolled over her. "I can do that."

She squeaked as he lifted her up off the ground. Before she realized his intent, he was carrying her into her house. He walked them right through the front door, kicking it shut behind them.

He plopped her on her kitchen table. She was suddenly intensely grateful that she'd purchased a high kitchen table. They fit perfectly. He wedged his body between her thighs, his hands sliding up the outsides and under her skirt.

"Nice skirt." He lifted his head to look her over. Reaching between them, he flipped the silky flounce along her collar. "And blouse. You dress like this for him?"

"I dressed like this for . . . a date."

"You look expensive. Untouchable." His gaze left a blistering trail as it roamed over her. "Not the kind of girl I usually touch."

But he had touched her. And then he said he wouldn't again. But he was now. So what were they doing? She didn't know how to respond. Her chest was too tight, an invisible fist squeezing her lungs. Fortunately, he didn't seem concerned with her reply. His hands kept moving, fingers diving under the outer edge of her panties, skimming along her hips and down to the crease between her thighs and crotch.

"So tell me about it." Gripping her hips, he yanked her closer, dragging her against the front of him, where his member already bulged against rough denim.

"About what?"

"Your date." The drawl of his deep voice scraped over her. "Did he kiss you? Touch you here?" He cupped her sex, his palm searing hot over her folds.

She opened her mouth and made a gurgling sound. She couldn't even form coherent words when he was touching her.

His thumb dipped, tracing the seam of her lips.

She gasped sharply.

"So slick," he said thickly.

And she was already wet. Embarrassingly so.

His thumb parted her, pressing into her wetness, easing a fraction inside her.

"Your bedroom?" He jerked his head toward the staircase.

She nodded jerkily.

Again, he picked her up like she wasn't the Amazon she knew herself to be and marched up the stairs, her legs solidly wrapped around him.

He didn't even hesitate to survey her room. Not that there was much to assess. He dropped her down on the bed and then stood back. He reached behind him and pulled his shirt over his head in a smooth move. He moved like some kind of jungle cat. Effortless and graceful. Her heartbeat quickened. It was crazy. This big beautiful man with his ripped-up body and dragon tattoo wrapping around his torso was nothing she had ever visualized standing in her room, over her bed, over her.

Her eyes locked on the stark beauty of his features, the intensity of his liquid dark eyes. She tore her gaze away. She fixed her stare on his chest, too overcome with nerves to look at his face again. But then she was just left staring at all that hard, golden skin and that did absolutely nothing to help her runaway nerves.

"Done staring, sweetheart?"

She nodded and shook her head, heat slapping her in the cheeks.

"Good. Because I need to get my hands on you again." He came down over her, his arms caging her in, hands tangling in her hair as his head dipped toward her. "And while I'm at it . . . my mouth, too." His lips descended and everything else was lost except this. Him and his blistering-hot lips.

His hands shifted to cup her face, each finger a searing imprint. She gasped at the hot press of his palms on her cheeks. His hands. His mouth. His tongue stroking her bottom lip. She was full of the taste of him, the sensation. His weight melted over her, sinking her deeper into the bed. There was no mistaking his power, his strength. It radiated off him in waves. It was heady and a little frightening.

He kissed her long and hard and deep, his lips coaxing and persuasive. He was a drug and she was addicted, kissing him back, matching his movements, growing bolder. Her lips went tingly-numb and still she kissed him. Hard. All her barriers just dropped away like insubstantial dandelion seeds lost to the wind.

"North," she moaned as he tore his lips away and dragged them down her throat. Her head spun. Somehow his fingers undid the buttons on her blouse. He shoved the fabric over her shoulders with a whisper of sound.

At least she was wearing one of her prettier bras. Not that he was about letting her wear it for very long. He reached behind her and unhooked the clasp in a deft, experienced move.

He tugged the bra down, freeing her breasts. She didn't even have time to feel self-conscious. He closed his lips around a nipple, tugging the peak into his warm mouth and rolling it between his teeth and tongue until it was pebble hard and aching. She gasped and arched. He turned and lavished his mouth on her other breast, leaving her thrashing and wild on the mattress. Her sex clenched and throbbed so intensely tears leaked out from her eyes.

She was barely aware of the hands sliding under

her skirt—and then he gripped the edge of her panties, stepping back from the bed so that he could pull them down her legs. Then she was wholly aware of things happening south of the border.

She propped up on her elbows, watching as he unsnapped the buttons on his jeans. It wasn't anything she hadn't seen before, but here, in the full light of her bedroom, it was new. It was all for her and it was *everything* and she couldn't even blink for fear of missing a moment of it.

He was fully aroused. His erection jutted forward, even more intimidating up close and personal. She wet her lips nervously, but even as nervous as she felt, her sex clenched eagerly, hungry and ready for that fullness inside her.

He reached into his back pocket and pulled out his wallet before sliding his jeans the rest of the way down. He kicked them aside as he pulled a square foil packet from his pocket. Of course he was prepared. A guy like him would be. He was good at this and she was about to find out just how good.

She inched back on her elbows, but he came down on the bed, crawling toward her with a predatory gleam in his eyes, his cock pointing in a straight arrow for her.

"What's the matter? Don't you want me to ruin

you?" The words should have sent a stab of alarm through her, but she only felt a hot bolt of lust.

She nodded almost savagely. There was no going back now. In fact, if she even tried to stop now she just might die.

"Then try not to look like you're about to be sick everywhere." His knees wedged her legs apart. His cock brushed the inside of her thigh. The bristle of hair scraped her tender skin.

She swallowed. God, she felt like a virgin. Everything about this was uncharted territory.

He stilled, all of him freezing except his fingers. They skimmed the side of her face. "You've done this before, right?"

She released a nervous puff of breath and nodded, replying too quickly. "Of course!"

He nodded in turn, but his gaze was dubious. "Good." He took the foil condom and ripped it with his teeth. She jumped at the sound. "You seem a little skittish." He reached between their bodies, rolling on the condom.

"I'm not." She swallowed and tried to steady her shaking voice. "I've done this lots of times . . ." Her voice faded at the bald-faced lie.

"Yeah?" He settled his elbows beside her head and pressed a lingering openmouthed kiss to her neck. "How many times?" There was a teasing quality to his husky voice that told her it didn't matter one way or another to him. He wasn't judging her. He just doubted she was telling the truth. And he would be correct. She might not be a virgin but she was hardly an expert at this kind of thing.

"Well, I never kept an exact r-record. I'm not you. But I've done it oh, plenty of times with my ex-boyfriend."

"Yeah?" His teeth sank down on her earlobe and heat shot straight to her core. She moaned, arching up against him. "You and this ex did this a lot?" he growled.

She felt him then, directly between her thighs, prodding and rubbing against her sex. The throb only intensified there. It occurred to her that it probably wasn't a good idea in this moment to appear more experienced than she was. He would have evidence to the contrary soon enough.

His mouth nibbled along her jaw and then he was kissing her again.

"Maybe not a lot," she admitted between messy, gasping, decadent kisses. "And it's been a while—"

He stopped rubbing and prodding. Her eyes flared as she felt the fullness of him pushing inside her. She stiffened against the sudden invasion, her hands flying to his arms. She'd never felt anything like him before. Not that her frame of reference was so extensive, but this was shattering. She felt stunned at the sensation. Her fingers dug into his biceps, probably leaving scars.

"It's definitely been a while," he growled. "God, you're tight, sweetheart."

She released a huff of breath, feeling herself stretch to accommodate his size.

"Almost there," he added, his voice strained, almost unrecognizable.

"Almost?" she choked. "You're not going to fit."

"Don't worry, baby. You're made for me." He slid all the way home with a groan, dropping his head into her neck, his voice rumbling against her skin. "Faith," he breathed her name against her skin. "You feel so good—"

She inhaled a bracing breath, adjusting to the sheer size of him throbbing in her.

He looked down at her. "Are you okay?"

"Y-yes. Just been a while." She inhaled and exhaled a few times. "And you're . . . different than what I'm used to." *Bigger.*

He grinned his sexy smile that made her stomach flip over. "You'll get used to me."

You'll get used to me.

And that only made her stomach flip again. Heat spread across her face, like ants creeping down her neck and chest.

She didn't have time to consider that and what it meant. There was only action and reaction. Pleasure and sensation.

She fidgeted under him, cutting off whatever he was going to say. She was past the point of needing time to acclimate to the size of him. Right now she just wanted friction and pressure. Inner muscles she'd never even known she possessed clenched around him.

It was all the prompting he needed. With a groan, he lifted his head and withdrew to plunge back inside her. She cried out, and then he was thrusting again, hammering deep, giving her no time to recover. It was a constant barrage of sensation.

And he didn't stop there. He bent his head, lifting one breast and drawing the nipple deep, sucking and scoring it lightly with his teeth.

Her sex hugged the pulsing length of him, and she moaned at this incredible fullness wedged so tightly inside her that she felt like he was a part of her. As though there was no deciphering where he ended and she began. She arched her throat on a moan.

"Ah, is this what you wanted?" he spoke against the curve of her breast.

She nodded and rolled her head, tangling her

hair under her. "Yes." This was everything she had wanted.

Her ruin and salvation.

"You *are* milking my cock, sweetheart," he panted.

She tossed her head in a wild nod and worked her hips under him, willing him to move faster, harder, to give her more. "Yes."

He watched her darkly as he pinched her nipple between strong fingers, sending an arrow of lancing sensation right to where their bodies joined.

She cried out.

He pulled out and then pushed back inside her. Still controlled. Still steady. He kept it up, creating an even tempo of friction that had her writhing and moaning beneath him.

"What?" His voice grew harder, louder in her ear. "What do you want, Faith?"

"Harder."

His eyes darkened. It was like he was waiting for her to say that.

His hands seized her hips and his pace increased. He pounded into her, the headboard rattling against the wall with his every thrust.

She shouted his name and clawed his back. His grip on her hips tightened, fingers hard and deep, biting into her flesh.

He lifted her by the hips until her backside was up off the bed, his cock diving deep, hitting that elusive spot until he shattered her. She came, her body jerking violently. He continued to hammer into her, relentless as a machine, crying out loudly. Yes, he was loud. And even in the throes of her passion that startled her. She had never heard him. Never with other women. If he had shouted like this she would have been able to hear it through the walls.

Something swelled in her chest as she took this as proof. She was different than the others for him.

Foolish or not, she believed that. She wanted to believe that . . .

His hands slid from her hips to grip her ass. He massaged the rounded swells like he couldn't get enough of the feel of her. He was still not finished with her. At this particular moment that felt like a blessing and a curse. Her vision glazed as he drove in and out of her and she felt the wave of another orgasm.

"I—I c-can't," she choked. "It's too much." It wasn't possible. She never had more than one before. She was lucky to have just the one. This didn't happen. It was too much . . . the pleasure almost bordering pain.

"Shh, sweetheart." He bent down and took her mouth in another blistering kiss.

"I can't . . . I never . . ." Her voice cracked and her fingers dug harder into his arms.

"Yes, you can. You'll see."

She arched, responding to something in the hard authority of his voice. He was raw power and strength and she had never had that in a lover . . . hell, never in a boyfriend. He was her fantasy. A man who could take command in bed and dish out all the hot, sweaty sex she could handle . . . *more* than she could handle.

Incredible sensations shot out to every nerve ending before firing back to that sweet spot he hit again and again.

She started to tremble as he pumped in and out, his big hands kneading her bottom in a way that just got her hotter and made that invisible fist tighten and twist low in her belly. She was close again. Strange little sounds fell from her lips. Strange sounds more animal than human tore from her throat. She dropped her hands and seized fistfuls of her comforter, her movements turning clumsy in her desperation.

Her second climax swelled up inside her, starting deep. She curled her toes into the mattress and pushed up, lifting her hips higher.

It was like he knew her. Knew every place to touch. Knew exactly what to do to make her body sing. One hand left her ass to find her clit, his fingers rubbing and pinching the oversensitized nub as he slid in and out of her.

That's all it took. At last the tension snapped. She shattered, coming again, quivering under him as his pace increased to a frenzy, their bodies smacking loudly.

"That's it, sweetheart." His breathing changed, too. His movements became less graceful, more urgent as he drove to his own release. He cursed, surging deep, holding himself still as he came inside her, releasing a guttural groan.

He gave another short thrust, his hand dropping to splay on her belly in a way that made her feel marked, her body claimed in a way that was new. New and not unwelcome.

Removing his hand from her stomach, he dropped onto his side beside her, breathing heavily.

Euphoria clung to her, leaving her slightly dizzy.

So this was what she had been missing.

The instant the thought entered her head she wondered how she would ever go without it—without *him*—again. Euphoria or not, she wasn't blind to the weirdness factor. She'd just had mind-blowing sex with her neighbor.

Oh, and he happened to be an ex-con.

She held very still beside him, unsure how to

react. What did one say in a situation like this? Would he get up and leave now? Would they resume like this never happened? Should she get up and put on her clothes and offer him a drink?

His arm reached out, wrapping around her waist and hauling her close, tucking her to his side. She snuck a glance at his face. His eyes were closed, but she knew he wasn't sleeping. His chest moved up and down too quickly. She waited several moments to see if he was going to say anything.

Nothing. After a while, she stopped waiting and eased from the bed.

"Where are you going?" His hand shot out to close around her hip.

She looked over her shoulder. "There's a yummy dessert downstairs . . ."

He sat up on one elbow. "Sounds good."

She smiled. "Wait here. I'll go get us some."

Bending, she slipped on his T-shirt, reveling in the cool cotton, in the scent of him. Feeling his gaze on her, she padded out of her room and hurried into her kitchen, where she cut a large wedge of tiramisu. Her heart raced and she felt giddy as she carried it back up to her room.

She had a great, strapping, sexy man in her bed and they were about to eat dessert together. It felt very . . . couple-like. A dangerously good feeling, but there it was nonetheless.

He was waiting with an arm tucked behind his head, propped up on two pillows.

She settled down next to him and handed him one of the two spoons she brought.

He sat up and took it, then looked at it as though he didn't know what it was. "Seriously?" He tossed it aside. It thudded to the carpet.

"Why did you do that—"

"We just had sex. We can share a spoon." He scooped up a bite of the creamy deliciousness and held it out to her.

She opened her mouth and he inched the spoon toward her but at the last second he swerved and fed it to himself.

"Hey!" She lightly punched his arm.

He laughed until the taste of the tiramisu fully settled on his tongue. "Damn. What is this!? It's amazing."

"Tiramisu. Remember?" She stared at him.

He stared back at her blankly. She giggled a little and added, "You don't know what tiramisu is? Where have you been living all your life? Under a rock?" The moment the words flew from her mouth she felt like an idiot. She closed her eyes in one long blink and reopened them to stare at his face. "Sorry," she mumbled.

He shrugged. "It's okay. I have been living under a rock for a solid part of my life. Pretty much literally."

She felt even more of an idiot right then. Yeah. He had been living under a rock. At Devil's Rock Penitentiary.

She moistened her lips, unsure how to talk about this with him, knowing she should. She wanted to. Really. "That must have been really hard. I can't imagine—"

"No." He cut her off. "You can't imagine. You couldn't ever imagine it."

His words weren't hard necessarily, just firm. Even so, they stung a little.

He held the spoon up to her mouth, grinning at her. "C'mon, baby. Your turn."

She opened her mouth. "Mmmm." She moaned at the first taste, covering her lips with her fingers.

A corner of his mouth kicked up as he spooned himself some dessert. "You make that same sound when I'm inside you."

Heat flamed her cheeks. "Stop."

"You're blushing now? After what we just did?"

"You're bad."

He snorted and scooped up another bite for her. "You already knew that before we fucked."

She winced. He paused and looked at her, not missing her reaction. "What? You can't hear it or say it but you can do it?" He laughed lightly. "You're such a good girl, Faith Walters. Too good."

She sniffed and started to pull back. "I'm not that good."

He plucked the bowl from her hands and set it aside. "Oh, baby, you're good." He grabbed her around the waist and rolled her onto her back. She yelped, unable to blink, staring up at him with eyes that felt wide and aching in her face.

His head dipped and he kissed her hard and long. He pulled up for air, speaking against her lips. "You, Faith Walters, are *very, very* good."

"Yeah?" She breathed raggedly against his mouth, shocked to feel him again, hard and ready against her thigh.

"Definitely." Lowering his head, he kissed her again until she wasn't blushing anymore. Until she wasn't doing anything except gasping yes and pulling him closer.

Because North Callaghan making love to her felt like the most natural thing in the world.

NORTH NEVER ONCE let himself fall asleep beside Faith. He'd surrendered to everything else his body craved, but not that. He clung to consciousness and that was something new. Those rare instances where he spent the night with a woman or a woman spent the night with him, he instantly conked out after sex, exhausted and replete, sinking into the tempting pull of oblivion. Not so with Faith. He felt wired. His mind awake, skin alive and jumping with awareness of the woman beside him.

She was the temptation, far greater than anything oblivion offered him. Unsurprising, he guessed. Everything with her was different; why not that, too?

His fingers walked over her skin. He drew small circles on her arm, his stomach churning and knotting in an unfamiliar manner. For the first time being with another woman, being with *her*, filled him with a sense of wonder. Like when he was welding and creating something from nothing. Correction. Creating something beautiful from nothing. God. He was almost poetic, and that was a joke. He was not a poet.

He stroked his hand down her arm and stopped at her wrist. He hesitated a moment before lacing his fingers with hers, letting their palms kiss while she slept.

As the air in the room faded to a murky blue, he tried to sort out his feelings when it came to Faith Walters. Moments ticked into minutes and the answer became no more clear-cut. When it was time for him to finally get out of bed, he had no clearer idea what those feelings were. He only knew that one night with her wasn't nearly enough. He wanted to do this again. Except doing this again meant talking . . . and that would lead to defining what it was they were doing. The define-the-relationship talk. No thanks. He didn't do those. The moment a woman wanted the DTR, he took it as his cue to go. Although that would be tricky business when he lived next door to her . . . And she happened to be the sheriff's sister. Yes, he had known that before last night. These had been the reasons he told himself to keep his hands off her.

Not that those reasons had stopped him. Still, he regretted nothing. He would change nothing.

But it had to stop now.

He had to stop.

He slid his jeans on and reached for his T-shirt. He pulled it over his head and caught a whiff of Faith. The coconut scent of her hair. He cursed softly. He needed to wash the shirt as soon as he could.

The sheets on the bed rustled and he glanced

down as she rolled onto her back, bringing the sheet with her and unfortunately covering up her nakedness. "North?"

Her voice was groggy with sleep and seductive as hell. Every fiber of his being screamed for him to climb back into that bed with her. To spend all day with her, touching and loving every inch of her body until he had her memorized.

He couldn't do that though.

"I gotta get ready for work. Go back to sleep," he said, his voice gentle.

She settled back into bed. She was exhausted. He'd kept her up late. She probably wouldn't even remember this verbal exchange later.

She'd asked him to ruin her, but she didn't really mean that. She didn't know what that meant. He knew. He'd seen it firsthand. He'd lived it. He still was living it. He had to leave her alone before he actually inflicted wounds that went too deep and became irreparable. Before they became scars.

Before it all became more than words between them.

Before he wrecked her like he did everything else in his life.

TWENTY-FOUR

NORTH SLAMMED OUT of his truck and stalked up to the front door. It happened from time to time. Occasionally the past came knocking. Like it had today. Only this time, his guard had been down. He'd been humming as he worked. *Humming.* His thoughts wrapped up in a long-legged brunette. Even if he had told himself to keep last night buried in last night like any self-respecting one-night stand, he could still taste her mouth. Still feel her against his hands. Her coconut-scented hair chased him as he moved around the garage.

He made a beeline for his fridge and popped open a beer. Collapsing on the couch, he found a ball game on TV and nursed his way through a couple beers, trying not to think about the customer who'd rolled in today and recognized his face. Apparently the man had been Mason Leary's second cousin. He had choice words for North. Not willing to risk his job, North had stood by and done nothing as the man called him every foul thing he could think of. If prison had taught him anything, it was how to take a beating—be it physical or verbal.

Still, it was a shitty day.

He heard Faith moving around next door. That didn't improve his mood. He glared at the wall and went and got another beer.

His phone dinged and he saw it was a text from her. An innocent Hey stared back at him. He ignored it. Dropping his phone, he fell back on his couch again.

An hour rolled past. She didn't text again. He figured she would get the picture eventually. Last night was a onetime thing. If anything, today's fiasco at work drove that home more than ever.

People like you should be in cages. You shouldn't be free and allowed to share the same space as the rest of us.

He shook his head, trying to chase away the words and the venom in which they had been uttered. It was harder than it should have been. He was going soft. That must be it. He had heard far worse insults in his life. Maybe he was getting too domesticated. His gaze slid to the wall separating him from Faith Walters again. Yeah. That must be it. Domesticity. He needed to purge it from his life. Stay hard. It was the only way he could protect himself.

His phone dinged again and this time it was a text from his brother asking him to join them for dinner. With a disgusted snort he tossed the phone down on the couch. Good people. Nice people. He had too fucking many of them in his life. Strangely enough, things were easier when he was at the Rock and he didn't have these types of people around him. When things were black and white and he knew where everyone stood—himself included.

He flipped through channels and found an old western he recognized as one of his uncle's favorites. He dropped the remote and left the channel there, watching as bad guys and good guys shot at each other across an open range. Life was simple back then. You knew who the bad guys were. You knew who the good guys were. You were either one or the either. None of this bullshit.

He was halfway through the movie and on beer number five when a knock sounded at his door. He stared at it for a moment, not moving. His gut told him to stay where he was. *Don't move. Don't get up.*

He stood.

He didn't bother looking through the peephole. Something told him who would be on the other side. It wasn't rocket science for him to guess.

He opened the door to find Faith standing there, dressed in a soft-looking T-shirt with a faded Bullwinkle across the front. Her shorts did nothing to disguise the sexy slopes of her legs. Her eyes were luminous in the dark of his unlit porch.

"Hey." She held up a plate of brownies. The rich chocolate aroma hit him full force and he was suddenly bombarded with the echoes of his childhood, of innocence. Before he'd destroyed everything.

"Brownies, huh? No scones."

Uncertainty flashed across her face for a split second before she managed to smile at him. "Brownies are more a guy thing if I'm not mistaken."

He tilted back his head and took a long slug of beer. Lowering his drink, he stared at her for a long while.

She shifted on her feet. "Aren't you going to invite me inside?" She lifted her chin a notch and he knew that her pride was on the line. It took her a lot to ask him that. This girl was not versed in one-night stands. She was not versed in men like him. He should do the right thing here. End things now before expectations set in and rooted. He knew that. He had planned to do that. Up until he opened this door and feasted eyes on her he would have.

He sucked in a deep breath, searching and digging for the words buried somewhere inside him where goodness and right still existed. *Go. Get away. Leave me alone. Don't come back.*

Screw it. Tossing his well-intentioned plans aside, he seized her wrist and tugged her inside, slamming the door shut behind her.

He plucked the plate of brownies out of her hands and set both his beer and the plate on his countertop.

"What are you—" she started to ask.

Turning around, he took her face in both hands and pulled her toward him. "I'm interested in a different kind of dessert."

He kissed her hard and fierce. She said something. Mumbled words fought between their lips, but he ignored them and kissed her harder—until she was panting and their hands were wild, groping and tearing them free of clothing.

When they were both fully naked, he grabbed her by the waist and plopped her on top of his kitchen table. Her wide eyes met his. "North . . ."

He heard the hesitation as clear as day in her

voice. "You're good, baby," he assured her, ignoring the whisper in his head that told him to stop, to not do this again with her. To her.

He reached for his wallet inside his jeans and quickly removed a condom, watching her, naked and quivering on top of his kitchen table as he tore it open with his teeth. His hand gave the barest tremor as he rolled it down his aching cock. He reached for one of her small rose-tipped breasts. He fondled her roughly. First one perfect breast, then the other.

Her head dropped back and she released a keening moan. One glance down and he could see she was already glistening wet and ready for him. It was the hottest thing he'd ever seen. *She* was. He grabbed her by the waist and pulled her toward him with a growl, until he was right there, poised and brushing against her sex. She choked out a sound that might have been a word. Her fingers grabbed him, nails scoring deep into his biceps as she urged him closer, her eyes so shining and radiant that he was certain he could find her in a room void of any light.

He couldn't wait a moment longer. He plunged into her with no ease or delicacy. It was base and primal and hard, and exactly what he craved. Maybe what he had craved for years. It felt more satisfying than anything he'd been chasing, anything he'd had, except maybe the last time with her.

She screamed and dropped back on the table, her arms flung wide and outstretched above her head in abandon.

A curse seethed between his clenched lips as she surrounded him, hugging him like a silken glove. He looked down at her, spine arched, upturned breasts flushed pink with desire. She was so pretty it actually hurt to look at her. Her lips were puffy and bruised from his mouth and her eyes looked so wide and guileless and slightly stunned as he worked in and out of her. He was corrupting her. He knew it, and while he hated himself, while he couldn't bear it, he couldn't stop either. Her sex pulsed and flexed around him, pulling him in impossibly deeper.

Digging his hands into her hips, he slid out from her and flipped her over on the table, lowering her legs to the ground. He spread her feet apart so that she was standing on the tile floor, bent waist down for him. As tall as she was, the angle was perfect—and so was the view of the sweet swells of her ass.

He stroked her, finding her slick heat, so wet and swollen for him. Her clit was distended and so sensitive she cried out when he gave it the barest graze.

"Too. Much," she gasped, squirming away.

"You can take it, Faith," he rasped, wrapping an arm around her waist. He bore down on the little nub, rubbing it in a fast little circle.

A shuddering sob racked her body, followed in quick succession by another one. She cried out, pressing her palms against the table and pushing back against him. "North!" she pleaded.

He answered her by plunging back into her tight pussy. A deep growl spilled out of him. He stroked a hand down her spine while still working his other one between her legs.

For each of his thrusts she pushed back, meeting him with similar force until they were both crying out, both shuddering. She exploded first, shrieking and grinding against him, her sex milking him, squeezing him like a vise as she hit her climax.

He followed fast behind with his own release, shouting like he never did. Like the man he wasn't. A man who wasn't burdened.

He draped over her for a lingering moment, his forehead resting against her back as his breath crashed out of him. She was bewildering like that, making him forget who he really was in a moment of passion. A dangerous thing. He could never forget.

He pulled out from her body and moved into

the kitchen, forcefully tossing the condom in the trash. When he turned around she was already on her feet. Hands shaking, she dressed herself. He leaned one hip against the table, cautioning himself not to touch her again when that was exactly what his body cried out to do. He swallowed back a sound of self-disgust. Needing to do something with his hands, he picked up a brownie and took a giant bite, schooling his expression into something impassive.

"Are you going to get dressed?" she asked with a nervous little laugh. Only a good girl like her could feel awkward after what they had just done. Especially considering it wasn't even their first time.

He shrugged, not even glancing down at himself. "I'm comfortable."

"That was . . . amazing." Her smile turned shy and definitely nervous. "Different."

Unease trickled through him. This was starting to feel too intimate, too much like what other well-adjusted couples did after they fucked.

"Of course it was." Of course she would be one of those that wanted to talk afterward and examine everything. This was insanity and he was a fool.

Her eyes narrowed slightly, evidently picking up something in his tone and words. "What is that supposed to mean?"

"You're you, Faith Walters. What we did was . . ." His voice faded and he dragged his hand through his hair with a pained sigh. "Tell me this. Why do you let me touch you? And kiss you? Why did you just let me have sex with you like that?" He gestured to the table. It hadn't been kinky necessarily, but it had been fast and hard and short on foreplay.

"What?" she demanded. "Having regrets now because I'm a good girl?" She air quoted that last bit, her face flushed with emotion. "Afraid I'm going to want to pick out china patterns now? Grow up, North. You don't have anything to worry about."

"Maybe you should do the growing up. I mean, what the hell are you doing here with me, Faith?"

IT WAS AN excellent question.

Searching his face, Faith was glad to finally have this out between them. It was time to talk about what they were doing with each other. Because she was beyond the point of pretending any of this was nothing. She'd just had the most amazing sex of her life with him—*again*—and now he was being a jackass.

He motioned wildly between them. "Why have you been letting this go on between us?"

"I don't know, but I'm starting to wonder." She

propped a hand on her hip. "And *this* what, North? What is it that we're doing?" She stared hard at him, waiting for him to say that it was more than sex. Because, God help her, it felt like *more* to her.

He laughed once, a harsh bark. "You need a definition?"

"I do!"

"It's called fucking but I have no idea why you've been doing it with me." His brown eyes glittered to black. "Do you have some stupid felon fetish? Is that what this is?"

She sucked in a sharp breath. "Are you trying to be an asshole on purpose?"

He kept right on talking. Like he hadn't heard her. Or he had and didn't care what she thought about him. "Your brother is right. You shouldn't be living next door to me. You should not—"

Her hand shot out, shoving him in the chest. She just reacted. It had always been like that between them though—from the very start. All impulse. All reaction.

She never minced words with him. Even after she knew about his history, she was never afraid. Never hesitant. Never tiptoed. Never behaved as though she should.

"Stop it! Don't say that. I get enough of it from my father and brothers."

"Maybe you should listen to them then. Leave me. Stay away from me."

She glanced around wildly. Spotting a marker on the counter, she stalked over and snatched it up.

"What are you doing . . ." His voice faded as she yanked off the marker's cap. Bending, she drew a great long line in front of her along the tile floor.

Standing back, she stared him directly in the eyes. "There."

He glanced from the line to her. "What the hell is that?"

"That's the line, North Callaghan. Remember?" She felt her nostrils flare as she exhaled a breath. "And I'm stepping over it." She made a great show of lifting her foot and crossing the line. "Now what are you going to do about it?"

He opened his mouth, for once speechless. Usually she was the stammerer, but here, right now, he was at a loss.

"What are you so afraid of?" she demanded, still searching his face. "Is this really an 'I'm not good enough for you' moment?"

"It's the truth." He stared grimly.

"Nuh-uh." She shook her head fiercely. "You're a coward, North Callaghan. Don't ever think you are doing this *for* me."

"Oh, I'm a coward. You're right about that." He

shook his head with self-disgust. "You don't get it. Every morning I wake up with this sick, twisting sensation in my gut." He clutched his stomach, clenching deep against his ridiculous abs, the tips of his fingers whitening from the strength of his grip.

He continued, "Most people wake up relaxed and groggy, their minds still lost to sleep or dreaming about their coffee or what they want to eat for breakfast. That in-between state, you know? Not quite awake and not asleep, when everything in the world is perfect and clean and fresh?"

She nodded. It sounded like many of her weekend mornings when she slept late.

"I never get that. I haven't had that since I was a kid in high school. The past never leaves me. Every morning I wake up and I feel sick all over again once I remember it all. I take that first big breath and it feels like fucking razors going down. Every day I feel that way. Every day I relive it. I'm broken. I ruin everything I touch. I have to leave you alone before I destroy you, too."

"North—"

He continued coldly, his words a steady rain of bullets. "If you knew anything about me, you'd be disgusted."

"Why?" she pressed. "Tell me. Talk to me."

"In prison, I watched—" He stopped and swallowed. "I stood by as men were . . ." His voice strangled and he stopped again. He looked away from her a long moment before looking back at her. When he did her heart stuttered at the deadness of his stare. "You can't help anyone in prison. Not unless you want a world of shit to rain down on you, too."

She slid a step closer. "So you're saying that other men were hurt and you didn't try to help them?" She stepped forward, reaching for him, eager to touch him and offer comfort.

He flinched and jerked back. "Don't say it's all right. The boy I was when I went into that prison might have committed a crime, but he had honor, humanity. He would never have stood by as men were attacked . . . as men begged for help, crying like babies as horrible, unthinkable things were done to them." He punched his chest with a fist. "I. Did. Nothing."

She touched his arm. "You can't blame—"

"Stop it. This was just sex. That's all it was and all it can ever be. Now if you're okay with that, fine. If not, you should leave."

She dropped her arm, everything in her wilting inside. She had believed all along that he wasn't a man who would hurt her—at least not physically.

And that still held true. Her heart, however, was another matter. Right now it was dying.

She gave herself a mental slap. Faith had always prided herself on being one of those women to steer clear of bad boys. She had seen so many women make poor choices when it came to the men in their lives. Boyfriends and husbands who abused them and their children, who failed to provide, who abandoned them. She had never been tempted by men with unsavory pasts, and yet here she was. She had been tempted. She had fallen for this guy who was not long-term-relationship material.

"Like I said," she finished, her voice strong and steady as she stared him down. "Coward." Turning, she strode across the room and grabbed the doorknob, yanking it open.

"Faith?"

She stopped halfway out the door and looked back at him.

"That line you drew on the floor of my kitchen?"

"Yes?"

"You did it with a permanent marker."

Fitting. She marred his tile floor. She laughed. "And you were so worried about *you* ruining things. Guess I did that." Shrugging, she exited his house, deliberately slamming his door for no other reason except that it felt good.

To feel even better, she slammed the door on the way back inside her own house. She paced the length of her living room. She couldn't believe she had been so stupid. She'd fallen for her neighbor and, of course, it meant nothing to him. *She* meant nothing to him.

Her family had been right. He was bad news, but not in the way he claimed. North insisted he was broken and not good enough for her and yet that hadn't stopped him from sleeping with her. She should have seen it coming, but she still felt used. How could she even look at him again?

She knew what she needed to do.

TWENTY-FIVE

*T*HE POUNDING WOULDN'T stop. She stopped amid packing up her kitchen, pushing herself to her feet. She stepped around the U-Haul boxes she had picked up after visiting with her Realtor yesterday. Mandy didn't understand, but after her initial questions, she didn't press Faith for an explanation. The house would go up on the market at the end of the week. In the meantime, Faith had decided to start packing. She could move back in with her father and sell the house while it was vacant. He'd be happy to have her until she found another house. She just couldn't stay here. Not any longer than she had to. She'd avoided seeing North so far, but she knew it was only a matter of time before they came face to face.

The pounding was enough to drive her crazy. After taking a quick peek out her front blinds to assure herself that it wasn't North, she yanked open the door and marched out to confront the offender. "Can I help you?"

The man pounding on North's door stepped back and looked at her. "Yeah. I'm looking for the guy that lives here."

The guy. It was assumed she wouldn't know him. And really . . . did she know him? Did she know him at all? She thought she had. Or she thought she was at least starting to. She thought that maybe they had something special. But she was wrong. She was wrong about him. She didn't know him at all.

She narrowed her gaze on the man, wondering if maybe he was North's parole officer . . . except he had a look to him that reminded her of North. Even though he was fairly clean cut, he had that edgy bad-boy vibe. And something else, too.

"He's not home." She waved to the street. "His bike is gone. You'll have to come back another time." She used the tone of voice that she adopted when dealing with difficult people. Wendy called it her pit bull voice.

The guy blinked, looking her over. "You know North Callaghan?" It was more of a statement than a question.

Knew him? That might be an understatement.

She knew him in the biblical sense, yes. She wasn't the first one able to claim that fact. However, something other women couldn't claim, something maybe no woman could claim, was that she loved him. But North didn't love her. The thought angered her more than it surprised her. She shouldn't have been so stupid to fall for someone so wrong for her.

God. She closed her eyes in a suffering blink. She loved him. She was an idiot. It was only physical to him, but she had gone and thrown her heart into the fray. If she hadn't already made her mind up to move, she sure as hell would now.

She hesitated before nodding at the stranger. "Yes. He's my neighbor. I know him." It seemed the smartest thing to leave it at that and say nothing more.

He stared at her a long moment before sighing. He ran a hand through his hair, ruffling the dark locks as he looked out at the street. She should move inside. She should be nervous. This guy that she didn't know, who seemed in no hurry to go away, should make her nervous.

He looked back at her then. "I'm his brother, Knox. He hasn't been answering any of my phone calls or texts."

She angled her head, studying him further. Same

dark hair. Same angular jaw. Good looks must run in the family. The tension in her chest relaxed a little. She stepped out from her doorway and stuck out her hand. "I'm Faith Walters."

"Faith," he murmured. She smiled, trying not to feel uncomfortable. "Maybe you could give him a message for me?"

She shrugged uneasily. "We're not really friends." Or friendly. *In fact, I'm moving because of him. Because I slept with him and I love him and he is incapable of loving me back.*

Knox angled his head and looked at her with growing interest . . . almost as though he could read her thoughts. She forced a smile. "I see. So. You don't see him?"

She shrugged again.

Knox's eyebrows lifted. "Huh." Now there was no denying the interest in that single sound. "You don't talk ever?"

"Well. We used to. I mean . . . not anymore. No. We don't." Her voice faded away. She sighed. In her attempt to not reveal anything about her relationship, or lack thereof, with North, she had probably already revealed too much. Clearly they weren't just neighbors. They were more compli-cated than that.

Knox's expression turned from knowing to sympathetic. He stared at her so long she shifted awkwardly on her feet. "You seem like a nice girl," he finally said. "Whether he realizes it or not, my brother deserves a nice girl in his life."

She swallowed against the sudden lump that had formed in her throat. She nodded, unable to pretend she didn't know what he meant. "Yes. I happen to agree with you." As conflicted as her feelings were for North, she couldn't disagree that he deserved love and forgiveness in his life.

Knox stared at her long and hard. "My brother is a good man. Not perfect, but a good man. He might doubt that, but I never have."

She nodded. "I know."

Knox smiled slowly. "I like you, Faith Walters."

She gave a rusty laugh. "You don't know me."

"I'd like to. My wife and I would like to get to know you. Hopefully, North will bring you around."

Her smile slipped away. "Yeah, sorry, but I don't think that's going to happen."

She sobered. There would be no getting to know each other because she was moving and even if she wasn't North wasn't about to bring her around his brother and sister-in-law.

All this talk about North being a good man didn't amount to anything if he didn't believe it himself. And there was the not-so-minor point that he didn't love her back. He wasn't capable of either of those things—loving himself or her.

"I THINK I'M going to have to cut you off."

North looked up at Piper standing over him, one hand propped on her hip. He glanced down at the single beer in his hand. "Little zealous, aren't you? This is my first."

"Yeah, but you're swapping eyes with Bambi after just one beer and that is not a good idea. I'm seriously questioning your judgment. You don't need more alcohol to muddle your head." She wrinkled her nose. "Trust me, my friend, even you don't want to go there with Bambi."

He looked over at the purple-haired dancer. She lifted her chin in his direction, the invitation clear. He'd come here tonight looking to escape—and because staying at his house meant he was only feet from her door. That didn't seem like a good idea. His resolve, when it came to Faith, had already been tested and failed.

Piper followed his gaze. "She's a nightmare you don't want in your life."

He lifted his beer and took a slow sip as the dancer squeezed her breasts and blew a kiss at him. "Funny. She doesn't look like a nightmare." Even as he uttered this, he felt nothing. Not the faintest stirring. Not the slightest temptation. The sight of the half-naked woman did nothing for him, which was a shame. He'd told himself the best way to get over Faith was to get another woman under him. When he left his house that had seemed like a fine idea. Unfortunately, that was no longer appealing. Staring at Bambi only made him feel empty inside.

"I thought you were seeing someone anyway."

He looked at her sharply. "What gave you that idea?"

She shrugged. "Just a feeling. You're not seeing Serena anymore."

He took another pull from his beer. "I'm not seeing anyone." Even as he uttered the words, the image of Faith filled his mind.

"Please. You got that look."

"What look?"

"The I'm-hung-up-on-someone look. What's her name?"

He shrugged. She nudged at his shoulder. "What's her name? C'mon."

"Faith Walters."

"Walters. Huh, like that jackass Sheriff Walters."

"Yep. That would be her brother."

Piper stared. "You're kidding. You're dating the Sheriff's sister?"

"We're not dating," he snapped, too quickly.

"Ohh." She rocked back on her heels. "You're in *love* with her."

"What? How do you get that? I told you we aren't dating."

"Riiiight. That's why you're sitting here looking at the dancers like you're suffering through a plate of liver and onions." She motioned to the men around them. "Do you see any of these other guys looking like they're in that kind of anguish? No. That would just be you."

He grunted a response.

She moved past him, patting him on the shoulder. "Dreams come here to die. Trust me. Forget about this place. Go home to your girl, North."

He sat alone for several more minutes, trying to convince himself that Piper was wrong, that if he stayed here long enough he would be able to forget about Faith—that he could lose himself in someone else and not want her anymore.

The purple-haired dancer stopped before his table. She twirled a bright lock of hair between her fingers and looked him over coyly. "Hey, there. I'm Bambi. Want to get out of here?"

He stood up from the table and dropped a few bills on the table for Piper. "Yeah. I do." Without another glance, he turned and left the club. Alone.

NORTH PULLED ONTO his street and stopped hard, his foot digging into the brake pedal as his gaze locked onto the FOR SALE sign in Faith's yard. She didn't . . .

She couldn't . . .

She was.

Sonuvabitch. He thumped his steering wheel. She was actually selling her house. She was moving. Because of him. Of that he had no doubt.

He sat there for a moment and simply stared, telling himself this was good; it would make things easier if he didn't have to see her every day. But his stomach only continued to knot and twist until he thought he might be sick all over the front seat of his truck.

No. No. *No.*

It was the only word to fill his head but it was enough.

No. Fucking. Way. It was supposed to be just physical. It wasn't supposed to be *this*. And yet it was this. Just like Piper accused. She had been right.

It hit him hard like a Mack Truck to the face. Everything he ever wanted he had either lost or was stolen from him. But not this. He wasn't going to lose again. Not her.

Once she was gone, once she had moved, he knew

it would finally and forever be over. He'd never see her again except someday far in the future when he bumped into her at a store or the county fair and she'd be with another man. Maybe this other man would be her husband. She'd be pregnant or have a baby on her hip and North would be forgotten like sophomore-year geometry. Her face would burn at the sight of him, the unwanted memory of a horribly embarrassing indiscretion.

Hell no.

He had done everything to wreck this and push her away, but no more.

He would finally attempt to save something. Again. He wouldn't stand by and watch as this was destroyed. He would attempt to save them. Hopefully it wasn't too late and there could be a *them*.

He hopped out of his truck and marched up to her door. He rapped sharply several times until the door opened.

She faced him, her expression stony. "North?"

"You're moving?"

She glanced over his shoulder. "That's what the sign means."

"You can't."

She frowned. "I don't understand why you care. You were very—"

"You shouldn't have to move."

"I'd be more comfortable living somewhere else."

He dragged a hand through his hair, tugging the ends hard. "I don't want you to go." He let go and splayed both his hands wide in front of himself.

"North, you don't need to feel guilty. This is for the best. We should never have gotten involved—"

"That's just it! I want to be *involved*! I want us together. Seeing that sale sign . . . thinking you could be somewhere else, somewhere away from me . . . I just can't handle that."

"*You* can't handle it? How good that you realize that now." Angry splotches of color broke out over her face. "Well, too bad, North Callaghan." She stabbed him in the chest with a finger. He winced. "*I* can't handle staying here."

"Faith—"

"No, North. Hopefully, the house will sell quickly and we don't have to do this much longer. Until then, let's just stay out of each other's way."

Before he could answer, she smoothly closed the door in his face, leaving him standing there, staring at where she once was, looking at the small circle of her peephole, pretty convinced she wasn't looking back at him.

TWENTY-SIX

He SPENT THE next week stealing the FOR SALE signs that kept popping up in Faith's yard. That didn't stop prospective buyers from showing up. He led a few of them astray, either telling them they had the wrong house or the owner had changed their mind and taken the house off the market. He did other things, too, all hoping to get her attention . . . and forgiveness.

He left flowers for her. It was the kind of thing nice girls like her deserved. He knew that. He figured he'd try. He sent texts. Serious ones. Naughty ones. Teasing ones. He tried everything to lure her out of her self-imposed exile from him. All attempts she ignored. He also resorted to parking in her driveway. That had always provoked her before. But nothing. She never rose to the bait.

He was running out of ideas. He had to do something.

He knew even if she sold her house, she would still be somewhere in Sweet Hill. But chasing after her when she didn't live next door would more closely resemble stalking. And considering who her family was, that would probably not work out in his favor. He had to figure something out. Soon.

FAITH HAD JUST entered her kitchen when she spied the Girl Scout walking down her shared driveway toward the sidewalk, dragging her wagon after her. Faith had taken to keeping her blinds open. Her FOR SALE sign was continuously being stolen from her yard—yes, she had a good guess as to the identity of the culprit—and she was hoping to stop that from happening again.

Running for her door, she was outside before the girl hit the sidewalk. "Hey, you there! Wait! I'll buy some cookies!"

The cute girl turned around, shielding her eyes from the sun with one hand. "Sorry ma'am! The nice man just bought everything I had." She pointed to North's house to indicate who the "nice" man happened to be.

Faith stopped and turned to glare in that

direction—at North. In his arms he held at least a dozen varieties of Girl Scout cookies. A quick scan revealed her favorites squeezed into the mix. Thin Mints and Caramel deLites crowded his muscular arms. She could think of a thousand and one characteristics for North Callaghan. *Nice* wasn't one of them.

"Really?" She threw her arms wide. "You're going to eat all of those yourself?"

His deep gaze burrowed into her. "I thought you might want them."

She scoffed. "Oh. So you bought them for me?" She eyed him dubiously. Was this like the flowers he had left for her? She didn't know what his game was for certain, but she assumed he felt guilty for the fact that she was selling her house. Or maybe he just felt like having sex with her again—although a man like him could get it anywhere, so that didn't necessarily smack of truth.

"I'm not much of a baker. This is the best I can do," he answered. "I mean I could try, but the results might not be to your liking."

"Why would you want to bake me anything?"

"You did. For me." He shrugged as though it was that simple.

She angled her head, studying him. He looked

so . . . earnest, but as she was learning with this man, nothing was simple.

"You're not me, North. You don't have to try to be like me." She hesitated and then added, "You doing this won't make any difference. I'm moving and we both know why." She stared deeply into his eyes, trying to convey that for whatever reason he was doing this he could stop. She needed him to stop. Because resisting him wasn't easy.

A stark look entered his eyes and then vanished. Hard determination glinted there. "Maybe I want to be a little more like you."

She shook her head. "You're you though. I'm not idiot enough to ask a man to change . . . to expect him to be someone he's not."

"Maybe I'm discovering that being what you want isn't such a leap, after all. I'm closer to that than I realized."

Hope warred in her chest. If only that were true. It was tempting to believe in the promise of his words. She still wanted him. That hadn't changed just because she got enough backbone to walk away from him. She couldn't let him sway her. He had only ever been honest with her, but right now, he was confused. Or misguided. He wasn't looking for long term. And she was. He believed

he destroyed everything he touched, that he was
haunted, burdened by the past, and could never be
clean enough for her.

She turned to go back inside her house.

"I want you all the time and it's wrecking me."
His voice cracked a little behind her as he declared
this.

She faced him again, her heart kicking against
her ribs at this declaration. She took a deep breath
and pushed it back down. "That's only lust. Find
someone else to—"

"No." He dropped all the boxes of cookies and
lunged forward, stopping just shy from touching
her. "Don't. You think if I could have moved on, I
wouldn't have? You've infected me, Faith—"

"So I'm a disease?" She didn't know whether to
be insulted or not.

He groaned in clear frustration. "Look. I'm not
good with these kinds of things. I've never told a
woman I love her before and I'm sorry I'm making
such a mess of it." He dragged a hand through his
hair, sending the long locks spiking in different di-
rections.

Everything inside her stilled and locked up hard.
She moistened her lips and whispered, "What did
you say?"

He spread his arms wide. "I love you and you

might be moving, but I'm not giving up on us, Walters. I don't care where you go. I'm going to be patient and work to convince you that—"

"You *love* me?" She fought hard to keep hope from overwhelming her. "What does that even mean to you, North? Do you even know?" Her voice trembled, and she had to stop herself from falling into his arms. He loved her? Could that be true?

"It means this." He waved between them. "Us? Me standing in front of you and offering you everything I have. *Me*. My heart. It's yours if you'll have it. It's real. It's more than physical, Faith." He inhaled a shaky breath, his eyes brimming with more emotion than she thought him capable of possessing. "It means I want forever with you."

She took a step back, staggered at his words—words she never thought to hear from him.

He continued, "I've been out for two years, but I've never felt free. I've never felt happy except in these moments with you." He gestured to his back fence. "I've found contentment when I weld, when I create things. There are times then when I can block out the world and find a quiet sort of peace doing that. But my feelings for you aren't quiet, Faith. They're loud and big and scary as fuck but that's because with you I feel joy and happiness. I want that all the time. I want you to feel that way, too. Please. Tell me that you can."

He finished his speech with a ragged breath, as though he'd run a great distance, and she supposed he had. It had been a long uphill run for him to get to this point. She knew that much about him. He was professing his love and asking for it in return.

She stepped forward and flattened a hand against his chest, directly over his heart, where it beat fierce and fast. This was not the man who, a week ago, thought himself dead inside and the ruiner of all things. This was no longer the man who blamed himself for not being able to save anyone, for not lifting a finger as others around him suffered.

He was finally stepping forward, finally willing to save himself.

She moistened her lips. "The reason I'm moving is because I do love you . . . and I can't bear to live next door to you without—"

He killed the rest of what she was going to say by dipping his head and claiming her mouth in a hard, drugging kiss. When he came up for air, his gaze devoured her. "You love me. That's all that matters, Faith. And as for moving . . . maybe you should sell the house."

"I should?"

"One home makes more sense for the two of us."

"You want us to move in together?"

One corner of his mouth kicked up. "Might as well. I don't intend to be anywhere other than your bed every night for the rest of my life." A flash of uncertainty crossed his face. "I mean, if you love me and if you think—"

Standing on her tiptoes, she kissed him again, letting him feel her certainty. She didn't want to spend another night without him. One house sounded perfect.

Still kissing, they backed themselves inside her house. He kicked the door shut after her.

"The cookies!" she cried against his lips.

"Forget them. I'll learn to bake," he promised.

EPILOGUE

"You know, visiting hours are going to end soon." Briar waved her fingers, gesturing that North needed to give up the baby he was holding in his arms.

North shook his head slightly, barely sparing a glance for his sister-in-law.

"North," Faith chided, laughter in her voice.

He grimaced, knowing he needed to let Briar hold the child, but little Max was only one day old and North was having trouble letting him go.

There'd been visitors off and on all day. Uncle Mac and Aunt Alice had only just left. He felt as though he hardly had an opportunity to be with the newest member of the Callaghan family.

Knox chuckled. "There's always tomorrow, Briar. And it's not as though you don't have your own baby waiting at home."

Briar looked horrified and swatted her husband's

arm. "I'm not leaving here without holding my nephew. Now give him up, North."

"Go on," Faith coaxed him from where she reclined on the hospital bed, looking radiant after giving birth to their son the day before. "It's okay. You'll be holding him a lot in the years ahead."

He carefully passed his small son into Briar's waiting arms and then moved beside his wife. Bending, he pressed a tender kiss to her lips.

A year ago he would not have imagined he could be this blessed. His brother and Reid might have found happiness and love, but he had thought such things could never be his. The love of a woman. Fatherhood. Happiness.

"That won't be enough," he said. "Holding him . . . and you. I won't ever get enough of it."

She grinned. "Good. Because you're going to be doing it forever."

His chest swelled on a breath as he gazed down at his beautiful wife. "Forever is exactly what I want."

My Fair Duchess by Megan Frampton
Archibald Salisbury, war hero and society expert, has received orders for his most challenging mission: teach Genevieve, Duchess of Blakesley, how to be a duke. But how can he keep his mind on business when she entices him towards pleasure?

It was impossible, unprecedented . . . and undeniably true. Genevieve is now a "duke," or, rather, a duchess, and Archie is supposed to teach her to be a lady. But what she really wants to do is run into his arms.

Perfect for You by Candis Terry
Declan Kincade has spent so much time chasing success he's forgotten how to live. Lately though, his all-business routine has been in disarray. Brooke Hastings is the best employee Dec's ever had: polished, capable, and intelligent. He's also just realized that she's smoking hot . . .

What's worse than never meeting the right man? Finding him, and working side-by-side while he remains blind to your existence. Until one temptation-packed road-trip changes everything . . .

REL 0217

*G*ive in to you

These unforgettable sto
to buy and give you hou

Go to *www.AvonImpuls*
have to offer.
Available wherever e-books are sold.

AVONIMPULSE

IMP 0811